CORNELL WOOLRICH

His name represents steamy, suspenseful mystery fiction . . . chilling encounters on the dark and sultry landscape of urban America in the thirties and forties. Author of more than 100 stories, novelettes, and books—many dramatized on such classic radio shows as *Climax* and *Suspense*, on TV's *Alfred Hitchcock Presents*, and in great films like *The Bride Wore Black*, *Rear Window*, and *Phantom Lady*—Woolrich is in a class by himself.

CORNELL WOOLRICH

"HIS WRITING GOES RIGHT THROUGH YOU LIKE A SHRIEK IN THE NIGHT. SOMETIMES YOU EVEN WISH YOU COULD FORGET IT, BUT YOU CAN'T."

Dorothy Salisbury Davis

CORNELL WOOLRICH

"HE CAN DISTILL MORE TERROR, MORE EXCITEMENT, MORE DOWNRIGHT NAIL-BITING SUSPENSE OUT OF EVEN THE MOST COMMONPLACE HAPPENINGS THAN NEARLY ALL HIS COLLEAGUES AND COMPETITORS."

Ellery Queen

CORNELL WOOLRICH

One of the truly great and truly original American writers . . . now coming back to readers everywhere from Ballantine Books.

Other Cornell Woolrich titles
Published by Ballantine Books:

THE BLACK CURTAIN

THE BLACK PATH OF FEAR

RENDEZVOUS IN BLACK

CORNELL WOOLRICH

The Black Angel

BALLANTINE BOOKS • NEW YORK

ISBN 0-345-30664-3

This edition published by arrangement with Doubleday & Company, Inc.

Manufactured in the United States of America

First Ballantine Books Edition: October 1982

INTRODUCTION
BY FRANCIS M. NEVINS, JR.

H E WAS THE POE of the twentieth century and
the poet of its shadows. For almost thirty-five years
this tormented recluse wrote dozens of haunting
suspense stories, the most powerful of their kind ever
written—stories full of fear, guilt, and loneliness,
breakdown and despair, and a sense that the world is
controlled by malignant forces preying on us. And
throughout his life he felt those forces eating away at
him.

Cornell George Hopley-Woolrich was born in New
York City on December 4, 1903, to parents whose
marriage collapsed in his youth. Much of his childhood
was spent in Mexico with his father, a civil engineer.
The experience of seeing Puccini's *Madame Butterfly*
in Mexico City at the age of eight gave him his first
insight into color and drama, and his first sense of
tragedy. Three years later, he understood that someday he too, like Cio-Cio-San, would have to die, and
from that moment on he was haunted by a sense of
doom that never left him.

During adolescence he returned to Manhattan and
lived with his mother and her socially prominent family,
and in 1921 he enrolled in Columbia College, with his
father paying the tuition from Mexico City. He began
writing fiction during an illness in his junior year, and
quit school soon afterward to pursue his dream of

becoming another F. Scott Fitzgerald. His first novel, *Cover Charge* (1926), chronicles the lives and loves of the Jazz Age's gilded youth in the manner of his current literary idol. This debut was followed by *Children of the Ritz* (1927), a frothy concoction about a spoiled heiress', marriage to her chauffeur, which won him a $10,000 prize contest and a contract from First National Pictures for the movie rights. Woolrich was invited to Hollywood to help with the adaptation and stayed on as a staff writer. Besides his movie chores and an occasional story or article for magazines like *College Humor* and *Smart Set*, he completed three more novels during these years. In December of 1930 he entered a brief and inexplicable marriage with a producer's daughter—inexplicable because for several years he had been homosexual. He continued his secret life after the marriage, prowling the waterfront at night in search of partners, and after the inevitable breakup Woolrich fled back to Manhattan and his mother. The two of them traveled extensively abroad together during the early 1930s. His only novel of the period, *Manhattan Love Song* (1932), anticipates the motifs of his later suspense fiction with its tale of a love-struck young couple cursed by a malignant fate that leaves one dead and the other desolate. But over the next two years he sold almost nothing and was soon deep in debt, reduced to sneaking into movie houses by the fire doors for his entertainment.

In 1934 Woolrich decided to abandon the "literary" world and concentrate on mystery-suspense fiction. He sold three stories to pulp magazines that year, ten more in 1935, and was soon an established professional whose name was a fixture on the covers of *Black Mask, Detective Fiction Weekly, Dime Detective,* and countless other pulps. For the next quarter-century he lived with his mother in a succession of residential hotels, going out only when it was absolutely essential, trapped in a bizarre love–hate relationship that dominated his external world just as the tortured patterns of the inner world of his fiction reflect the strangler grip in which his mother held him.

The more than 100 stories and novelettes Woolrich sold to the pulps before the end of the thirties are richly varied in type, including quasi-police procedurals, rapid-action whizbangs, and encounters with the occult. But the best and the best known of them are the tales of pure edge-of-the-seat suspense, and even their titles reflect the bleakness and despair of their themes: "I Wouldn't Be in Your Shoes," "Speak to Me of Death," "All at Once, No Alice," "Dusk to Dawn," "Men Must Die," "If I Should Die Before I Wake," "The Living Lie Down with the Dead," "Charlie Won't Be Home Tonight," "You'll Neve See Me Again." These and dozens of other Woolrich suspense stories evoke with awesome power the desperation of those who walk the city's darkened streets and the terror that lurks at noonday in commonplace settings. In his hands even such clichéd storylines as the race to save the innocent man from the electric chair and the amnesiac searching for his lost self resonate with human anguish. Woolrich's world is a feverish place where the prevailing emotions are loneliness and fear and the prevailing action a race against time and death. His most characteristic detective stories end with the discovery that no rational account of events is possible, and his suspense stories tend to close not with the dissipation of the terror but with its omnipresence.

The typical Woolrich settings are the seedy hotel, the cheap dance hall, the rundown movie house, and the precinct station backroom. The dominant reality in his world, at least during the thirties, is the Depression, and Woolrich has no peers when it comes to putting us inside the life of a frightened little guy in a tiny apartment with no money, no job, a hungry wife and children, and anxiety consuming him like a cancer. If a Woolrich protagonist is in love, the beloved is likely to vanish in such a way that the protagonist not only can't find her but can't convince anyone that she ever existed. Or, in another classic Woolrich situation, the protagonist comes to after a blackout (caused by amnesia, drugs, hypnosis, or whatever) and little by little becomes convinced that he has committed a murder or other crime while out of himself. The police are rarely sympathetic, for they are the earthly counterparts of the malignant powers that delight in savaging us, and their primary function is to torment the helpless. All we can do about this nightmare world is to create, if we can, a few islands of love and trust to help us forget. But love dies while the lovers go on living, and Woolrich is a master at portraying the corrosion of a relationship between two people. Although he often wrote about the horrors both love and lovelessness can inspire, there are few irredeemably evil characters in his stories, for if one loves or needs love, or is at the brink of destruction, Woolrich identifies with that person no matter what crimes he or she might also have committed. Technically, many of his stories are awful, but like the playwrights of the Absurd, Woolrich uses a senseless tale to hold the mirror to a senseless universe. Some of his tales, indeed, end quite happily (usually thanks to outlandish coincidence), but there are no series characters in his work, and the reader can never know in advance whether a particular story will be light or dark, whether a particular protagonist will end triumphant or dismembered. This is one of the reasons that his stories are so hauntingly suspenseful.

So much for the motifs, beliefs, and devices at the core of Woolrich's fiction. In 1940 he joined the migration of pulp mystery writers from lurid-covered magazines to hardcover books, and with his first suspense novel, *The Bride Wore Black* (1940), he launched his so-called Black Series, which influenced the French *roman noir* and the development of the bleak Hollywood crime movies of the forties, which the French have labeled *film noir*. Julie Killeen, whose husband was killed on the church steps moments after their marriage, spends years tracking down and systematically murdering the drunk driver and his four cronies whom she holds responsible for the beloved's death. Eventually she is herself stalked through the years by homicide cop Lew Wanger, and when their paths finally converge both hunters find themselves in the presence of the malignant powers.

The second novel in the cycle was *The Black Curtain* (1941), the masterpiece on the overworked subject of amnesia. Frank Townsend recovers from a three-years' loss of memory, becomes obsessed with the determination to learn who and what he was during those missing years, and finds love, hate, and a murder charge waiting for him behind the curtain. Next came *Black Alibi* (1942), a terror novel about a killer jaguar menacing a large South American city, while a lone Anglo hunts a human murderer who may be hiding behind the jaguar's claws.

The fourth novel in the cycle, which you are about to read, is the one I consider the best of the Black books, and one of the strongest, most wrenching and bizarre works in the Woolrich canon. *The Black Angel* (1943) deals with a terrified young wife's race against time to prove that her convicted husband did not murder his girl friend and that some other man in the dead woman's life is guilty. Writing in the first person, from the wife's viewpoint—a huge risk indeed for a hopelessly introverted man who never knew a woman intimately—Woolrich makes us feel her love and anguish, her terror and desperation, her obsessions that grow to madness inside her like a cancer as she destroys herself to get her man back from Mister Death.

The roots of the novel extend deep into Woolrich's past as a writer and a man. Ladd Mason's description of the girl Patsy, who was his first love, is a substantially accurate portrait of Woolrich's own first love, a girl on whom he had a teen-age crush before he understood his own homosexuality, and whom he discusses at great length in his unfinished and unpublished autobiography, *The Blues of a Lifetime.* The basic storyline is a kind of extension of Woolrich's 1932 novel *Manhattan Love Song,* in which the narrator Wade was on the brink of leaving his wife for the mysterious and enigmatic Bernice Pascal when Bernice was murdered and Wade wrongly convicted of the crime. But the prior work from which Woolrich borrowed the most for *The Black Angel* was a very early and never-since-reprinted pulp story that deserves discussion in detail.

In "Murder in Wax" (*Dime Detective,* March 1, 1935) Woolrich recycled the situation with which *Manhattan Love Song* ended—indeed the dead woman's name is Bernice Pascal in both works—but this time he explored it from the viewpoint of the defendant's wife. "He always called me Angel Face," the story begins. But this is a hardboiled angel indeed, the first and one of the strangest in the gallery of women Woolrich wrote about in the first person. While her husband is waiting to be executed, she finds a matchbook monogrammed TV in the lining of his jacket and concludes at once with no evidence at all that her husband had picked it up in Bernice's apartment. Hoping to pin the murder on the mysterious TV, she tracks down Bernice's address book and finds the name and number of one Tommy Vaillant. She proceeds to enter the man's life as destroying angel, complete with hidden tape-recording apparatus, making love to him and waiting desperately for the moment when he will let his guard down and talk about his connection with Bernice. When he does, she is ready—and manages to edit the tape so that his damaging but inconclusive admissions sound like an outright confession to the murder. Then, just before taking the doctored tape to the police, she tips off Tommy to leave town and avoid arrest. "I—I sort of like you, Tom," she tells him. In an O. Henry twist at the end of the story, which contradicts a good deal of what has gone before, we learn exactly why she let Tommy escape *and* how she knew her husband was innocent, namely that she herself killed Bernice.

The destroying angel motif was one of Woolrich's favorites, and in 1940 he used it again in *The Bride Wore Black:* This time at the center of an episodic novel in which, for reasons not revealed until the end, the angel figure invades the lives of a variety of emotionally vulnerable men and destroys each of them. That is also the general nature of the action in *The Black Angel,* except that this time, by telling us in the first chapter of the forces by which the loving-destroying angel is driven, he makes it possible for us to empathize with her and shudder at what she does to herself and others in the holy name of love. The outline of the story comes largely from "Murder in Wax," but every person and event is reshaped into something new and different and unspeakably haunting.

The novel was immensely successful and, like every other book in the Black series, was picked up by other media almost at once. Without bothering to credit Woolrich for the source novel, CBS Radio's *Suspense* for October 19, 1944, broadcast a thirty-minute adaptation by Robert L. Richards entitled "Eve," starring Nancy Kelly. Small wonder Woolrich wasn't credited: the play touched base with the book only at rare moments. (A short-story version of the radio play was published in *Suspense Mystery Magazine*, December 1946.)

Far more successful, indeed to my taste the best movie ever taken from a Woolrich novel, was the Universal picture *Black Angel* (1946), directed by Roy William Neill, who had been responsible for most of that studio's Sherlock Holmes films with Basil Rathbone and Nigel Bruce. June Vincent starred in the title role, with Dan Duryea as a Martin Blair transformed from a heartbroken drunk into what amounts to a surrogate for Woolrich himself. Broderick Crawford played Lieutenant Flood and Peter Lorre was

Marco, the film's substitute for the lovestruck gambler McKee. Neill and screenplay writer Roy Chanslor made an extremely free adaptation of the Woolrich novel, but one that somehow stayed so true to the dark spirit of the source that it stands out as one of the finest examples of *film noir* ever made in the United States. It was Roy William Neill's best picture, and his last. He died the year it was released.

In the 1940s it was customary for movies to be adapted into radio plays as it's common today for them to be adapted into paperback novels. Soon after *Black Angel* came out, a sixty-minute radio version was aired on ABC's *Hour of Mystery* on June 16, 1946. Not to be outdone, CBS' *Suspense* produced a sixty-minute expansion of the earlier half-hour version of "Eve" and broadcast it on January 24, 1948, with June Havoc in the lead. An hour-long live TV drama based on the movie and starring Marilyn Erskine and John Ireland was aired March 28, 1957, on *Lux Video Theater*. But there have been no adaptations since, at least not in the United States, although Woolrich's work diary indicates that at one time he thought or was approached about turning the novel into an opera libretto, to be titled "The Tape-Recording Angel." Certainly the book has enough emotion for several operas.

The Black series resumed with *The Black Path of Fear* (1944), in which the narrator runs away to Havana with an American gangster's wife and the pair are stalked by the vengeful husband, who kills the woman and frames her lover, leaving him a stranger in a strange land, menaced on all sides and fighting for his life. And in the cycle's final novel, *Rendezvous in Black* (1948), Woolrich once again took up the destroying-angel motif but with the sexes reversed: A grief-crazed young man, holding one among a small group of people responsible for his fiancée's death, devotes his life to entering the lives of each of that group in turn, finding out whom each one most loves, and murdering these loved ones so that the person who killed his fiancée will live the grief he lives.

During the early forties Woolrich continued to write stories and novelettes for the pulps, and dozens of his huge backlog of earlier stories were adapted for dramatic radio on series like *Suspense* and *Molle Mystery Theatre.* As the novels increased his reputation, publishers issued numerous hardcover and paperback collections of his shorter tales, and many of his books and stories were made into *films noir* of the forties (although the most famous Woolrich-based film, Alfred Hitchcock's *Rear Window*, was made in 1954). As if all this activity were not enough, Woolrich continued to write more novels, too many for publication under a single byline, so that he adopted the pseudonyms of William Irish and (his own two middle names) George Hopley for some of his most suspenseful books.

The Irish byline debuted in *Phantom Lady* (1942), in which an innocent man is sentenced to die for the murder of his wife, while his two best friends race the clock to find the apparently nonexistent woman who can give the husband an alibi. The second Irish, *Deadline at Dawn* (1944), is another clock-race story, with a desperate young couple given until sunrise to clear themselves of a murder charge and escape the web of the city. In *Night Has a Thousand Eyes* (1945), as by Hopley, the suspense rises to unbearable pitch as a simple-minded recluse with uncanny powers predicts a millionaire's imminent death by the jaws of a lion, and the doomed man's daughter and a sympathetic cop struggle to avert a destiny that they suspect, and soon come to hope, was conceived by a merely human power. *Waltz into Darkness* (1947), also written as Irish, is set in New Orleans around 1880 and tells of the hopeless love affair between an unbearably lonely man and an impossibly evil woman. And in the last Irish novel of the forties, *I Married a Dead Man* (1948), a woman with nothing to live for, fleeing from her sadistic husband, is injured in a train wreck, is mistaken for another woman with everything to live for who was killed in the crackup, grasps this heaven-sent chance to start life over with a new identity, falls in love again, and is destroyed by malignant powers along with the man she loves.

Despite overwhelming financial and critical success, Woolrich's personal situation remained as wretched as ever. His mother's prolonged illnesses seemed to paralyze his ability to write, and after 1948 he published very little: one minor novel under each of his three bylines in 1950–51 and a few short stories. That he was remembered at all during the fifties is largely due to Ellery Queen (Frederic Dannay), who reprinted a quantity of Woolrich's pulp tales in *Ellery Queen's Mystery Magazine*. But Woolrich and his mother continued to live in comfortable isolation, for his magazine tales proved to be as adaptable to television as they had been to radio a decade earlier, and series like *Ford Theater, Alfred Hitchcock Presents*, and *Schlitz Playhouse of Stars* frequently presented thirty-minute filmed versions of his stories. Indeed even the prestigious *Playhouse 90* made use of Woolrich, turning *Rendezvous in Black* into a feature-length teledrama (broadcast October 25, 1956) starring Franchot Tone, Laraine Day, and Boris Karloff.

When his mother died, in 1957, Woolrich cracked. Diabetic, alcoholic, wracked by self-contempt, and alone, he dragged out the last years of his life. He continued to write but left unfinished much more than he ever completed, and the only new work that saw print in his last years was a handful of final "tales of love and despair." He developed gangrene in his leg and let it go untended for so long that when he finally sought medical help, the doctor had no choice but to amputate. After the operation he lived in a wheelchair, unable to learn how to walk on an artificial leg. On September 25, 1968, he died of a stroke, leaving unfinished two novels, a collection of short stories, and an autobiography. He had prepared a long list of titles for stories he'd never even begun, and one of these captures his bleak world view in a single phrase: "First You Dream, Then You Die." He left no survivors, and only a tiny handful of people attended his funeral. His estate of nearly a million dollars was bequeathed in trust to Columbia University, where his literary career had begun, to establish a scholarship fund for students of creative writing. The fund is named for Woolrich's mother.

"I was only trying to cheat death," he wrote in a fragment found among his papers. "I was only trying to surmount for a little while the darkness that all my life I surely knew was going to come rolling in on me some day and obliterate me. I was only trying to stay alive a little brief while longer, after I was already gone." Trapped in a wretched psychological environment and gifted, or cursed, with an understanding of his own and everyone's trappedness, he shaped his solitude into stories that will haunt our descendants as they haunted our forebears. He could not escape death, but the world he imagined will.

ANGEL WITH WHISK BROOM

He always called me "Angel Face." That was his name for me when we were by ourselves. That was a special thing, from him to me. He'd bring his face down close to mine and say it low. He'd say he wondered where I got it, that angel face. And things like that your husband says to you.

Then all at once it stopped. And before I knew it, it was weeks since I'd heard it. I waited for it to come again and wondered why it didn't. Then that stopped too.

His blue suit was missing from the closet, and that was strange. That was my job, to send things to the cleaner. I worked my way a little deeper in along the hangers. To the left, his side of the closet.

His gray one was missing too, and that was stranger still. Two suits at once? That was all he had, except the one that he was wearing.

If there hadn't already been one or two little things before this it would have been different. It would have been just a case of a couple of his suits gone from the closet. But there had already been one or two little things before this. And that made it something else again.

A lie now and then where there was no reason for a lie. There was the evening he'd spent with one of the fellows, had a few beers too many. No harm in that. I'd told him so. I'd said, "I didn't ask you, Kirk. You're the one is telling me." Then, only a week or so later, when his companion of that particular night happened to be up in our apartment and I laughingly referred to the incident, why did he develop such a blank, puzzled look and give such a cagey, noncommittal answer? Until Kirk gave him a little signal on the side, which I pretended not to see, that seemed to work wonders with his powers of recollection.

Then there was the powder compact. He'd picked it up on the street and left it in the pocket of his overcoat. He saw me looking at it and he told me how he'd happened to find it. People do lose compacts. Even solid gold ones inscribed "To Mia from Craig."

But then, on the very next day after that, no compact any more. I asked him what had become of it. "Oh, I got rid of it," he said offhandedly.

But it had been gold, hadn't it? I tried to suggest.

"Nah," he disabused me. "I thought so too, but I had a jeweler test it for me. It was just gilt metal. So I left it there."

But would they be likely to stamp the symbol "14K" on anything that wasn't gold, as they had on this? I wondered privately. I didn't tell him that I'd glimpsed that on it. I don't know why. When you have an uneasy feeling that happiness is beginning to slip through your fingers you hang on as tightly as you can; you don't give it an added push away from you.

Little things like that, they made this matter of the two suits something else again, at sight.

But more than anything else, no "Angel Face" for weeks now. Only Alberta, that formal Alberta, never previously used, when he had anything to say to me.

They say everyone has to go through it at least once. They say the best is to let it ride, seem not to notice, and it will work itself out. They say. Try and do it sometime—when you're twenty-two and it's your first experience with it.

I'm a coward, I guess. I didn't tell Kirk I'd been to

the jeweler where he said he'd left the compact, to try to reclaim it or at least make sure that it *wasn't* gold and he wasn't cheating Kirk. "What compact?" the jeweler said. "Nobody's been in here with any compact." He might have been lying; I couldn't tell. Maybe I didn't want to know for sure.

What an odd name, Mia, I thought on the way back.

I saw her later. I couldn't tell for sure that it was the same person. It might have been somebody else with the same first name. But it was such a rare name. It seemed impossible that there could be more than just one person in the entire city with just that name. It was a publicity picture on the theatrical page of the evening paper. You know, that sort of thing they use at random to fill up space and not because of any intrinsic news value.

I remember I clipped the thing out, with the sort of morbid curiosity that makes you do those things, and slipped it under the lining paper in the bureau drawer, where no one but me was ever likely to find it.

It mightn't have even been the same person, for all I knew. But that was such an unusual, such a seldom-encountered first name.

I didn't try to talk to him about it. I was afraid to risk it. I buried my head in the sand like an ostrich, hoping it would blow over, go away, I wouldn't have to face it.

And now this business of the suits, and here it was anyway.

I turned away from the closet, white in the face. I went to the storage one in the hall, where he kept his valise empty and unlocked between business trips. I crouched down beside it, and the latch tongues wouldn't open; they were locked. I put my hand through the grip and tried to lift it clear of the floor, and it nearly pulled my arm out of joint, it weighed so much. Everything in it already, ready to go.

I let it down with a thump. It seemed to swim around a little, like a big leather boat, on the lake my eyes made. I said to myself: "It's not what you think. It's just a business trip for the firm." But then why hadn't he told me? He always told me. He always let me do the packing for him.

I wondered when he'd found the time to do it. Probably that very morning; I'd found him up ahead of me. But more than that, even, I wondered how he'd found the heart to do it.

Something I'd once heard came back to me: "They're all cowards about having a parting scene. They'll grapple with an armed burglar barehanded, but there isn't one of them that won't slink out sooner than face a final good-by with a woman."

I found myself by the phone, and I'd just finished dialing his office number. That whispered plea you heard in the waiting silence, that was me. "Make it a business trip. Oh, please, don't let it be anything else."

I asked the big boss's secretary. She was nice. I'd met her once or twice. And, luckily, Kirk didn't happen to be in just then; that gave me the excuse to ask her instead.

"You don't happen to know just how soon he'll be going away again for Mr. Jacobs, do you? I forgot to ask him before he left this morning, and I happened to be going over some of his clothes just now and wondered if I should put them away in tar paper or wait a while in case he needs them to take with him."

I wondered if that sounded as lame to her as it did to me.

"You don't need to worry about that," she said. "He won't be going out again for months to come. Not until late spring. Everything's dead right now. I heard Mr. Jacobs say so yesterday."

It was like something cold trickling into my ear from the receiver. I said a thing or two after that, but it was only sheer momentum that kept me talking; there wasn't really anything more to say.

I didn't even say good-by. She did, in a way. A way that showed she was no fool. Just before she hung up I heard her murmur almost compassionately, "Don't let it get you too much, honey."

I don't remember what I did for a while after that. I think I just sat there on the telephone bench. Then outward movement came back again, slowly at first, in spurts and starts that finally worked themselves up into a flurry of action ending in a crashing exit.

I went in and opened the bureau drawer. I turned back the dust-paper lining and picked up that thing I'd taken out of the papers weeks before.

I knew what she looked like by heart by this time. That scrap of newspaper she was on should have been worn ragged by now, the number of times I'd pulled it out and looked at it when I was alone in the place.

She looked as lovely as only a publicity photograph can make them look. Probably one and a half times as lovely as she really was. She was brunette, as the Rachel powder in the compact had said she would be. Her eyes were wide and languorous, and her lips had a sullen, pouty look. She looked good to stay away from, but then I'm not a man; probably it worked in reverse with them. She was indicating a rose on her shoulder with one slender, upcurved hand. What supported it, the rose, was uncertain. There wasn't a sign of anything, until the lower frame of the picture cut across her just a moment too late. The caption below it read: "Mia Mercer, one of the attractions appearing nightly at Dave Hennessey's Hermitage."

This time I didn't put it back. I hung onto it. I didn't want to hang onto her photograph; it was him I wanted to hang onto. I took it out to the kitchen with me and propped it up against something. I reached blindly all along the upper-case cupboards until I'd located and toppled down that bottle of ceremonial gin of his. I didn't know very much—yet—about the procedure of using it. That was his province, not mine. He was very good at fixing it with things like mint and lemon, but I didn't want cordiality now; I wanted courage. I let out a little into the jigger glass and gulped it down. I thought some plaster had fallen off the ceiling and hit me on the chest for a minute.

I sat there staring at her picture and hating her hard. I let a little more out and gulped that. The plaster didn't hit me this time. I started to feel a slow glow inside me instead. I sat there and stared at her some more.

I guess it was the gin made me decide to do it. It must have been. The gin made everything seem so easy, so plausible. I would have shrunk from it, unstimulated. It would have seemed like something out of *East Lynne* or *Camille*. The gin made it seem logical, perfectly natural, and by no means a futile thing to do.

I went in and started to get dressed. Dressed for calling, that is. I took more pains dressing for her than I ever had dressing for him. And yet he was the one I was dressing for, in a roundabout way. I had to be careful. Enemy eyes.

Finally I was ready and I got out fast. I knew if I didn't go quickly I'd never have the nerve to go at all. The two jiggers of gin were wearing off, so I stopped just long enough to gulp a third and last to see me through.

Then I went out and closed the door behind me, and for the first time in four years I didn't give a damn what there was going to be for supper.

2

VISITING ANGEL

THEY'D TOLD ME OVER at that Hermitage place that this was where it was. It was one of those re-modeled private residences that have been converted into apartments. But of the expensive, not the cheap, variety. It was the type of place that offers extreme privacy. No attendants in the lobby, an automatic elevator. The door was the self-locking kind. Yes, I thought bitterly, she'd want extreme privacy.

I went into the small forward vestibule and found her name beside one of the small door buttons, but before I could put my finger to it a delivery boy bearing an empty box came out. He politely held the door for me, so I got in without having to telegraph my punch and run the risk of being refused admittance from below.

A moment later I was standing before her inner door on the second floor. And now that I was there I wanted to be back home again; I wanted to be anywhere but where I was. By that time the false courage of the double jiggerful of gin had had time to wear off, and I saw this for the preposterous, unlikely to succeed thing it was again. The only reason I didn't turn around and scuttle off again before she had time to come out and confront me was that, now that I was right there out-side the door, it seemed senseless not to wait long enough at least to find out if I had the right person or not. I was almost certain I did have by now. I didn't like a remark they'd let drop at that Hermitage place when I'd been there just now. Miss Mercer had turned in her notice only two or three days ago. She was going away on a short vacation, she'd said. Yeah? I thought bitterly. On whose time?

The hopelessness of the thing I was trying to do came over me again. I put my hand distractedly to my forehead and thought, "What do I expect to get from this? What good will it do?"

She was taking a long time to answer. My courage was oozing out of me by the minute. If I had to wait much longer for the showdown I wouldn't be able to open my mouth at all. This was one of those things you had to do at white heat. Once you stopped and let yourself cool off you couldn't go through with it any more. I rang again, longer, harder, louder.

She wasn't in.

I gave the knob a twist only as a symptom of frustration. The door wavered loosely inward an inch or two. It must have been off the latch the whole time. I widened the gap and put my face to it. I could see a strip of room about a foot wide, splashed with a lot of vivid turquoise-blue color.

I cleared my throat. I even spoke aloud. I said, "I beg your pardon?" No one answered.

Not finding her in at the moment emboldened me. I forgot about my recent inclination to retreat. I stepped inside, closed the door softly behind me, stood there for a moment like that, with my hand resting on the knob. Then I lingeringly took it off, and entry was complete.

Enemy territory, I thought.

I took it all in. I thought: "So this is how they live when they—live like this." It was a decorator's job, that outside room. Almost like a stage setting. Swell to look at, from the door like this, but no good for living in. Too florid. It was flooded with this acutely vivid turquoise-blue color: upholstery, carpet, drapes, lamp shades. Either she or the decorator had a passion for it. Then all over, like flecks of blood, there were dabs of vermillion.

I shook my head, not so much in moral condemnation as in common, ordinary, everyday sense of value. It wasn't worth it; it was no bargain; she was being overcharged. My way was the better way of the two; worry about a bill now and then, but at least be able to usher your company out when you felt like it, lock the door after them for the night. Every room, I felt to myself, looking around, ought to have at least *one* ugly or dilapidated piece of furniture in it. That makes an honest room of it, not a bandbox like this.

I moved a little deeper inward. My own reflection glided unexpectedly across a mirror I hadn't noticed and gave me a guilty little shock, until I'd swerved and recognized myself. I looked out of place here, even in a mirror. The suburbs trespassing on the bright-light belt. Washington Heights taking a peek in on Sutton Place. "Angel Face," he called me. Well, maybe, but a sort of insipid, timid angel right then. Those eyes couldn't have looked mysterious if they'd tried, only sort of—guileless, I suppose you'd call it.

An arched opening into the next room came slipping toward me as I slipped toward it. Through it I could see a section of boudoir, and if the note in here was turquoise blue, the note in there was a sort of lush coral pink. It was drenched with it, even the satin-quilted walls.

I could see the foot of a coral satin chaise longue sticking out, with a rumpled coverlet on it and a discarded bedroom slipper or mule lying under it toe up. She must have dressed in a hurry.

I shifted back and forth outside there, without going any nearer at first, until I could scan both of the side walls from where I was. There was no one in there. This was just a reflex precaution; I knew I would have been heard and challenged long ago if anyone had been in there.

I lingered outside a moment or two longer. For some strange reason it seemed less reprehensible to be caught trespassing in her living room than to be caught tres-

passing in the sanctum sanctorum of her boudoir. I
roamed aimlessly around, looking over at the door by
which I had entered every other moment. I strayed here
and there, touching this, tapping that, poising three fingers in tripod formation on something else as I passed
by. That was the only outward sign of the tension I was
under.

Everything was monogrammed. That seemed to be
another fetish of hers. There must have been a time she
hadn't had much of anything, and now that she had
plenty of everything she had to show whom it belonged
to; she couldn't let the observer take it for granted.
She'd thought up a symbol of two *M*s overlapping one
another, so that they looked like a single capital with
four downward stems. She must have stayed up all one
night to arrive at *that* brilliant inspiration, I reflected.
A sixth-grade school kid could have rigged up something more original in ten minutes flat.

It had been sprinkled around wholesale. My only
surprise was it had been left off the steam radiators
and windowpanes and such. It was on cigarette boxes
and on the cigarettes inside them and on matchsafes and
worked into the corners of cushions and—

Suddenly the telephone began to ring someplace right
there in the room with me. They use the expression
"jumping out of your shoes." I didn't jump out of mine,
but if they weren't actually clear of the plushy carpet
for a moment they felt as though they were, with the
frightened heave I gave.

I stood perfectly still for a minute, waiting for it to
quit. It didn't. It kept on and kept on, until finally I
couldn't stand it any more. What made it worse was I
couldn't locate where it was at first, even by the sound.
It was someplace near by, right in the same room with
me, but there was no sign of it.

I went looking around high and low for it, with furtive, trembling haste. It seemed to grow clearer over in
a certain corner where there was a turquoise-lacquered
object that might have been a chest of drawers. I

clawed at the mid-section of it, and a little slab came down in desk formation. There it was behind that, lacquered turquoise to match everything else, and bleating like something smothering to death. Beside it was a little address book, with its pliable leather cover dyed the same inevitable color and stamped with the same inevitable monogram.

I lifted the receiver finally, to try to silence it in that way. Then, because I already held it in my hand, I put it to my ear, stood quiet with it like that.

A man's voice said instantly, and with a sort of hurried intimacy, "Hello, Mia?" And then over again, because there was no answer from my end. "Hello, Mia?"

That voice. I would have known his voice anywhere. I put my free hand down on the desk slab and braked myself against it while I curved over weakly above it, like when you have a pain in your stomach.

"Hello?" he kept saying. "Hello, Mia?"

The colors in the room ran a little; a drop or two of turquoise seemed to swim around in my eyes. In this damn place you even shed turquoise teardrops.

I didn't have the heart for any cheap surprises, for any punishing triumphs. I didn't want to be cruel to him. He was being cruel enough for the two of us. I put it down again quietly, almost tenderly.

I didn't have to worry about whether I had the right person or not now any more.

Crazy thoughts without logic took turns slashing at me. "Why do they get you to learn to love them, if this is how they're going to treat you after you do? Why do they come around you when you're seventeen and aren't doing anything to them, are just minding your own business, getting along all right without them, if this is how they're going to act when you're twenty-two? Why don't they leave you *alone?*" I sobbed deep inside where it couldn't be heard. "Why don't they leave you *alone* if they don't mean it?"

I walked haphazardly back toward the arched opening leading to the next room again. I think I thought it

was the outside door. Then when I noticed what it was
I stopped, to turn and go the other way.

But in there, on the vanity table in a crystal frame, I
could see her picture smiling mockingly at me, as if to
say: "You see? Aren't you sorry you came around here
now? If you hadn't you still wouldn't have been sure."
And hate came on, and bitterness came on, and I
strode forward, to go to it and pick it up. I suppose to
smash it, or some other equally childish thing.

I didn't watch where I was going and I stumbled over
something as I made my way around the foot of the impending chaise longue.

A foot, a leg, projecting from the other side of it.
What I had taken to be a discarded boudoir slipper
until now. Even from where I was standing at the moment, but for the hideous clarity of that one unmistakable silk-clad limb, it still looked like a tumbled mass
of boudoir pillows, perhaps a discarded negligee and
a chaise coverlet, all intermingled and allowed to fall in
a neglected heap to the floor, there in that one place.

I suppose I gave a smothered scream. I don't remember. I got down waveringly and edged aside one of
the pillows. Coral sateen it was, and so soft, so harmless. But someone had smothered her to death with it.

Though no man was the breath of her life, one of
them had taken the breath of her life away, and she was
dead.

I was sorry I'd tampered with that concealing pillow.
For that grimacing, suffused mask with the protruding
tongue didn't look at all like the photograph in the
crystal frame over there any longer.

I got up again, cold and sick and frightened. I'd
never seen a dead human being before. I couldn't seem
to turn my eyes away. I retreated stealthily backward, a
step at a time, as if afraid that if I dared to turn my
back on her she'd rise up and come after me.

When I had regained the archway between the rooms
and had at least a head start, then panic came on briefly.
The panic of any young, unversed, not very bright

thing. I made several confused half turns, this way and that; then I located the door and sped for it, my frightened mind screaming: "Let me out of here! I want to get out of here! I don't want to stay in this place—with *her!*"

Then at the last moment, just as I'd reached the door, the thought of Kirk came to me, and some sort of protective instinct—I don't know what it was—brought me up short, held me there a moment.

They mustn't connect him with her. They mustn't know he'd known her or— I turned and saw the phone standing there across the room with the slab let down before it the way I'd left it. And next to it that little private address book of hers. I went running over and picked it up and leafed through it. There it was, on the *M* page, big as life. His name and office number.

First I was just going to tear the page out bodily and leave the rest behind. Then I realized that maybe they would notice that; it would look too incriminating. So I thrust the whole booklet into my handbag intact and snapped it closed on it. They weren't going to find *his* name around here, not if I could help it.

I looked around questioningly. There wasn't anything else out here that I could see that might involve him, and not even for his sake could I have gone back into that—that other room a second time.

I told myself I'd better get out of here fast myself. Somebody was liable to come along at any moment and—

Even so, I knew enough not to bolt out without reconnoitering first and thereby running a risk of blundering head-on into someone on the outside. It's uncanny how quickly your instincts, if left to their own guidance, will adapt themselves even to the most bizarre, unlooked-for situations, as though you were used to meeting those situations every day in your life. Accordingly, instead of throwing the door open forthwith, I stood there listening intently beside it for several moments before making any further move.

It was because I stood there motionless like that, and with my head tilted at just a certain angle, that I had a chance to become aware of this fleck of color against the creamy expanse of the door. It was in the seam, the opposite one where the hinges were located, and it was just over the lower one of these, as though it had sidled downward until the hinge had blocked its further descent.

Even after it had caught my eye it meant nothing; there was not enough of it to convey any meaning in my present state of tension and anxiety to get out. Only, as I turned the knob and slowly drew the door inward from its frame, motion, and motion of a dab of color, caught my eye back to where it had been again, and I saw that it had fallen out with the reverse widening of the seam at that end and now lay on the floor, a postage-stamp-size square from where I stood. I reached down and picked it up, and it was only then that I could make out what it actually was.

It was simply the pasteboard cover of a match folder, or rather half the pasteboard cover of a match folder, torn off, then folded still again to smaller size and thrust into that seam to serve as a wedge. Its purpose obviously had been to retard the swing of the door slightly so that, though it might give the appearance of being closed, the latch tongue would fail by a fraction of an inch to meet and thrust into the socket meant to hold it. In other words, it could be reopened later and at will from the outside, simply by turning the knob, as I had done myself.

It had clung to the seam during three entire passages, I felt sure: the entrance and exit of whoever had done this to her, and then my own entrance just now, only to be finally dislodged when I disturbed the door a fourth time, to leave. Until now, apparently, it had simply slid lower down within the seam until the hinge blocked it off.

To my novice's mind it seemed for a minute a great, a dazzling clue, but then as I breathlessly unpleated it my excited hopes died again and I saw that it was nothing, told nothing, except what was implicit in its being there in the first place.

It was one of hers. It had the ubiquitous *M* on it. It was blue, but of a darker shade than the turquoise she favored so. It must have been a leftover from some previous color scheme that had preceded the turquoise deluge. I was about to throw it back again where it had been, let them find it for themselves, make what they could of it. And then the thought of fingerprints occurred to my unversed mind, and because I had already handled it generously and had a layman's typical awe of that mystic science, I thrust it instead into my handbag with the address book.

I peered out through the eye-width gap I had made ready in the door. There was no one in sight. I stepped quickly outside and closed the door after me. There was a staircase beside the elevator, and I chose that in preference to the car, as being both quicker and more secretive. There was no one below either. It was a tactfully serviced building.

I opened the street door and came outside, and with the first fresh air a sense of unreality that I had been where I had been, had seen what I had seen, came over me overpoweringly. I walked quickly away from that bad place without looking back. I was frightened and sick and all the things you are after such a thing, but over and above everything else there was a persistent refrain running through my mind: "I have him back again now. *She* can't take him from me ever, ever again."

For a moment I was glad he wasn't there yet when I got home. For a moment or two only. I needed time, a little time to myself, to get over this thing, to pull myself together after it. I had the creeps. My hands were cold and clammy, and every few minutes I'd tremble uncontrollably, then stop again as suddenly. I took off the carefully selected outfit I'd worn and put it away out of my sight. It hadn't been appreciated.

I began to feel better, grow calmer, as soon as the outward vestiges of the horrible expedition had disappeared from view. And then suddenly, just as I was about to brew myself a cup of black coffee to complete the restorative process, fright struck again. But this time full-fledged, direct, and personal, here in the place where I lived, and having to do with me and him. Not the childish fright of some stranger's dead body in a strange place into which I had had no right to venture in the first place. Suddenly I realized what the real thing was to be frightened of.

He might go over there and become hopelessly enmeshed. I must get hold of him, warn him not to go near there, to stay away. He had already tried to reach her on the telephone right while I was in the place. He might have repeated that again, since I'd come away. And then, that failing, he might go there himself in person.

Even while I dropped what I'd been doing as suddenly as though I'd been burned, fled out to our telephone, I couldn't understand how I'd failed to take this into account until now. I had even taken the precaution of removing her address book with his name in it, yet it had never occurred to me to take the greatest precaution of all: to forewarn him. My mind must have somehow slipped a cog. Just because I was aware of what had happened to her I seemed to have taken it for granted that he was too. How could he be, until he'd gone there and stumbled on her, just as I had myself?

I was dialing so fast the slotted wheel made a blur beneath my hand. I shouldn't have waited this long to try to reach him. I still couldn't understand what had made me overlook such a glaring necessity. I should have called him the moment I was out of there, from the first corner drugstore I'd happened upon.

The office girl down there got on again.

My voice was a spasm of sound that had no words in it, only a thought transfer. "Kirk—Mr. Murray—quick!" At last she got it.

She said, "You just missed him. If you'd called only a minute sooner! He passed me on the way out just a moment before you—"

I let my eyes fall slowly closed, sipped in my own breath.

My voice came back again, frayed uncontrollably. "Frances, go after him; see if you can get him back! It's desperately urgent! I've got to speak to him before he leaves that building!"

I knew that place down there; there was a long walk out to the elevators.

She took fright from my fright. "Wait, maybe I can still catch up with him out in the hall!" I heard the clatter she made getting away from the switchboard, even heard the diminishing patter of her footsteps across the floor. He must have still been in sight outside as she flung open the outer office door, because I even heard her call his name. It came back hollowly and from a distance, as something does echoing down a long, empty hallway. "Mr. Murray!"

There was a wait that I thought was never going to be over. The hell with mutual embarrassment; the hell with diffidence; we were down to essentials now; we were down to bedrock, he and I. I'd say, "Kirk, stay away from that woman! Don't ask me whom I mean or how I know! Listen to me now, if you never listened to me before. *Don't go near there!*" And then I'd have to tell him, "She's dead—something's happened to her!" And then, because he'd have to have some direction given to him in that first moment of shock, gently, understandingly, without reproach: "Come home to me; come home where you belong—I'll have some supper for you, and we won't talk about it."

We wouldn't either. No, we wouldn't. Just bring him back to this phone for me now, and I wouldn't talk about it again, even in my heart.

Her steps came back. I could hear her breathing fast from her efforts even before her voice sounded. She was

going to say, "Here he is, Mrs. Murray. I just caught up
with him in ti—"

She said, "I saw him getting on down the hall and I
called to him, but he didn't hear me in time. And before
I could get over there the operator had closed the door.
It must have been an express car; they won't come back
for you no matter how you pound on the glass afterward." And then those oh, most inadequate of words,
when spoken to someone in her death throes: "I'm
sorry, Mrs. Murray."

There was no way I could reach him in time now. He
was going there to that place, and there was no way I
could stop him. The slender thread had snapped. I'd
been given my half an hour's grace, from the time I left
there until the time I got back here, and I'd thrown it
away. And thrown him away with it. And thrown myself away with him.

In the twilight I stumbled around there, like a dimly
focused figure moving through the steam room of a
Turkish bath. That was what it was like inside me,
anyway, no matter what it was like on the outside.
More terrible than anything else was the knowledge
that while I floundered here helplessly, dying by inches,
unable to interfere, to prevent, he was moving steadily
through the streets—on foot, or in a cab, or on a
subway—toward that grim destination. And in my
overheated fancy I could see a grinning death's-head
waiting for him behind that boudoir door, bony arms
stretched out to clutch him in a more terrible embrace
than hers had ever been in life, to twine about him and
never let him go.

Once it occurred to me I might have saved him by
reporting it to the police myself, if I'd only done it in
time. Then at least he would have walked in there after
them, not ahead of them. I could see why I'd shied
away from this until it was already too late, though.
I'd been afraid of bringing on the very thing I wanted
above all to avoid: his involvement. And now it was

too late; I daren't do it now any more; it might only succeed in bringing them there right on his heels.

Dusk had inked into night now, and I still didn't light the lights. What for, what did I want to see? Lights are to see something by, and the only thing I wanted to see was his face. They couldn't show me that because it wasn't here.

A light green circle with twelve slanting eyes, like a kid's outline drawing of a face, peered at me from where the clock was. And all it did was hurt, and hurt, and hurt some more. For a little while there'd been a slim chance that he *might* have intended coming back here first after all; even if only to pick up his packed valise, even if only to say, "Alberta, I'm leaving you." But that slim hope was long since gone now. The eyes on the clock had killed it. It was long past his time for coming home now. He hadn't intended coming here first. It was already the hour for me to do the dishes. It was already the hour for him to tune in the Bob Hope program and sit in there laughing with that choked sound he made when he was laughing to himself.

And the rooms were dark. There was no laughing sound in them, no odor of cigarette smoke. I was alone, a lost, frightened thing straying around, my whole world crumbled away all around me like the shell of an egg.

Once I took the clock and lifted it and squeezed its cold round shape between my hands and shook it as if to wring some pity into it, pleading with it: "Oh, make him come—*please* make him come! Give him back—"

It just tittered, "Tk—tk—tk."

Sometimes I stood by the window, cooling my heated face against the glass. Sometimes I sat still, pressing my eyes against my hands. Sometimes I got up and moved around from room to room, in and out and in again, but never going anywhere. Sometimes I would go to the door and swing it wide and stand there looking for him, as if hoping the draft would sweep him in to me. But it never did; he never came.

It seemed to have been going on for so long. This couldn't be the same night, could it? This must have been some trick arrangement of a week of nights, a month of them, lumped solidly together without any days in between.

Then finally, like an unmistakable warning inside me, came the point at which I knew I couldn't stay on in here any longer. Oh, I'd said to myself I couldn't stand it a hundred times over already, but that was just saying it; this was the real feeling now. This was the strange calm, the lull, that precedes hysteria. I knew if I didn't get out, even if only to roam the streets, I'd begin screaming his name out in another minute, and the neighbors would all open their windows and—

I jammed on my hat in the dark—the first, the last, the only time I ever did it that way. I found my way to the door; I wrenched it open—and there he was, standing right on the other side of it, nearly filling the narrow frame.

It was uncanny; it was almost like mental telepathy. I put my hand up and I touched him where the necktie went down into the vest. He felt so good. So good and solid and *warm* and *present*. I'd never known that gladness was a lot like gin; they both burned like the dickens inside you.

Hysteria deflated into a couple of bedraggled whimpers that crept out and slunk off, as if ashamed of themselves, and that was the end of it.

I reached out with my other hand and threw the switch and lit him up. Lit him up from in front, from inside our place, as well as from that dim light way down the hall.

He'd been standing there like that, in that funny way, looking for his key, I supposed. He almost never could find it at the moment he needed to use it. I could even hear the faint clash of metal as he fumbled for it in his pocket.

He'd been in a fight. As if I cared! He could have been in ten, so long as he'd come back to me now. His

lip was split, and there was a cut over one eye, and a
strand of his hair hung down in a dank fishhook over
his forehead. The only thing that was strangely missing
was the whiff of alcohol to go with it.

I reached up and fondly pushed the fishhook back in
place, but it came right down again. I put both my arms
around his neck, tight, and hid my face against him and
took a great big deep sigh.

I kept waiting to feel his arms close around behind
me, but they didn't. "He's still off me a little," I thought
ruefully.

But I didn't care; he could be sore at me all he
wanted, if he'd only stay with me while he was being
sore.

He shoved me unexpectedly back before him, and
when I looked up in surprise I saw it wasn't he but the
two men who were with him, one on each side, who had
shoved him.

I hadn't seen them until now; the doorway wasn't
terribly wide—and then there'd been *him* to look at.
There was a glistening little chain from his hand to one
of theirs, even though he was holding it in his pocket,
trying to hide it from me. And his other one—well, the
second man was holding that down at his side, with the
cuff all twisted around like a wringer.

But it was that chain; I couldn't take my eyes off it.
It hurt; it was wound so tight around—my heart.

He said to me quite gently, "Don't be frightened,
Alberta. It's all right."

One of the strangers, close beside the two of us said,
"It's all right, is good."

But we only had eyes for one another, even after
they were inside with him and the door was closed. We
stood there, the two of us, in a frightened little world of
our own, with nobody else around.

He said, "They think I—" He stopped and started
over again. "Well, look, there was a—"

"I know, I know about it. It wasn't *you. Tell* them.
Kirk, not you. Tell them."

"Yeah, tell us, Kirk," one said.

We didn't hear them; we didn't even know they were there. One had wandered off, anyway, to look around the place.

"How did you know? The radio—?"

"I was there," I said. "I was right there when you—"

I saw the start of surprise he gave. He reached out with his free hand and touched the extreme corner of my mouth in a sort of caress. But one finger lay across both lips at once, the upper and the lower, so I knew what the caress was for.

A voice from somewhere outside the two of us said, "What'd you just say, lady?"

Kirk said quietly, "She didn't say anything."

His foot slid out a little along the rug, unnoticeably, and touched mine warningly. I had sense enough not to look down.

"She said she heard it on the radio," Kirk said.

"Tell them, Kirk," I kept repeating futilely. It was the only thing I could think of to say.

He smiled at me a little. "I have been, for hours past. It doesn't seem to help." The point was he was coming back to me, more and more every minute; I could feel it. Not from this police business, from *her*, I mean.

"You don't think so, do you?" And when my swimming eyes had told him the best they could, he said: "Well, I have that much at least."

I had him back again.

I turned to the one who had stayed right beside us. He'd had to, because of that little steel chain. "He couldn't have, don't you see?" I even plucked at the chain, childishly trying to get rid of it, but that only brought both their hands up at once in a double gesture that was somehow horrible. "He couldn't have," I kept on saying. "He was at his office. He was at his office until after six. I phoned him there; he'd just left; the girl'll tell you—"

It was like talking to stone. Even his eyes were stone.

They were fixed on me, but they gave no sign of mobility.

The other one came in from the hall. He was carrying Kirk's packed valise with him. "Yeah, here it is," he announced quietly.

The one with us said, "We better let him go, Flood. She says he couldn't have done it." He didn't even crack a smile. He had refined cruelty down to a science. Or maybe he didn't even know he was being cruel at all.

Flood said, with a touch of lazy compassion, a sort of passive tolerance at best, "Aw, don't rib her, Brennan. I've got one of my own home. I know how they are."

"Yeah," Brennan marveled, as though I wasn't within hearing of them at all. "Ain't it wonderful the way they'll go to bat for these guys? They don't even know what it is, where it is, or anything else about it, but right away it couldn't have been him because they say so." He sucked something and it made a pop inside his cheek. "All right, ready? Let's go."

I flung my arm convulsively around Kirk's neck, as if to hold him there with me. Across his shoulder I pleaded to the one called Flood, in whom I thought I'd detected a soft spot: "But he was still at his office after six, don't you see? *I* was over there myself at her place; I was there, I tell you, around five, and she was already—"

Kirk's cuff mate gave me a withering look; he was plainly disgusted by such a transparent prevarication; that was an insult to their intelligences. "Sure," he said dryly, "you were over there. You had tea with her, I suppose. They were going away together tonight, and you dropped in for a sociable farewell visit. Or maybe to help her pack."

And even the one called Flood—I could see by the way he looked at me he didn't take it seriously either— just felt sorry for me. He tried to let me down as gently as he could. "I'm sorry, Mrs. Murray," he said, "that wouldn't help much even if it were so. You see, she—it happened between one and two in the afternoon. We have experts who can give us the time on these things. And Murray here"—you could tell by the tightening up when he pronounced the name and glanced aside at him his feeling sorry ended with me, didn't extend to Kirk— "Murray here may have been back at his office by the time you phoned around six, but he admits that he was over there at the Mercer place just around that very time. In fact, he was seen leaving the building at a quarter of two, so there's no virtue in his either admitting or denying it."

Kirk's breath said, soft beside my ear in rueful tenderness, "Don't say that any more, about you going there. Please, for me, won't you? Thanks just the same." I saw that he didn't believe me himself, now that he'd thought twice about it, any more than the other two did. Masculine minds seem to run in the same groove in certain situations.

"I couldn't get in; she didn't answer the bell," he went on. "So I waited a minute or two, and then I went away again." But this was to them, over the top of my head, not to me. He was ashamed to address me directly about it because of the implication.

Brennan suddenly raised his own hand. To show me Kirk's hand, by bringing it up automatically like that along with his. There were a number of varying red streaks on the back of it.

"Her cat did that," Kirk said, continuing to address them. "I've told you where those came from over and over."

Brennan said to Flood: "She wouldn't let him in, but her cat raked his hand."

"It was outside in the hall; it had gotten out in some way. When I tried to grab it, it slashed at me and ran away. It acted like something had frightened it. But it was always running out like that, beating it up to the roof and places, so I let it go—"

"Good alibi, that cat," Brennan said. He let their hands drop again. "But not good enough. Come on." He gave his wrist a directional jerk that tautened the links. Kirk had to turn in answer to it. It did something to me, to see him turn in involuntary obedience like that. The way a dog does on a leash.

I tried to draw his face down to mine, press it to me, but his cheek slipped away and was gone; I couldn't hold it.

They were taking him out the door. "Ah, wait," I pleaded. "Won't he need something? Let me give him something to take with him."

I ran into the bedroom, looked around blindly, snatched up something at random from underneath one of the bed pillows. I think it was a pair of striped pajamas; I'm not sure.

I know, I know; it was a silly thing to do, but I'd never had my husband taken away from me for murder before; I hadn't learned the proper decorum.

I ran back with them, and when I got there the door was standing open and the hallway beyond was empty. They hadn't waited; they were gone.

I stood there in the open doorway, and the rolled-up pajamas dropped disconsolately to the floor at my feet and lay there.

3

ANNOUNCEMENT OF WIDOWHOOD

I COULDN'T BELIEVE IT was all over and done with already as I sat there in Benedict's office waiting for him to come back. The long dragging months seemed to have flashed by like minutes. I had a childish notion that they'd left something out, that they'd rushed things through more than they had a right to, more than they did with others. Benedict said no, and the calendar said no, but it couldn't be that this was the last of it, that there was nothing more after this. Why, it was only yesterday that he was still sitting there across the table from me, grumbling: "Gee, what d'ye *do* to this coffee? You could plant geraniums in it!" Why, it was only last night, wasn't it, that they'd taken him away from me, and I'd come running to the door a minute too late, and a pair of his rolled-up pajamas had fallen to the floor and remained there at my feet?

And now it was over already. It had been since that hideous day last week. This, today, was just anticlimax, the finishing touch. That was why Benedict had been able to persuade me to wait here in his office instead of going down there and being present in the chambers. He'd wanted me to stay home altogether, but I couldn't have endured that. At least here, at this halfway stop, I could hear it a little sooner—what I knew already.

Benedict's office girl was a sympathetic young thing. She sat there beside me on a hard little wall bench in his reception room with her arm around me, offering me a drink of water from time to time. I guess she didn't know what else to do for me. She kept talking away a blue streak, trying to be encouraging.

"It's just a technicality. I know it frightens people so, but it isn't final; it isn't irrevocable. It's just a legal phrase that's automatically spoken in all these cases. Honey, I've seen Mr. Benedict get more people off on appeals and reversals. Haven't *you*, Mort? How about it, Mort?"

Mort was a young law clerk who worked in the office. He was sympathetic too. He'd go away and then come back again at intervals. He wasn't talking quite so much and so sanguinely, I noticed. Maybe he knew more law than she.

"He wouldn't even let me take the stand. Don't you think maybe that would have helped?"

"But, honey, what could you have *done?* What could you have *said?* Don't you suppose he would have been the first to call you if it would have helped any? He never overlooks a witness that he thinks will help a case. And he never uses one that he thinks will weaken it. Does he, Mort? Mort, does he? Nobody saw you come or go there that day; that was the unfortunate part of it. The jury wouldn't have believed you any more than the arresting detectives did. They would have thought you were just making it up to try to shield your husband, and the sympathy that you aroused for yourself would have worked in reverse; it would have alienated them against him even more than they were already. That's why he tried to keep you away from the proceedings as much as possible and made you wear a veil and sit far back in the courtroom where you wouldn't be noticed. You see, you're too appealing, too attractive, honey; and you have to admit he *was* mixed up with this other woman, *was* going away with her, even if it was only for a spell. You were a bad risk; you would have hurt our side more than you helped it, just by being who you are, looking like you do. You were the injured party, but the—forgive me for saying this, honey—the injury was done you by the very man my boss was trying to defend."

"Let him injure me some more," I thought dismally; "I only want him back. Let him injure me to his heart's content."

"And then even if Mr. Benedict hadn't felt that way about it himself," she went on, "Mr. Murray particularly asked him not to call you unless he had to; that was his wish. He didn't want you to get all smeared up in it if it could be avoided."

That was true. Kirk had told me the same thing himself.

I kept watching the door, watching the door, waiting for it to open. "Shouldn't he be back by now? Does it always take this long?"

"He'll be here any minute now, honey. Just be patient."

Finally it did open, and there he was, carrying a brief.

I tried to read his face from all the way across the reception room. My eyes fastened on him in mute appeal and followed him as he came on toward me, and then past, and swung out the little gate in the partition railing and passed through. He avoided my gaze with an air of studious preoccupation. He didn't seem to see me until I had risen and he couldn't pretend not to any more. That alone should have been answer enough.

Then he said, "Come inside; come into my office." And to the girl, "Why did you let her sit out here, Ruthie? Why didn't you have her wait inside?"

The girl said, "She didn't want to be alone in there, Mr. Benedict. She asked if she could sit with me, and I had to be out here to answer the switchboard."

He held the private-office door for me and I went in. I felt a little bit as though I were going to my own execution here and now. There wasn't very much doubt of what he was going to tell me. It was just the word itself that was so awful. And the attaching of a date to it.

He couldn't look at me at first. He fussed around with the papers he'd brought back with him as long as he could. I just waited, with my eyes burning at him.

He sighed finally and said: "Now don't take it hard. The other day was the real test, and you stood it like a major; you were wonderfully brave."

He wouldn't have said that if he could have seen me afterward, at home by myself, with the corner of the pillow stuffed into my mouth, I thought.

Wasn't he going to say it ever? Was he just going to stand there like that all afternoon? "Is it—?"

"I'm appealing it, of course."

"He didn't give him—the other?"

"He couldn't; there was no recommendation of mercy."

"Say it. I can stand it. Only say it quick and get it over with."

But he still wouldn't name the word; I had to myself.

"The chair? The electric chair?"

He looked down at his desk in assent.

It exploded in my mind. *My husband has been sentenced to death.* That thing we all obey, all live under, the law of the state, has decreed he shall be taken from me in full health, and his body attached to—

I closed my eyes briefly, opened them again. Because what there was to be seen on the outside was less fearful than what there was to be seen on the inside.

He was worried about me. I was sitting down, so he must have thrust forward a chair. He tried to take out a bottle of liquor he kept for such emergencies in one of the desk drawers. I motioned to him not to. "Don't be afraid," I murmured half audibly.

"It isn't over yet. You're taking the typical layman's point of view," he tried to say. Or something like that.

I motioned that aside too. Of course it was over. The damage was already largely done. The sentence had already been partially carried out on both of us. In our hearts, if nowhere else. How could we both be ever quite the same again? What good would his appeal be by the time it was finally submitted? They'd never give me back quite the same man that had gone up there to that place where they kept them. They'd never give him back the same wife that he had left behind.

After a while, in a carefully controlled voice that wasn't like my own at all, I asked: "How did he take it?"

"With his head up, looking him straight in the eye."

"I should have been there, somewhere close by, at such a time. He was all alone in that room, poor boy."

"He said he was glad you weren't there to hear it. He thanked me as they took him out for not letting you come."

A moment or two went sluggishly by. "I guess I'll go home now," I said forlornly. "There's nothing to wait here for any more."

He got up and came outside with me. He said, "I'll take you downstairs and put you in a taxi. Do you want Mort or the girl to ride home with you to your place?"

"No," I said. "I'll be all right. I'll have to get used to going around alone from now on, I guess."

After he'd closed the cab door on me and given the driver my address, and just as he was about to turn away, I reached out quickly through the open window and clutched him by the sleeve. "When? Tell me the date."

"Now, why do you want to—?" he protested.

I wouldn't let go his arm. "I've got to know. Please tell me."

"The week of May sixteenth."

I sank back against the seat. And all the way home the thought that rode with me was: "I'm only twenty-two, and yet they're going to make me a widow in less than three months."

4

FAREWELL SCENE

IT'S HARD TO SAY good-by for good at any time or any place. It's harder still to say it through a meshed wire. It crisscrossed his face into little diagonals, gave me only little broken-up molecules of it at a time. It stenciled a cold, rigid frame around every kiss. And nothing should come between the kisses of a man and his wife.

He said things that went right through me. "Everyone's entitled to be forgiven at least once. Even a dog; they give a dog three bites—"

"You are, you were, you have been, long ago, oh, long ago."

"That was just—well, it must have been one last wild oat left over. I would have been such a good husband from—then on. If they would've only let me. I would have been the best-behaved guy anyone ever had around her. I would have brought you candy or flowers every night when I came home and I would've never kicked about the coffee any more."

"Don't," I sobbed. "You'll bring me flowers; you'll bring me candy; you'll kick about the coffee all you want, *all* you want. You will, you will again, you'll see."

He smiled as though he had his doubts. "But in case, in case I don't, afterward, after it's over—Angel Face, you won't let anyone else bring you flowers home at night or kick about the coffee, will you? Don't let anyone else—I know you're young yet—but that belongs to me."

"Never," I panted despairingly, "never anyone else but you. It'll be you or no one at all. Kiss me again. Again. Again. Oh, just once more. Another. They don't stay *on*. Kirk, how can we make them last?" Forever is such a long time.

"There's something else I want to tell you. I've always wanted to, ever since that night. This is my last chance; I have to now; there's only a minute left. You remember that night?"

How could I ever forget it?

"I only went there to tell her I was backing out. That the trip was off. Even the first time, at two. Before I knew what had happened, before I knew it had been taken out of my hands. I'd been thinking it over. I knew it was you, had always been you, would always be you. The other thing was just a week-end spree, a binge, no different from a kid playing hookey from school for one afternoon—and coming home all rashed up with poison ivy afterward, so he don't do it again in a hurry! Only, I was supposed to meet her at the station, and I couldn't just let her stand there waiting and not show up. I didn't want to do *that* to her; she was a woman, after all. So I went over there to try to break it to her ahead of time. No one answered at two, the first time I was there. I went back to the office and I tried to reach her on the phone a couple of times in between. Then when I still couldn't get her I went back again at six, when I left the office. What I'm trying to tell you is I went over there—to tell her it was off."

He ran his thumbnail ruefully along the wire, like harp strings. "I don't expect you to believe me; I wouldn't blame you if you didn't. It must sound like sour grapes at this late day. But, Angel Face, it's true. I wasn't going with her. That's all I can say."

I leaned my forehead tenderly against the wire toward him. "Darling," I said, "I've always been able to tell when you were lying. And I've always been able to tell when you were telling the truth. And I still am, now. So don't be afraid. I believe you."

"Thanks." He sighed gratefully. "That'll make it a little easier."

They came over to take him inside again. So this was it now, and words became just empty sounds. "You'll be back. This isn't good-by. Now remember that—I'm just saying so long to you for a while. Take good care of yourself, darling—until—until I see you again. Oh, wait, just let me kiss him once again—"

"Get ready with some more of that bad coffee, darling, so I'll have something to growl at when I—"

"I'll be waiting with it."

"So long for a while, Angel Face."

Isn't it pitiful how two people can kid themselves when they know they're both lying?

The wire stencil that had framed our kiss was empty; his lips were gone. The murmur of his voice hovered about it for a moment more, as if I were still hearing him say it, though I wasn't any more. "So long, Angel Face."

I had that much back again, at least. He always called me that. That was his name for me when we were by ourselves. That was a special thing, from him to—

5

REVERY BY MATCHLIGHT

THE FLAT WAS GONE now, and in its place there were the four cramped walls of a furnished room. I wouldn't have wanted the flat any more, even if there had been money enough to hang onto it; I would have run into him a thousand times a day, from every chair, from every corner of it. I would have heard him wheezing in the shower, howling for the towel that was never there; I would have heard him chuckling over there in that corner where the radio used to be; I would have heard him snoring over in the other bed, late at night—

Life was simpler here in this place. Life was a shot of novocain. Life was carpet slippers all day long, and a bathrobe, and hair that wasn't combed. Life was a rickety iron bed that wasn't slept on, just was wept on. Life was a can punched open maybe once a day, not from hunger, just from a sense of duty. Life was a knock on the door and an "Are you all right in there, lady? This is the landlady; I ain't seen you in three or four whole days now, and I just wanted to make sure there wasn't nothing the matter."

"I'm all right. Sure. I'm great. Don't worry if you don't see me or hear me, even for a week at a time. I'm still here; I'll still be sitting in here."

"Do you want me to get you a paper, help you to pass the time?"

I screamed it, but she didn't hear it because I

screamed it inside of me. "I don't want the time to pass! It's going too quick already! I want it to stand still! I want it to *freeze!*"

"No, thanks, there isn't anything I want to read about or know about."

Life was like that.

I reached the low point of the whole thing, the bottom-most dip of the graph, the night someone from the Police Property Clerk's Office came around to return his things. They give them back to you, it seems; they give you back everything but the main thing: who was in them. That they keep; that's theirs, to plug into the lighting system and then throw away.

This was just routine, the usual procedure when they send them up to *that place,* but I didn't know that, and at first sight of them hanging over his arm, empty, it gave me a horrible twinge, as though—it was over and he was gone already. I took them and I signed something and thanked him and closed the door. And if I let out all the stops afterward, that was just between me and those clothes of his.

I knew, though, as I lay there, face burrowing into the folds of his jacket, that I could never be so utterly, heartbrokenly, abandonedly forlorn again as I was there in that little room, with just the light bulb overhead to see me. From then on, whether there was hope or not, whether there was a chance or not, the curve was bound to be upward. Things could never look so dismal to me again. You can only cry like that once. Once and for one man. I gave him that. That was my testament of love.

Afterward, I remember, I was sitting dully on the edge of the bed, stroking the empty sleeve of his coat across my lap and slowly pulling myself together after the recent drenching outburst. The things that had been in his pockets that last night were in a couple of little manilla envelopes, fastened to a buttonhole of the coat. I detached them and emptied them out. The money he'd been carrying and his wrist watch and his key holder, and even his seal ring, were in one. And less valuable things in the other. A chromium pencil (that had always been out of lead) and a business letter or two and a laundry ticket with a Chinese character on it, standing for shirts that were still waiting for him somewhere and that he'd never call for now.

It was like a poignant rosary of the commonplace, to pay out these things one by one before my eyes.

And a battered package of his brand of cigarettes, with still the same two leftovers in it that must have been in it that night. Oh, they were so honest, these police! They wouldn't touch a convicted man's last two cigarettes. But they'd send him, for something he hadn't done, up to meet his—

And a pair of those lucky-number counterfoils from the last time we'd been to a show together. You know the kind. You detach the stubs and drop them in a box on your way in. And then a week from Thursday, if that particular number happens to be drawn— The remark he'd made that night came back to me: "I never had any luck with one of these stunts yet!" He hadn't been lucky in more things than that, poor boy.

The envelopes were empty now. The pitiful collection was all spread out on my lap. No, wait—one last thing. It came sidling out at a shake of the envelope.

Nothing. The ultimate in valuelessness. A folder of matches. Even that they'd conscientiously returned to me. Everything, everything but him himself they'd seen to it that I got back.

It was one of *hers*, in the bargain. I recognized it by the turquoise cover, the inevitable double *M*. One superimposed on the other, so that it really looked like a single *M* with double outlines.

That, I couldn't help thinking, was rubbing it in a little, although most of the sting was gone at this late day. He must have picked it up to use the last time he was there and then absent-mindedly put it into his own pocket instead of returning it to wherever it had been lying. As anyone might be apt to do. And here it was now, in my palm. About all that was left of her pitiful, ephemeral glamour. That had expressed itself, thought the quintessence of elegance was to stamp initials wholesale all over everything—on match covers and highball glasses and, I supposed, lingerie. I didn't hate her. I found, tonight, I never had. I'd been badly frightened for an hour or two that day. And ever since I'd just been sorry for her. Still, I got a peculiar mordant satisfaction from shredding the remaining match or two that were all that still clung to this battered token. Striking them, to flash transiently for a moment, like she had. And then—she was gone now. She was gone like this: *Phwit!* And there it was, on the floor, something to be thrown out.

A little thing came into my mind. I don't know how or from where. And as I thought of it, dwelt on the thought of it, it grew bigger and bigger, until it was crowding everything else out. I had seen one of these match covers up there myself. It had been wedged into the seam of the door, to keep the latch from closing fast. I had noticed it as I was standing there waiting to slip out, and I had picked it up, unfolded it, thrown it down again. It was just like this one; it had an *M* on it, and the pasteboard was blue on the outside.

But here was the little thought that grew bigger and bigger: It *wasn't* just like this one.

It had been blue, but not turquoise, a far deeper shade. And the *M* on it wasn't a double-lined *M*; it was single-lined.

Why would she go to the trouble of selecting a certain trick monogram—naïve though it was—and then have it scattered around on everything in sight, if she was going to allow a variation of it, a symbol that didn't quite match, to appear on one item? It wouldn't have been in character. To her, monogramming spelt chic, and not to have carried it out identically on everything at once would have been a flaw.

Besides, this very cover in my hand now showed she had carried it out on her matches as well as on everything else. Therefore, that other cover that I'd seen up there was *not* hers.

That initial was somebody else's. It stood for somebody else whose name began with an *M*. And that somebody else had killed her.

There was a triple coincidence there that had kept me from realizing that fact until now. Both names, hers and her killer's, began with the same letter. Just as Kirk's own did, for that matter, although it would never have occurred to him to go around carrying his initials on match folders and things; he would have laughed at the idea as it deserved to be laughed at. And, secondly, this unknown seemed to have the same crass flair she did for having his things personalized with an initial. And, thirdly, it happened that the piece of pasteboard involved was blue, though of a quite different shade from the tone she had seemed to dote on.

And in my excitement of mind that day, following the shock of the discovery I had just made, these discrepancies hadn't made sense to me.

They did now. Somebody whose name began with an *M* had been to see her that day, had detected something he didn't like, had fixed the door so that he could return and catch her off guard, and when he had—

Oh, if I only knew all the people she knew whose names began with *M!* Wait, there had been a book. Hadn't there been a list of names, an alphabetical calling list, I'd snatched up and taken with me that day, at the last moment, in my flurry of panic-stricken departure? I hadn't thought of it since; I hadn't seen it since. But that latter fact alone argued that, if I had taken it, it was still around somewhere.

I got out my handbag and started plumbing its depths and crevices. The woman never yet breathed who could be absolutely certain, at any one given time, of all that her own handbag holds. There is always some overlooked thing, some mislaid thing that she has lost track of, to be found lurking in its myriad compartments and zippered slits.

There was in this one too. But not what I was looking for. And yet I was certain I had brought that thing away with me. I could remember its soft leather turquoise cover, its stepped page margins, as well as I could that single-lined *M* on the match cover. I had all but torn the lining out of the bag, and there was no use kneading it any further. I sat there with it dangling disheartenedly over my knee.

Then I remembered that I'd gotten myself together rather carefully that day, to try to create a certain desired impression on her. I must have carried the other, the special, the dressy one. I'd forgotten I owned it. I hadn't used it since. That had been the last time clothes, accessories, meant anything to me. I'd been down to elementals from then on.

So I got it out and looked in that. And at the first touch of my fingers, as I unsheathed the mirror, turquoise flashed up at me like a patch on the black lining.

I opened it at the *M* page. My fingers had stopped being steady any more. I thought: "*Someone* in this book killed her. The name is in this book. On this very page I'm holding open here. It's looking right at me, staring me in the face. And I'm looking at it. But I can't tell which one it is."

Marty .... *Crescent 6–4824*
Mordaunt .... *Atwater 8–7457*
Mason .... *Butterfield 9–8019*
McKee .... *Columbus 4–0011*

"I'm looking at it," my mind repeated, "and I can't tell which one it is."

But I was going to find out.

I didn't even know his first name, or rating, or which precinct house he was attached to. So if there'd been more than one of them by that last name I might have got hold of the wrong one. In fact, I didn't know anything about him. Only that he'd been a little less brutal, a little more human, that night that they'd brought Kirk back to the apartment. And I had to have someone to turn to; I couldn't go the thing alone.

So I walked into the precinct house that was the nearest to where she had lived and I asked for him. "Is there a Flood here?"

"Wesley Flood, on Homicide, that who you want?"

"I—I guess so."

"Name, please?"

"Just say a young lady."

They showed me into some room at the back, and he saw me in there. It was he. He couldn't place me for a minute, I could tell. Then he remembered. "You're Murray's wife; that's it!"

I told him wanly, yes, that was it.

He looked me over surreptitiously, I guess to see how I was taking it, standing up under it. I caught a flicker of sympathy in his eyes, though I suppose he didn't realize it showed. I really didn't want that; I wanted advice and coaching.

I told him what I'd found at the Mercer apartment. I told him what I thought it meant and what I intended doing about it.

He heard me through. Just sat and listened attentively. There was no mistaking his expression, though. Finally I had to say, "You still don't think I was up there that day, do you?"

"Possibly you were—"

"Well, here's the book. Look, right here. Her book."

He leafed it, tapped it a couple of times against his thumbnail, handed it back. His attitude was unmistakable: it was over; it was water under the bridge. Whether I had been up there or not didn't matter any longer. Hadn't in the first place. The case was closed.

He tried to talk me out of it at first. "Look, even taking your point of view, even granting that Murray— that your husband—isn't guilty and that there's someone else still at large who is, don't you see you may be starting from a wrong premise altogether in basing something on this book and on that match cover you say you saw? There's no hard-and-fast rule that the name of everyone she knew *had* to go into that book. It could work the other way around, couldn't it? Those she knew well, those she knew best, mightn't be in it at all. She'd be so familiar with their numbers she'd know them by heart, wouldn't have had to write them down. Only those she knew less well would be in the book."

I thought of Kirk's name. She'd known him well enough to try to vamp him into going away with her, and his name was in the book. I didn't tell him that; there was still an ache in that old wound.

"There have been murders committed before, you know," he went on, "by people having no telephone numbers to their name at all. What I'm trying to tell you is this: there's no certainty—"

"But nothing's ever certain, is it? Only that you people have the wrong man."

He lidded his eyes deprecatingly. "Ah, you'd only get all muddied up. You're too nice a person, Mrs. Murray. Don't try it. You're not her type; you won't know how to handle half of these people."

"I'll have to learn."

Maybe it showed on my face. Maybe he saw what he'd be doing to me by dampening, taking away this one incentive I had left. Maybe he thought it would be kinder after all to let me start out on a hopeless, foredoomed quest than on no quest at all, to just sit counting the days as they went by, crossing them off one by one on the calendar of my mind until that red-letter date, sometime during the week of May sixteenth, was reached.

All I know is he suddenly changed. For no apparent reason, because of nothing that I had been able to say to convince him. "Try it, anyway," he consented abruptly. "Go ahead and try it."

I'd intended to anyway, whether with his benediction or not. But I did need someone to angel me, even if against his own convictions.

"Will they—do you think I'm running any risk of being recognized from the trial?"

"Well, I didn't know you at first, and I'm supposed to have a mind trained to remember faces. You didn't take the stand, and you were kept pretty much in the background. I'd say if you change yourself around a little you'd have a pretty good chance of not being recognized."

"Now, what sort of evidence will I need for it to be any good? Documentary, or will it just be enough if there's some slip made in the course of conversation, or what sort of requirement will there be from the police point of view?"

"There wouldn't be any documentary evidence in a case like this," he let me know. "You don't find murders written down in black and white, like bank statements. If you can get anything you come to me with it, even if it's only a rumor, a piece of idle gossip. That'll be enough from this policeman's point of view. If there's anything to it at all we'll see that it gets turned into something documentary; you leave that to us."

He saw me to the door. "You go ahead, and luck to you. Keep in touch with me; you can always find me around here." But then at the very last he couldn't resist adding, out of sheer kindliness, I suppose: "Will you do one thing for me, though? Don't get your heart too set on it. Don't take it too hard if it doesn't—work out the way you expect it to."

I knew he didn't really believe Kirk hadn't done it. He didn't expect me to uncover anything, because he thought everything there was to be uncovered had already been uncovered. Pity was making him seem to abet me. He thought it would be easier on me if I had some will-o'-the-wisp to chase than just to sit still waiting for the switch to fall.

I knew that as I left him; I could read it in him, on him.

"I'll show him too," I vowed. "I'll show them all."

* * *

"I stayed up all night rubbing soap on my finger," I told the pawnbroker, "but I can only get it up as high as the joint, where it is now. It won't go over it."

He tried it a couple of times with his bare hand. "You could have it filed off," he said.

"I know I could, but I don't want that done to it. I thought maybe you have a pair of pliers or some sort of instrument handy you could get it off with. I don't care how much it hurts; it's got to come off."

"I'll see what I can do," he said. He came back and put a drop or two of oil on my finger just above it and then got a good firm grip on the ring with a pair of nippers. Then he braced my arm by holding it pressed tightly under his own and started to tug way at it.

It made it; it came off and flew across the pawnshop, and he had to go after it.

It looked so funny and raw there where it had been until now. It had left a little circlet of pink behind at the base of my finger. It was the first time it had been off since I was seventeen.

He polished it and examined it and said: "You want to sell it outright or just pawn it?"

"I'd rather just pawn it. I—I'll want it back someday."

"Five dollars," he said.

"But it's pure gold; it's—"

"I know, but how much gold is in a wedding ring? Seven-fifty. And not because of the ring, because I've got a heart where I got no business to have one."

I held out my hand. "Just let me look at it once again before you take it." I tilted it so that I could see the engraving on the inside.

K.M.—A.F., 1937.

My brother-in-law pretended not to know my voice at first. Well, maybe he really didn't recognize it at that. I hadn't see them for over three years, since they'd moved out to Trenton.

I said, "This is Alberta. I'm speaking from the city."

His voice dropped still further, became wary. "Oh—uh—yes," he said. "Alberta, how are you? We got your note and—uh—been meaning to answer it. You see, how we're fixed here is—well, the house is rather small, and on account of the kids, I don't see—"

"But you don't understand. I didn't ask to be taken in. I thought I made that plain in my note. I don't want anything done for me; I'll look after myself. All I'm asking you to do is lend me a sum of money. I'll pay you the usual rate of interest on it, and you'll get it back, every penny of it—"

"Is it for—? Are you still trying to help *him?*" The way he said that, you had to hear it to know what I mean.

"Is Rose there? Let me speak to her a minute." I'd never liked him much anyway.

"She—uh—just stepped out to the store." The timing was faulty; there was too much slack in the answer. As when you turn your head to confer in pantomine. I could see the signs going on, as thought I were right in the room with them. Signs of interrogation and signs of refusal.

My own sister. No, because I was the wife of a condemned man now. I might bring notoriety into their home. They had their children's welfare to consider, their friends, their standing in the community.

I said with a sort of passive, low-wattage dignity, "All right, Harvey. Never mind. I'd better get off now."

"You can reverse the charges," he said patronizingly.

I needed that money bitterly, even the little the call was going to cost. I knew it was a foolish thing to do. And yet it wasn't pride or sulkiness. It was a compulsion of the very blood itself. I could no more have accepted that small sop from him now—

"No," I said with calm firmness. "It's been worth it to me. The experience alone—"

I hung up. I never saw either of them, or spoke, or heard from, or thought of them again.

6

Crescent 6–4824 .... Marty

IT HAD A LINE drawn through it, and I wondered why. It was the only one on that whole page to have a line drawn through it. I'd noticed a name here and there, on other pages, with a line drawn through the number and a new number superimposed—and that was understandable, a change of location. But never a line drawn through both name and number alike, as with this one. Wherever they went, though they changed numbers, they carried the same names with them; those remained unchanged.

Then what was this?

It could be death, I knew. And I dreaded the thought of tracking down a dead man. Or it could be a severance of relations. I hoped, of the two, to find it was that. One thing was sure: that line meant something, was there for a reason, had not just been drawn through it idly.

It came due at its appointed time, and its appointed time was now, five-thirty of a porcelain-blue evening. Hours had gone by in the preparations leading up to it, preparations that could not be seen by the eye, gave no outward sign, could have been mistaken for silent pondering or absent-minded reverie, but were active within me nevertheless.

At the very end, as the moment for it drew nigh, I drew nearer to it by degrees. The telephone, I mean.

I walked back and forth before it, murmuring to myself, memorizing a lesson under my breath. Sometimes
looking up at the ceiling, sometimes down at the floor,
as I did so. Turning every few paces and retracing my
steps. Back and forth, back and forth, whispering under
my breath.

"If the voice is young, sort of vital, resonant, the
opening wedge is: 'You don't know me, but I feel as
though I know you; I've heard so much about you.'
Then go on from there. The key is flirtatious, coquettish.

"If the voice is dry, lifeless, worn out, the opening
wedge is: 'I have some information which I feel may
interest you.' The key is a suggestion of pecuniary or
personal advantage.

"If the voice is brisk, businesslike, impersonal, then
the best approach is likewise direct, impersonal, without shadings or overtones. 'My name is so-and-so; I
would like to speak to you personally for a few moments.'

"If the voice is indeterminate, cannot be analyzed,
fits into none of these categories, then the third approach, the direct, businesslike one, is still the best."

I had stopped parading now. I had it memorized.

I sat down before the instrument and braced myself,
one hand stiffly to each end of the small table it sat
on.

I thought of *him*, as I did each time. "Wish me luck,
darling; maybe this will be it." I took a deep prepara-
tory breath. The dial wheel oscillated beneath my finger, and my thoughts oscillated with it. "If the voice is
young, vibrant— If the voice is dry, reserved— If the
voice is businesslike—"

"Hello?" There wasn't enough to tell by.

"Is Marty there?"

"Marty who?"

"Just Marty."

"You'll have to give me the last name."

I'd known I would; I'd been afraid of that, but I
didn't have it to give.

I parried evenly with the question I'd prepared myself. "Who is this I'm speaking to, please?"

"This is the desk of the St. Albans Hotel."

"Oh—" So all the rehearsal had been wasted. "Well, I have no second name. I'm trying to reach someone whom I know only as Marty. Couldn't you help me just from that? Couldn't you tell me if you have anyone registered with you whose first name is Marty?"

"I don't see how," he said rather ungraciously.

In this, from beginning to end, there was to be no acceptance of defeat. I knew already it must be that way. My mind was made up. There would be no such thing as a refusal, a slight, a rebuff. Or rather, they would have no power to hinder me.

"I don't see how I can help you. I'm rather busy at the moment."

I made my voice pleasantly reasonable. "This is important to me. It's not a frivolous matter. It's a serious matter. If I come down there myself, instead of taking up your time on the phone, won't you please try to help me trace this person?"

His own voice relented. "If you drop in I can have someone look over the registers for you."

It was a pleasantly prosperous-looking place, a residential-type hotel. Just under the upper brackets of ultra-smartness, perhaps, but spelling a sort of solid, substantial, middle-class affluence. That was likely to prove a point in my favor, I realized immediately as I stepped in. This type hotel attracted a very small percentage of transients. It would have a far slower and less continuous turnover than an ordinary commercial hotel, and the guests individually would be far more likely to be known personally to the management and to be recalled by name even after they had gone.

They were courteous to me. Sight at firsthand evidently improved my status. The assistant manager himself came out to me.

"I'm sorry, Miss—?"

"Miss French."

"I'm sorry, Miss French. As the desk already told you, there is no one registered with us at the moment whose given name is 'Marty' or Martin. I've had someone go over the register. Are you sure that's all the information you can give us?"

"I'm afraid that's all."

"Could you give me an idea of what the person looks like?"

"I'm afraid not," I had to admit. "You see, the person is not known to me. But it's very important that I get in touch with him. And this first name and the address here are the only clues I have." At least I was able to impress him with my earnestness, if nothing else; I could see that.

"I'm sorry, I'd be only too glad to help you." He stroked his immaculately shaven jowls. "But I don't see how I can."

I did, and I didn't hesitate to make the suggestion. "I don't like to impose, but if I wait out here, couldn't you have someone go back through your back registers—just for a short distance—and see if such a person was here formerly?"

"Well—" he said. "Well—" And then, "Just a moment."

He left me sitting out there while he went in to give the order to someone. So I knew I'd won that point, at least.

It took quite some time, and while I was sitting there I tried to form a composite impression of this mysterious "Marty" by piecing him together from the other habitués of the place. Not, I knew, that there was any guarantee he need necessarily resemble the others just because he had formerly dwelt there; he could have been a different type altogether who simply had happened to live in the same building for a while. But there *is* a degree of truth after all in the old saying about birds of a feather, and I felt he would not have lodged here at any time if he had not had a certain something in common with those I now glimpsed about me here and there passing through from the elevators to the street and vice versa, stopping for a moment at the desk or to chat with an acquaintance in the lobby.

This, then, was how he would be if he ran true to form: a man already past the financial hazards of the twenties and entered now upon the prosperous calm of early middle age, when money, if it is to be made at all, has already been made. That is to say, not that the process of making it is discontinued, but the system of making it is set, runs more or less under its own momentum, releasing the individual from a great many of the earlier strains and stresses. He would be jovial, complacent, a little self-assertive (and entitled to be). Beginning to round a little at the waistline, but not enough as yet to worry about it overmuch. Hair beginning to thin a little, but that would still be a secret between him and his barber. He would stroll about, preceded by an expensive Havana cigar, and he would have an appreciative eye for the female stranger that would grow stronger as time went on. Not one of them failed to look me over, though not in a blatant, disconcerting manner.

Well, that would be about him. A little of all that would enter into his personality, and then there would be other elements, of course, particular to him as an individual.

The assistant manager had come out to me again. He had something jotted on a card that someone had evidently transcribed from the register at his behest.

"I wonder if you could mean either one of these?" he said. "I had them go back three full seasons. Unfortunately—or perhaps I should say fortunately—we seem to have had a scarcity of guests with the given name of Martin during recent years. Now there's a Martin Ebling who was with us some time ago. He left as his forwarding address Cleveland; that was at that time. Whether it's still valid, of course, I don't know. Then the other is Martin Blair. He left as *his* forwarding address another hotel here in the city." His lip curled in a sort of professional disdain. "The Senator. I think you'll find that farther downtown." He sounded as though it were some sort of blemish that was liable to erasure from one day to the next.

I took them both down and I thanked him and left.

It was only when I reached there and gone in that I fully understood that lift of his lip.

"I wonder what happened to him?" I thought. "From the St. Albans to the Senator." It was more than a step down; it was a vertical drop.

They didn't look you over here; they practically disrobed you optically. With them the process of *not* making money was all that had carried over from the twenties, continuing all the earlier stresses and hazards. In partial compensation they had retained youth's slimness of waist and, on the average, their hair was thicker. Why this last should be, I don't know, unless it was because they couldn't afford to have it cut and singed and treated preventively as often, and therefore lost less of it. Or perhaps only with peace and perfect security comes the beginning of decay. They stalked around sucking cheap cigarettes, and there was something lean, avid, wolflike about their movements.

Not that they were all carbon copies of one another, you understand; it's just that that was the general atmosphere of the place. They were even more self-assertive than the other group, but with this difference: no one listened.

The clerk had a badly decayed front tooth and eyes that had looked on everything vicious there was under the electric lights.

"Marty Blair," he said. "Yeah, I remember him." The memory was unwelcome. His eyes creased at the corners, and his mouth did too.

"Is he still here?" I asked.

"He was put out a long time ago. We got tired of carrying him." He chuckled scornfully. "Once wasn't enough. We had to keep putting him out over and over.

He kept trying to sneak back in again each time, even after the door was locked. Finally we wore him out." He gestured with his hand in dismissal. No pity there, no mercy.

I wondered what *he'd* been trying to hang onto so desperately, to keep coming back like that each time. Respectability, I guess; even the tattered shreds of it that were still to be found in this place.

"Then you don't know where he went?"

He eyed me bleakly. "Wherever they go," he said, "when they're down and out for the tenth count. The Bowery, I guess."

"The Bowery?" I said helplessly. "How do you look for them along the Bowery?"

"Once they hit that," he said, "they're usually not worth trying to look for any more. Nobody bothers. That's a living graveyard."

It was just the words of a song to me; I had so much to learn about everything. "I'll never go there any more," something like that.

"But suppose he still *was* worth trying to look for, then what would I do?"

"Just go in one smokehouse after the other until you see him in one of them—if you can recognize him any more."

I didn't even know what he'd looked like to begin with.

"Lady, you've got yourself a job," he said when I'd told him this. He was too world-wise and weary to even ask me what I wanted him for, what I was trying to find him about. It was bound to be just a variation of some tale he'd heard before. For him there was nothing new under the electric lights. And I wondered if I'd ever be that way myself someday.

"He was just an ordinary guy, a dime-a-dozen guy," he said. "Gee, this is going to be hard. But I helped put him out myself two or three times, so I think I can— Thin and tall, kind of. Light hair, light brown hair. That's about all I remember."

Thin and tall. Light brown hair. He was right; I had a job.

They were looking at the backs of my legs from all over the place; I could feel them, and I wanted to get out. "Thanks," I said.

"Lots of luck, lady," he said mournfully.

Nothing new under the electric lights. It must be terrible, I thought to myself, to know as much as he did about the less appealing aspects of human nature.

Flophouses, they were, I guess. They called themselves hotels; their signs offered rooms at twenty-five or thirty-five cents a night, and there were scads of them along there. The entrance was always one flight up, never on the street level. And in the background you would see a long bare room with these hopeless figures sitting around, reading papers, or just rocking back and forth, rocking themselves slowly into their graves. Figures that had once been human beings.

It wasn't a matter of outward appearance, of the clothes they wore. This was a thing that came from inside. A living man could have been in worse rags than they wore, and he would still be a living man. One of them could have been put into the swankiest apparel to be found and he would have still remained—what he was. A lamp with the wick burned out. A bulb with the filaments worn out. Something still intact but that no longer gives off light.

There were so many of them along there. End to end they were placed. Because, after all, that is the one thing that must continue, even in this twilight world—sleep. At first, when I'd come back again each time the following night, I was never quite sure of where I'd left off the night before; they all looked so alike. I found myself overlapping a little. So I brought along a little piece of chalk and I marked a little check, a pothook, on the doorway of the last one as I was quitting for the night. And then when I came again the following night I knew where to begin. At the next one after that.

Over and over and over. Up the dimly lighted stairs

to the little niche or cubicle with a slab before it that served as a payment desk. And then the wordless gasp that always followed when they looked up and saw who it was that had been making that toilsome ascent. And then the inevitable blanket dismissal before I was even able to open my mouth. "Sorry, miss, we don't accommodate ladies."

"I know, but I'm looking for someone. Marty, his name is Marty. He's tall and thin, light brown hair. Blair's his other name, Marty Blair."

Yet I found, for one thing, that it was easier along here to ask for him just by his given name. This was a place where the second name dropped away again. Whether it was that they were ashamed and kept it to themselves, or that there was no longer any need for it now that they had all reached this common level, they seemed to be known to one another more by their first names and, more than that even, by nicknames that the Bowery had fastened on them.

He'd look through the haphazard, pencil-scrawled book of admissions they kept, and sometimes he'd call to someone sitting nearby for information: "Is Porky's real name Martin, any of you know?"

They'd scratch their heads and finally someone would say: "No—Marvin, I think I once heard him say. He ain't who the lady wants anyway; he's short, fat little guy. Don't you 'member him? He was in here only a couple nights ago, had the bed right across from mine."

Over and over, over and over. While the el rumbled by and you had to wait until it had finished passing before you could make yourself heard.

"We don't take women."

"I know, but I'm looking for someone. Marty, his name is Marty. Tall and thin and light brown hair."

Down the stairs again, around into the next doorway, up the stairs.

"No dames. We only got dormitories here, so you may as well go on down again."

"Marty, his name is Marty; light brown hair."

Down the stairs, around, and up.

"Marty, light brown hair—"

One of the newspaper readers over by the window looked up, cackled: "I bet I know who she means, Haggerty. Heartbreak. That guy that's always talking to a dame that isn't there."

I stopped, came back a step or two.

The man behind the slab looked around, asked the "reading room" in general: "Anybody here know his right name?"

"Blake or Blair, something short like that; I think I once heard him tell it to somebody."

"Blair." I nodded. "It's Blair."

He shuffled forward, offering his services. But indirectly, via the clerk, afraid to address me personally. "I can show you where you'll mostly find him. Down at Dan's place; it's only a little way from here."

The clerk had had a better look at me by now. "You better not go there, miss. I'll send one of these fellows for you, have him bring him back here."

"No, it's all right; I'd rather go myself."

I'd never been in a Bowery drinking place before. I'd heard the phrase "the lower depths"; I don't remember where. I think I'd read it once. This was it now. The lowest depths of all, this side the grave. There was nothing beyond this, nothing further. Nothing came after it—only death, the river. These were not human beings any more. These were shadows.

And there was one thing more pathetic than themselves, more eloquent of what had become of them. It was the hush that fell when I went in. That bated breathlessness. I went into many places after that, but never again did that same thing happen in just that way. Men in a barroom will often fall silent when a woman comes in. This was not that. This was not admiration or even covetousness. I don't know what to call it myself. It was the memory of someone in each man's past,

someone like me, long ago, far away, come back to
mind again for a moment, before the memory darkened
again and went out—forever. It was life's last afterglow
glancing off the faces of the dead as I brushed by them.

I went up to the bartender. "Is there someone in here
named Heartbreak? I'm looking for someone called
Heartbreak."

His jaw hung slack. He forgot to go ahead with what
he'd been polishing. He just looked at me and looked,
as though he'd never got through. I didn't get it at first.
He just worked there; he just catered to the dead; he
wasn't one of them. He shouldn't feel that way.

"Heartbreak?" he said half incredulously.

"Yes, Heartbreak."

He murmured something to himself that sounded like
"So there really *was*, after all—"

Then I got it a little. What was it they'd said back at
that flophouse? That he was always talking of or to a
woman who wasn't there. They hadn't believed there
was such a woman until now. Now, seeing me, they
thought I was she. They thought I was his dream come
down to the Bowery to seek him, to take him back to
life with me.

They were wrong; I wasn't she. But I had an idea of
who she might be.

He'd found his voice at last. He pointed. "That's
him, back there. See him, all the way back against the
rear wall?"

I saw a head, inert on one of the plank tables. One
arm half folded around it. The other dangling lifeless,
straight down toward the floor. I saw two empty thim-
ble glasses, one before him, one before the empty chair
beside him.

I turned to the barman uncertainly. "Do you think I
can—? How do you wake them up when they're like
that?"

"Want me to go back and shake him a little for
you?"

"No, I—I'll see what I can do myself. Just keep the rest of them away from that table." I fumbled in my bag, handed him a coin.

"What would you like, miss?"

"Nothing. That's just for coming in here and sitting with him for a while."

I made my way back toward where he was, that hush following me like the wake of a boat. Those who were in my way sidled aside to let me go by, then closed in again behind me. Every head in the place, probably, was turned to look after me. I didn't know about that; I didn't care. I reached him, and I stood there for a moment looking down at him, feeling a good deal of uncertainty within me. I didn't even know for sure that he was the one; I only had another nondescript's guess for it.

I sat down gingerly on the chair beside his, turned sideways toward him. He didn't move. You wouldn't have known he was alive at all. Even his breathing didn't show.

I touched him on the shoulder finally, waited.

That was no good.

I tapped him on it, pressed down heavier.

That was no good.

I tried to shake him.

That was no good either. His hand that was on the table fell around the other way, open side out; that was all.

The bartender came back to my assistance at this point, unasked, bringing a mug of cold water. He must have been watching.

"Stand up a minute, so you don't get any of it on you," he counseled. He pulled back his shabby collar a little, baring the nape of the neck. Then he expertly let the water trickle in a thin but continuous thread down on it. The effect must have been needlelike to be able to penetrate those layers of unconsciousness.

He stirred a little finally, grunted, rolled his head unwillingly out of the way of the annoyance. He blew his breath out flatly along the top of the table with a sort of hollow, snorting sound.

The bartender drew his head up and back by the hair, held it that way, leaned around in front of it. "Open your eyes, Heartbreak. Someone here wants to talk to you. The lady here wants to talk to you."

They remained furrows, plowed deep into his face.

The barman passed the head by the hair grip to one of the men standing gaping around us. "Here, hold him like that a minute till I get back." He returned behind the bar for something.

The man held the head aloft, but it was I he kept looking at the whole time with a sort of owlish gravity, not the patient.

"I get that way meself quite often," he offered tentatively. I don't think it was the content of the remark itself that mattered to him as much as the mere fact of having addressed me at all; he wanted to save that, like they did string and bottle caps and this and that. Things that other people don't value, but that helps fill up the emptiness of having nothing for them.

The bartender came back with something cloudy in a tumbler. Spirits of ammonia, maybe; I don't know.

"Here's a drink for you, Heartbreak. One on the house."

The eyes flickered, tried to open. They never quite made it, but at least they did flicker valiantly in the attempt. My mind said to me: "This man would be better off dead. Why do we think death is so cruel? It's life that is cruel. Death is man's greatest gift from Nature. Animals don't have this happen to them."

The bartender got it down him, apparently. I couldn't see—his back was between us, but the tumbler came back empty.

He held his head a moment longer, then he let go of it. The head fluctuated, weaved in a halolike orbit, but it stayed up.

The bartender withdrew, driving the gallery of onlookers that had hedged us in back before him. "Go back to your own places now, you men. Don't nobody come near this table, understand? This lady wants to sit here." And to me in parting, "I'll keep my eye out. Just call me if anybody crowds you or tries to put the touch on you."

"Thank you," I said.

I sank unobtrusively into the chair beside that erect, unseeing head, and the place and all the faces faded from view, the noise and the smoky haze, and we were alone together—me and the crossed-out line from somebody's book. Not just a cheap woman's book, the book of the recording angel himself. The Book of Destiny.

I waited for him to look around at me and see me there beside him. I wanted the reaction to come from within him, unforced. He was staring straight ahead into the nothingness that faced him. That always faced him day and night. What was he seeing there, I wondered; murder?

She had done this to him; it must be she, of course. The thing was, had she done it living or dead? Which had come first, the descent or the crime? The descent, almost certainly. She was only dead months. He'd already left the St. Albans, started on the downward way a year or two ago. He'd even been dispossessed from the other place, the Senator, the last rung of the ladder over the pit, well before it had happened. Then, perhaps, had he gone back, sought her out, and wreaked retribution on her for what she'd done to him? It appeared plausible.

He moved slightly, and I saw him looking downward at the floor around his feet. Looking around for something on that filthy place where people stepped and spat all day long. In a moment more I had guessed what he was looking for and I opened my handbag and took out the cigarettes I had provided myself with and held the package ready, with one protruding, as my first silent overture.

His eyes stopped roaming suddenly, and they had

found the small arched shape of my shoe, planted there unexpectedly on that floor beside him, and the tan silk ankle rising from it.

I watched, breathless, afraid to move. He stared steadily, and then pain clouded his eyes, and he turned his head aside toward the wall, but still bent downward as it was. The dream was too old; it had fooled him too many times for him to believe in it now.

Then he turned back again to see if it would be gone, that hallucination on the floor. It wasn't. I could see a cord at the side of his neck swell out as he kept himself from looking up to where the face should be but, he knew, wouldn't be. He was afraid to look up. He shaded his forehead with one trembling hand for a minute. I heard him murmur: "You'll go away if I do."

I edged out my forearm, with the cigarettes in my hand, a little farther along the rim of the table toward him, and that caught at his eyes and he saw that. He closed his eyes to give it time to vanish. He opened them again, and it was still there.

"Ah, Mia, don't," he pleaded. "Don't kid me like this!" And he ground his hands into the sockets of his eyes to rub the apparition out of them.

Thus he gave me her name, and I knew that the quest for "Marty" at least, was at an end. The quest if nothing else.

I spoke to him softly, reassuringly, as to a child, as to someone very sick who must not be frightened, whose confidence must be gained. "Yes, I'm here," I said. "I'm real. I'm really here."

The voice, I guess, disabused him. He made a confused turn of the head, and we were looking at one another at long last. The bum and the widow.

He pawed out toward me tentatively and still half fearfully, without quite reaching me.

"You're Marty, aren't you? Marty Blair."

I saw, by the little start of remembrance he gave, that he hadn't been hearing the name for a long time past; it had just come to him it was his own. Or rather had once been his own.

"Here, have one of these," I said soothingly. I even had to put the cigarette to this mouth, strike the match for it. He seemed too dazed, incapable of moving, of doing anything but just looking incredulously at me.

Then finally he said, "But you're in *her* seat." His eyes went to the empty jigger glass that had been before it on the table the whole time. "And what'd you do, finish off *her* drink? I always buy one for her every time I come in here. Even when I can't buy one for myself I always see that she gets one at least. Then sometimes she don't feel like it, and she lets me have it afterward."

I didn't know what to say. "She won't be here to-night, Marty. She couldn't come. That's why she sent me instead. I'm a friend of Mia's, Marty. I'm a very good friend of Mia's."

I waited to see what the name would do to him. It did plenty. The pain was livid, like an incision made across his whole face.

I gave him a little time. I would have sent for another drink for him, but I was afraid it would send him off into the dark again. Finally I said, gently as I could, "You think quite a lot of her, don't you, Marty?"

He smiled at me in a pitiful, helpless sort of way. Gee, that smile was an awful thing to behold. It was—I don't know how to say it; did you ever see a dumb animal run over and crushed out in the middle of the street, so that its hind part is paralyzed? It no longer feels any pain, but it drags itself up on the curb to expire, and it offers a convulsive, fanged grin just before it does.

I said to myself, "He could have done it. It could have been he very easily." It was in that smile just then, that terrible smile he gave. Pain, festered love that no longer knows what it's doing, no longer can distinguish between the rights and wrongs of murder.

Then after the smile came the answer to what I'd said. Totally unexpected, like something bursting in my face. He said quietly and without inflection, "I was her husband; didn't she ever tell you that?"

Even in the first shock of discovery my mind found time to note the tense he'd given it. "Was," he'd said.

I didn't have to be so careful with him as I would have with a normal person; his faculties were still tinctured with smoke. "Yes, I know that," I said demurely. I looked down at the table to try to keep his suspicions allayed. "Weren't you ever—was there a divorce, or something like that?"

"No," he said, "I just got left behind—after she started having friends and all—"

"When was the last time you saw her?" I kept looking down. I traced an imaginary line along the soiled table with the tip of my finger. Then I traced another one over the other way.

"I see her every night. The smoke clears away and there she is. She sits next to me, and I buy her a drink. She comes with me into every one of these places—"

"Yes, but when was the last time you *really* saw her?" I urged with gentle persuasiveness. I smiled a little, trying to show him that I didn't refuse to accept her on his plane; it was just that I wanted to know a little more about her on the other plane.

I waited, but he didn't answer.

"You used to go up and see her sometimes, too, didn't you, as well as having her come down here to see you?" And to make it stick I added: "She told me you did."

"Yeah," he said, "I used to. I used to lots. It hurt too much, though. So mostly I didn't go in; she didn't know about it. I just watched her windows from across the street in the shadows, in the rain and in the snow—"

I kept drawing that imaginary line over and over. His eyes were on my finger now, hypnotized.

"And then when they went away I'd go away—kind of happy—because she was by herself again."

"They?" I breathed, scarcely stirring my lips.

"Whoever it was. I couldn't see him; I was never

near enough. But you could tell by the way the lights would go out, and then a little while later somebody would come out of the doorway."

"And then you'd go away happy."

"I had her back again."

He stopped. I kept tracing that line, as though I were slowly drawing something invisible out of him. "Only mostly," he resumed abruptly, "they didn't come out again. I had to go away first. The cops would make me. And that hurt." He pushed in the side of his stomach. "The smoke would take care of that, though."

And murder? I thought.

I couldn't talk to him any more there. The stuff was too fresh in him. I'd made a good beginning. But I had to get him back on my plane again, where I could gauge his reactions better.

I said, "Marty, I want to do something for you. Would you like to sleep in a bed tonight and not just in a doorway or on a bench?"

He looked at me and said, with a pathos that was wholly without artifice, "Some people do, don't they?"

"You can, too, tonight. Would you like to, Marty? If I buy you a bed in a room all to yourself, will you promise me not to drink until—until I come down and see you tomorrow?"

He was able to walk without any noticeable convulutions. He'd learned how to; he'd had so much practice at it. By keeping his feet close to the ground, scarcely lifting them at all, he was able to make his way along, both straight and fairly steadily, at a sort of hangdog shuffle, head and shoulders bowed somewhat forward; that was all.

I took his arm. We must have made a strange-looking couple, leaving that place. A woman and a dead man.

I appealed to the barman on the way out. "I want to take him someplace to sleep where—where he'll stay put until tomorrow morning."

He didn't make the mistake of misinterpreting, at

least; but then, sizing the two of us up side by side, how could anyone have very well?

"Try the Commerce, over on Broome Street," he said. He let a little spurt of beer into a glass, added something to it I wasn't quick enough to identify, and swished it around surreptitiously. "Here, give him this to drink a minute first."

In the place on Broome Street I paid a dollar for a room for him and then went upstairs with him, at least as far as the door. I told him to take off his things and get some sleep and waited outside in the hall for a few minutes. Then I sent the boy in, quietly, and had him bring out his shoes to me. They were almost unidentifiable: shapeless slate crusts. I had him take them down below with us and wrap them in a bit of paper and told him to hold them there. Not to give them back to him under any circumstances, even if he should try to claim them before I could get down there.

"I must find him here when I come back tomorrow, and without any liquor in him."

"I don't know," the man behind the desk said doubtfully. "I've seen some of them that wouldn't let a little thing like bare feet stop them."

"Then if he tries to get out tell him that the room hasn't been paid for and he'll have to wait for me to come down and bail him out. Whatever you do, keep him here."

I went uptown again, back to the other world. I lay there all night long without sleeping, thinking about it, thinking it out, thinking it over.

Had he done it? Hadn't he? That fanged, hideous grin he'd given at one time. Why, that had been almost a replica of the death grimace I'd seen on her own face that day in the apartment. Was that the brand of murder, the symbol of it, transferred to his own countenance from hers? No, that was metaphysical nonsense.

He was her husband. He'd been mad about her in the colloquial sense first. And now he was mad about her in the literal sense. Set out a chair, a drink, for her each

time he sat down himself. They called him Heartbreak
down there in the nether world. There'd been a line
drawn through his name in her book, and he'd waited
outside in the rain, in the snow, watching her windows,
to claim her back again each time somebody left. Until
one day, *that* day—hadn't it occurred to him there was
a better way of claiming her forever, with never another
vigil necessary, with never another dispute about his
title to her?

It must have been that way. It was as plain as this
hand that I held out before my face in the blue pallor of
the early dawn.

"Marty, I know what you did to Mia." Suddenly, like
that, in the middle of something else. No, that was no
good. He'd deny it; that was only to be expected, even
from someone in his condition. But what was the best
I could hope to get, even if it were true and I'd hit the
nail on the head? A frightened, furtive flash across his
face. Why, for that matter, even if it weren't true I
might produce the same thing simply by the mere fact
of making the accusation at all. No, I had to have more
than that to go to Flood with.

I already had for him a splendid motive, an exquisite
motive. I already had for him an incriminating vigil
outside her windows that the police had never brought
to light or even suspected so far. Now all I needed, I
felt, was a guilt reaction of one sort or another from the
suspect himself, but a substantial one, one that would
hold water, something more than just a frightened look
or a stammered denial; given that, and I had enough to
go to them with, they could go on from there.

Suddenly, in that clarity which sometimes precedes
sleep, I thought of another way of eliciting this reaction
I was after, a way preferable and more reliable than a
mere verbal trap. The accusation or denial must come
from him, naturally, but it must be unforced, unsug-
gested; he must not realize that he was presenting it.
Then it would be valid; then it would be substantial
enough to hand over to Flood.

I would accuse *somebody else* and watch and see what he did.

And on that note my eyes finally dropped closed, their linings carmine against the rising sun.

I carried the wrapped shoes up to the door and knocked. There was no answer, and for a moment I got frightened and thought I'd lost him all over again. But I remembered there was no fire escape outside the window, they'd told me. I opened the door and looked in.

He was there. He was dressed. He was sitting on the bed with an inert sort of resignation, his hands dangling down between his legs. I closed the door after me and put the shoes down next to him on the floor and then stood there looking at him a moment. He looked at me in turn.

"Then there *was* someone like you sitting talking to me last night," he said finally.

"Yes, there was. How'd you sleep?"

He looked back at the mattress, as though to inquire of it rather than of himself. "I don't know," he said lukewarmly. "I'm sort of used to angles, like benches give you. I kept missing them."

"You better put those on."

He didn't ask me what I'd wanted of them; he didn't seem interested. "I wondered what become of them," he said indifferently.

I looked at him closely. I was seeing him for the first time in the daylight now. And although I was there to kill him myself, the full impact of what *she'd* done to him only came to me now as I got this better look at him. She'd killed him a thousand times to my one. He'd been a fine-looking man once; you could still make out the traces of it here and there in the shape of his head, particularly the back of it, the proportion of his features, a turn his head gave now and then. He'd been intelligent too; his eyes told that. No longer by what was in them, but by their lingering outward characteristics of color, size, and width.

She'd done her work well, all right. She'd gutted him. I couldn't help crying out to myself as I beheld what she'd left of him: "Out of all the thousands and thousands of fine constructive women in this world, what evil star made him pick her out? What *got* him about her? Couldn't he see, couldn't he tell——?"

And the answer, of course, was self-evident. What gets any of us about any of them; what gets any of them about any of us? The image in our minds. Not the reality that others see; the image in the mind. Therefore, how could he see, how could he tell, how could he free himself, when the image in his mind all along, and even now, was that of a lovely creature, all sunshine, roses, and honey, a beatific haloed being, a jewel of womankind? Who would even strive to free himself from such a one? Watch out for the image in your mind.

He straightened from the lacing of his shoes at last; it was a difficult job, because the punctures the laces were to go through were warped and askew and all but obliterated, and he had to coax the lace tip through each one by moistening it and drawing it to a point; he straightened, and then he got to his feet.

I said, "They're sending us up two cups of coffee and some rolls. I told them to."

He drew his finger uncertainly across under his nose and mumbled: "Gee, you're being pretty nice to me."

I let him be for a while out of common, everyday humanity, until at least he had some coffee in him. I didn't know why I should give quarter like this, unless I may have felt that I was aiding my own purpose by waiting until his system had become stabilized at least.

The coffee came, and we busied ourselves with it for a while: he sitting slumped on the edge of the bed, holding the mug clasped between both hands and down low almost over the floor; I standing taking mine from the top of the derelict object that passed for a bureau.

It came to me how strange the picture must be that we made, had anyone been there to see it. The huntress and the hunted, for that was what it amounted to, eying one another watchfully across this dusty, shabby, sun-blinded room, while we silently sipped at the nauseous contents of the thick mugs. The ravaged man he was; the strange, inscrutable woman I was. The silence in the room. The distance maintained between us. The eyes that watched their opposites gravely, even over the top of the thick crockery. It made what should have been an act of amenity into a sort of wary deadlock, where neither moved, waiting for the other to move first. By that I don't mean physical movement, of course.

He put his mug down to the floor empty. I thrust mine aside, three quarters full. I passed him cigarettes that I had brought with me.

Then I returned to where I'd been, put my elbow to the bureau top. I said, "Would you like a newspaper? Do you ever read the newspapers?"

He shook his head. I wasn't sure whether the answer was meant for both questions, so I repeated the one I was actually interested in having answered. "Do you ever read them much?"

"No, I never bother. There's nothing in them that has to do with me." He looked at me some more. Then he asked in a passive, detached sort of way, "What do you want with me?"

"I knew Mia, you know."

A hunted look came over his face; he turned it aside for a second. Or maybe it was a haunted look; I didn't know.

He wasn't going to go on, so I had to.

"She meant a lot to me. I thought maybe there was something I could do for you."

"What?" he asked. It wasn't said challengingly. Just inertly.

I shifted unobtrusively around until I could watch his face in the dingy mirror, and yet, in looking at me, he wouldn't guess at once that my eyes were on him.

"When I last saw her—oh, about three or four weeks ago—she asked me to—"

His face hardened, took on a sort of brutal aspect, especially about the mouth. "She's dead," he said.

I went on in the same quiet voice, as though he hadn't spoken. "I know that. But how do you know it? I thought you didn't read the newspapers."

No guilt appeared, though. Only a shuttering of the eyes, an expression of blank groping, as though he were trying to remember himself how he'd come to know about it without reading it in the papers.

I gave him time. "I thought you didn't read the newspapers? Then how did you know?"

He looked at the wall opposite him, and it wasn't to be found there. He looked at the ceiling, and it wasn't there. He looked at his empty hands, and it wasn't there.

I gave him time. "You said you didn't read the newspapers. How did you know, then? How did you know?"

He felt his forehead with the back curve of one hand, and it wasn't there. Wasn't in there.

"How did you know, then? How did you know?"

"Don't," he moaned in a helpless sort of way. "Each time you say that it drives it away again. I'm just going to get it and it drives it away again."

"Did you go up there, maybe, and see her lying there right after it happened? Don't be afraid; there's no harm in that." I shoveled my hands toward him in ingenuous protest. "Isn't that it, Marty? You happened to go up there and found her lying there just the way she was, with one of her own silk stockings twisted around her neck, choked to death; isn't that it?"

"No, she was—smothered to death with a pillow."

I said, without making the tactical error of altering the unexcited, casual tenor of my voice: "You see, you did go up there; that's how you knew. That's all right;

there's nothing to be nervous about in that. You opened the door and you saw her lying there the first thing, right from where you were, on the floor in that front room of hers, so you quickly closed it and went away again. Nobody's blaming you for—"

He said with a sort of childish querulousness, "She wasn't in the front room; she was in the room behind, the one she slept in."

"You see, you know the whole thing," I said quietly. I began treacherously touching up my hair via the mirror. "You say you don't read the newspapers, so you must have gone up there and seen it for yourself. By the way, how'd you get in?" I tried to make my voice sound admiring, flattering to his dexterity.

He began to shake his head, imperceptibly at first, then more and more confirmedly, but with a puzzled expression continuing on his face. "I didn't go up there," he murmured. "I didn't do that, because she wouldn't-a wanted me to. The last time I did she threw me out; she told me never to come around again. She was ashamed, I guess, on account of I looked so dirty and—well, you know. She said she'd call the cops if I ever came near her again. She said, 'Go to the Salvation Army, you bum!' I just watched from across the street after that." He sighed, but he kept on shaking his head.

The denials and retractions were starting in now, I said to myself. But he'd said enough already, more than enough.

I looked in my bag, at the cigarettes that were still there, and pretended not to see them. I closed it with a definitive snap. "We need some more cigarettes," I said. "I'll go down and get them in a minute." I was going to phone Flood. I had enough for him now. It was a job for him from here on. He'd warned me not to look for any documentary evidence. Well, what more could there be than this? He'd said he never read the newspapers, yet he'd known she was dead, and he'd known more than that: he'd known the exact method and even the very room she was lying in. He admitted he'd maintained an endless vigil across the street and been tortured by a cancerous love. What stronger motive could a man have ever had than what she'd done to him?

Flood would know how to get the rest of it out of him in short order, where I didn't. By this time tomorrow, maybe by tonight even, it would all be over.

"You want me to wait here for you?" he asked in that chronically helpless way of his.

"Just stay here where you are; I'll be right back." I opened the door.

The blat of a cheap, defective little radio in one of the adjacent little cubbyholes came welling in from outside.

He quirked his head almost idiotically and blinked. He started to shake his head again imperceptibly as before. This time up and down and not across. "That's how," he murmured cryptically.

"What?" I said from half over the threshold.

"That's how I heard. I remember now. I didn't read it in the papers and I didn't go up there. It came in over the radio at the Silver Dollar place. They got a radio there by the cash register, and there was some kind of a fight that night they wanted to get, so they had it turned on, waiting for it. I just about got there, and I didn't have any soup in me yet, so I understood the words that was coming out of it. I can still remember 'em by heart too. I only heard 'em once, but I can say them right through to the end, just like they came out. Sometimes they say *themselves* over, without me doing it myself at all. They're coming now, and I can't stop 'em. 'An attractive young woman was found murdered in her apartment by the police this afternoon. The victim was Mia Mercer, a brunette about twenty-eight years old, who had recently worked as an entertainer at the Hermitage—'"

His face puckered into a white cicatrice and went slowly over and downward out of sight, but the words continued to well from it unchecked. That voice. You had to hear it to know what grief can really do. No sobs, no huskiness, nothing so warm and alive as that. The monotonous sing-song of Chinese children reciting their lessons, meaningless, arid, a parrotlike duplication.

" '—She was last seen alive Thursday night, when she returned rather late, but it has been established that the murder did not take place until one or two o'clock today. The police are already holding a suspect, whose name is being withheld for the present, and they expect to—' "

I closed the door and came in again. I went over to him and placed my hand across his mouth and sealed it up, silencing that terrible, unbearable, mechanical flow of misery that was pouring from it like from a machine, a machine without intelligence or awareness of its own. I said to him what he'd said to me before: "Don't." I was a woman after all.

Acting can reach great heights of persuasiveness. But sincerity, when there is no acting at all, can reach even greater.

He'd got himself a stay, but not yet an acquittal.

Many hours had gone by. We were still there in the room together. It darkened early, that room, earlier even than the grubby world outside. It was dim already with imminence of dusk, while the afternoon sun still rode high elsewhere.

His voice was a lazy thread stitching through the silence.

"She was in a little blue dress that night; I can see it yet. It's funny how you go someplace and never think you're going to meet someone there who will change your whole life around from then on. You go to some dance or party, just because you've got nothing better to do, and you think by the next night after you won't even remember about it any more. And here ten years later you can still remember everything about it as clear as if it was just the night before. You can't remember any of the other nights around then, or even the months or years, but just that one night; you've saved it whole, the way it was."

His voice stopped. I waited without using my own, afraid if I did he would become too aware of me, wouldn't go on again. He was talking to himself more than to me. I was just the sounding board against which his voice projected itself. Presently he'd gone on again.

"In a little blue dress that sort of swung out wide from here down. She couldn't have been more than eighteen, and I just stood there looking at her."

Like me, I thought, like me. I'd first met Kirk at a dance like that too.

"And I can even remember the piece they happened to be playing just then too. 'Always.' Every time I've ever heard it since, it meant her in a little blue dress, the first time I ever saw her. It was our song, hers and mine, while we were together, and now that we're not, it's just mine, I guess.

"I guess I would have stood there all night like that, just looking. That would have been enough for me. But then the fellow that had taken me there, he came back to me and said: 'What's the matter? What're you going to do, just stand there? Don't you want to dance or nothing?' I said, 'Yeah, but only with one girl. That one over there.' And I showed her to him. He was one of these fellows don't stand back about anything; he laughed and said, 'That can be arranged easy enough,' and grabbed my arm and hauled me over to her then and there, without paying any attention to who she was with. And I went on from there under my own—" He couldn't find the word.

"Evil destiny," I supplied silently to myself.

"So that's how you first met her," I said. "That's how she was when you first met her."

The room was getting cloudier all the time. He was sprawled diagonally on the bed, back on his elbow, picking at the covering as he spoke. I was seated there on a chair drawn up close beside him. It's back was toward the bed, and I was straddling it in reverse, my arms folded along the top of it and my chin resting on them.

He and the bed were between me and the door. It would have been impossible for me to get out of the room in time, in case anything—

I'd been downstairs just now, a few minutes ago, and I'd told them to send somebody up and have them knock on the door in ten minutes' time. No sooner, no later. Seven minutes of the ten were up now.

The two pillows on the bed, pillows such as she'd been smothered with, were lying there undisturbed. They were within easy reach of him, the way he lay. The window looked out on a blind surface of shaft wall, and we were alone in the room, cut off, isolated. He didn't know someone was coming up to knock on the door outside in three more minutes. For all he knew, no one was coming near here for the rest of the night.

I dropped my wrist a little on the inside of the chair back, glanced at it. Two and a half minutes.

"I know who did it, Marty," I said quietly.

His eyeballs rolled upward at me like marbles, stayed that way, peering from under his upper lids. Finally he said uncertainly, "Yeah, that guy they've got up there now; everybody knows."

"No, no, I don't mean him. I know who *really* did it." I kept my lashes inscrutably down. "I'm the only one who does. Here's something that no one knows, no one but me, and now I'm telling you. *I was there at the time it happened.* I was in the place. I saw him, and he didn't know it; he didn't see me."

A pulse in his cheek started to throb. I saw it begin, and then I kept my eyes off it from then on. A cord running down the side of his neck stood out more distinctly than it had a minute ago, I thought, but I wasn't quite sure.

I knew what he was going to ask next, but I had to

wait for him to ask it before I could answer it. He took quite a while, as though he had a hard time getting the words to come.

"Why didn't you—tell someone sooner?" He swallowed in the middle of it. I saw the obstruction go down his throat.

"Maybe I didn't want to get mixed up in it."

"Are you—sure you really saw him doing it?"

"I saw him crouching *over her*, right in the act."

"Why didn't you scream or holler, try to save her?"

"I was afraid he'd do it to me too, if I did; I was afraid of my own life. I stuffed the corner of a towel in my mouth to make sure he wouldn't hear me."

"How'd you happen to be up there? How come he didn't see you, if you were right in the place when it happened?"

Tension was suddenly in the room with us, crowding the air in it, like a slowly expanding gas, making it resist when we tried to breathe it in. And yet we were both so quiet, almost motionless. He plucking at the counterpane. My face brooding over the chair top.

"I'd dropped in on her. That was nothing; I'd often done that before. For no particular reason, just to kill time. We were pretty chummy, you know. We were fiddling around there, doing nothing, like two women will at that hour of the day. She wasn't even dressed yet."

I remembered that much from firsthand observations.

"It suddenly occurred to me I wanted to take a shower. I don't know why; I just felt like it. She said go ahead, help myself. I went in there and left the bathroom door open just about an inch; I took off my things and got behind that thick green glass door. I left that open about an inch too. But I never got to turn the faucets on the wall. I was standing there strapping on one of these rubber caps that we women use, without making any noise, I guess. I had a little trouble adjusting it—it was hers—and that took several minutes. All of a sudden I thought I heard a man's voice out there where she was. I tiptoed out of the closet to close the bathroom door, so he wouldn't be able to look in. Before I even got over to it, it was already happening. I heard her fall to the floor in the room outside. I grabbed a towel and put it around me, and I stuck my eye to the crack of the door and looked out. It was only wide enough for one eye. I saw him pressing down hard at something on the floor there, and I knew what he was doing. I hid way back in the shower closet, where it was dark, for a long time afterward, until I was sure he'd gone."

"And you saw him?"

He said it very low. As close to him as I was, I could hardly hear it. His lips just moved a little. About a minute was gone now; about one and a half were left.

"I certainly did. I saw him right in the act. I saw him from head to foot."

"And you've never told anybody?" This time even his lips didn't move; the air in front of them just vibrated, that was all.

"I've never told a living soul. I'm the only one who knows it."

The hand that had been plucking the counterpane flattened on it in a directional pat. "Come here," he said. "Come a little closer, over here by me." His eyes stayed down, didn't look up at me. "Get on the bed here next to me."

My heart hurt as though a surgeon were taking stitches in it. Those two harmless-looking pillows there, side by side— His hand gave the bed another persuasive pat, and then another.

I forced myself up from the chair by pushing my arms against the top of it, and then I moved around it toward him until my knees brought up against the edge of the bed.

His eyes stayed down. He repeated that flat-handed pat atop the bed. Meaning "Down; down here beside me." I glanced at the pillows and then back to him. I put my knee to the bed and sank down on my side.

Our heads were very close together now, though our bodies lay extended in opposite directions, his form overlapping one side of it, mine the other.

His hand reached upward toward the head of the bed and drew one of the pillows out of position by its corner, and he started shifting it down toward me like that, flat along the surface of the bed.

I looked steadily up the ceiling. I thought: "In another minute a great white mass will drop down over me, obliterating everything."

"And you're sure you saw him?" his voice murmured close to my ear.

"I saw all there was to see of him. What do you want? Why did you ask me to come closer to you like this?"

And now the pillow would leap up and then come hurtling down.

Instead he inserted it under the back of my head and took his hand off it; left it there, as a partial support for my head, a resting place. Perhaps it was a form of bribery; I don't know. "Tell me who he was," he said in a husky whisper. "I want to know. I've got to know."

And if it had been he, he wouldn't have to know; he *would* already know.

The tension slowly siphoned from the air and left a sort of vacuum behind it. I felt all limp and starchless. My forehead was damp. I closed my eyes in momentary exhaustion.

The knock on the door came while they were shut like that. The test period was over. Marty just turned his head, not understanding. This was to have saved my life. "Yes," I called out weakly. A hotel boy looked in, and I told him to get some cigarettes or something; I don't remember.

I tried to analyze my own feelings. He stood acquitted now. What further, what greater certainty could there ever be than this? And yet to my surprise, along with the sense of disappointment, of frustration, that was rightly there, there was a sneaking, almost shame-faced sense of relief. I thought to myself with wonderment: "My God, I must actually have developed a liking for this poor devil to feel the way I do about it." Or maybe it was just a sense of sportsmanship, a repugnance at the idea of delivering the final blow to someone who was down already.

I got up presently and went over toward the tarnished glass framed over the bureau. My legs were still a little rocky under me from my recent crisis. "I may as well go now," I reflected; there was nothing for me here any more. I had as much proof as I could hope for.

I was forgetting him. I was forgetting I'd left him in mid-conversation, so to speak. I was forgetting that what to me was a topic over and done with to him was a topic broken off short. He got off the bed in turn, came up behind me. I felt his hand on my arm, but I didn't turn; I continued adjusting my hat.

"Tell me who he is; tell me."

"Why? What satisfaction is it to you to know? There's a man in jail for it already, and they're going to execute him for it soon—"

"That isn't enough; that's no good to me. I'm not the state. Whaddo I care who the state kills for it? I'm the one who loved her. I want to know who really did it, whose hands *really* did it! You can't transfer a thing like that from one guy to another. The one who really did it stays the one who really did it, no matter who the state takes it out on!"

"I don't know."

"You said you did. You said you saw him."

"I just said that."

"You're trying to back out now. You think I'm just a Bowery bum, not worth telling it to. I want that one thing from you, d'you hear me? That one thing. I want to know who that guy was that you saw kill her."

I went toward the door. He came around the outside of me and got there first, got between it and me.

"I'm not going to let you out of here. You know, and you're not getting out of here until I know too."

I tried to paw him aside. He didn't actively raise hands to me, menace me; he just bore my hands down, stayed there. I'd conjured up this tatterdemalion jinni myself out of a bottle of alky, so to speak, and now I couldn't exorcise him again.

"I wasn't up there, I tell you!"

"You said you were, and I believe you the first time. You knew her place too well, even that green glass shower door she had up there! Now who was it you saw? You're going to tell me."

He reached around behind me and caught my arm at the wrist. He started bending it up toward the shoulder, the wrong way. It's painful. It's a method little boys are fond of. It's effective, nonetheless.

We were struggling full-tilt now, even if still only passively. He'd retained a good deal more vigor than I'd suspected, and it occurred to me even in the midst of my present preoccupation that if he'd reacted positively to that other previous test a while ago I would have stood very little chance, knock on the door or no knock.

"Don't! Let go, you're hurting me!" I winced. "You fool!" I could have screamed, but I had more to lose than he by raising a great clamor, attracting attention to the two of us.

I couldn't stand it any more, and just saying I didn't know was no good; he wouldn't take that for an answer.

"You going to tell me? You going to tell me?" he kept breathing into my averted face.

I couldn't think of a name; I couldn't think of an address.

"All right, I'll tell you where you can find him; I'll tell you where he is. It's on the third floor at—" I gave him a name and address at random. "Now let me out of here!" There was water in my eyes from sheer physical pain.

He stood aside, and I clawed the door open and ran

out into the hall. As I hurried along it, rubbing my numbed arm to bring the circulation back and glancing resentfully back a couple of times, it occurred to me that it was just as well that the name and address I'd given him just now, under stress of improvisation, were my own. Under the circumstances there was no telling what he might take it into his head to do.

It's hard to sit waiting in the dark, waiting for a doorknob to turn stealthily, waiting for a blurred form to come creeping in on a death-dealing errand. The night outside was very quiet, and the room within was quieter still, and the only sign that I was there at all was the red bead of my cigarette, brightening and dimming, brightening and dimming, while a clock close by me ticked away.

This, in a way, was the third and final test he was being subjected to, though I hadn't intentionally planned it. The first had been his familiarity with the details of the crime; a firsthand familiarity. He'd neutralized that by his claim of having absorbed them over the radio. But that was just a verbal statement, and there was no way of checking on its truthfulness. So the burden of that test still lay more against than for him. The second had been his failure to make any attempt to silence me, when presumably I alone held knowledge damaging to him. Ergo, the knowledge I presumably held had therefore *not* been damaging to him, had nothing to do with him. So he had passed that one with flying colors. But the score was still one for, one against. Now, quite fortuitously, a third and final test had come up, and this would cinch it. Two out of three. Now he had the definite knowledge of who had killed the thing he valued most. Someone named "French"— he would see that name downstairs in the entryway— who lived in this same house I did, who lived on this same floor, who lived in this same room I was in now. He'd wanted that knowledge badly, badly enough to brutalize me in order to elicit it. The thing was, what had he wanted it for? What did he intend doing with it?

I had my own ideas about that, and that was why I was sitting huddled in a chair now, at three in the morning, instead of occupying the bed where I rightfully belonged. A chair drawn into a corner as far from both bed and room door as I could manage to get it, and with its back turned outward to serve as a screen for my lumped, tucked-under body.

I'd already been undressed and in bed for the night, lying there in the darkness, over two hours ago, when a sense of disquiet, of impending danger—call it a premonition if you will—began to assail me more and more strongly. Why had he wanted the exact name and whereabouts of her killer so badly, once I had convinced him I knew them? It wasn't just for the morbid satisfaction of it alone; it wasn't just so he could lacerate himself still further as he sat the nights away in smokehouses with "her" by his side. He didn't have to have an actual name and address for that; the pronoun "somebody" would have done just as well.

I'd pulled the light chain beside me and sat up at this point. I'd thought: "I better get up out of here, not lie here in this bed; otherwise I'm liable never to wake up in it again in the morning."

That was it, of course; that was what he'd wanted it for.

I put something over me and sat in a chair for a while with the light on. But then I realized that in that way I was only postponing it until some other night, some future night, when I would no longer be on guard. It was better to attract it at once, get it over with, while I was expecting it, was it not? And finally, it was the definitive test. If he came near here on a bloody errand he exonerated himself once and for all, beyond any lingering shadow of a doubt. Surely if he had done such a thing himself he would not attempt to wreak retribution on someone else for having done it. Even madmen didn't do that. Even they retained awareness of the parentage of their own crimes.

True, he couldn't get up here from the street. But that would only delay him a night or two; eventually he'd succeed somehow or other. And I didn't want this thing to be postponed. So I crept down the two flights of stairs and reversed the latch plunge on the outside door so that it could be opened from the outside. If he tried it now, tested it in any way, it would open for him just as any ordinary door.

I went up again to my own place and carefully closed the door without locking it. From a hook on the back of the bathroom door I unslung a laundry bag full of soiled articles of apparel. I carted it over to the bed and put it there where I had been lying myself a short while before. It was squat and lumpy in its natural contour, but I kneaded it and stretched it and its contents into a longer, more columnar outline that more closely approached a torso. Then I carefully arranged the coverings over it and put out the light, and in the dark it looked like someone lying there.

I knew there was still some risk attached to remaining in the place at all, no matter how well I secreted myself; yet I must be an eyewitness of whatever took place, for the test to be a valid one, and I couldn't sit crouched on the upper stairs all night peering down through the banister rails. So I drew a chair over into the far corner and got down behind it and took up my vigil—waiting for the love that had turned to death.

He might be lurking down there in the shadows of the street right now, watching these windows as he had once watched hers. He'd seen the light go out behind them, and now in a little while he'd venture forth and creep up to the door and suddenly vanish within, like something whisked away.

It was very quiet inside and out. There was a half-moon, enough to dust the air with pollen without bleaching it. I had the shades drawn down to three-quarter length, and the oblong boxes of light that came in below them reproduced themselves just high enough on the door slantwise to them, to take its knob. The knob was glass, and when it turned it would blur, create a momentary pinwheel of light. And then another way of knowing would be this: the third step from the top on the stairs outside was faulty; it would creak. I'd learned to skip it whenever I ascended them myself. But he wouldn't know.

It was four o'clock now, and I'd been sitting like this ever since shortly after one. I thought about them, the two of them. And, for that matter, the two of us: Kirk and myself. What a strange way for their love story to end up. A harmless, fluffy little girl of eighteen on a dance floor one night ten years ago, waltzing to the strains of "Always." And a boy comes in and looks at her, takes just one look, and from then on he's in love. And another boy and another girl, somewhere else, a thousand miles away, maybe, who didn't know either of them at the time and didn't even know one another yet. The girl, as a matter of fact, still a child in a middy blouse and bangs, probably chewing her pencil nightly under a lamp while she pored over her algebra homework. And now, ten years later, the first girl is already dead; murdered and infamous and vile. And a derelict, a stumble bum, who was once the boy, is about to creep up the stairs of a strange house, to murder someone he has never seen before, in the depths of the night. And the second boy is a shaven-pated, hollow-cheeked inmate in a penitentiary, awaiting execution for something he didn't do. And the second girl, the "little" girl, is hiding behind a chair in the dark in that same strange room, waiting to watch, to look on at a murder that is to be no murder, that is to be the act without the deed.

How strange, it came to me then, are the patterns of human experience! The meaningless life lines that start out singly and so simply from here, from there, draw slowly toward one another over a period of time, until finally they come together, mesh, to form into a design that never could have been guessed at, foretold, by what had gone before. And the completed fabric is the sum of all the threads that have gone into it.

If another boy hadn't gone to a dance one night and seen a girl there, floating in a blue dress to the strains of "Always," the boy I'd married would not now be in a cell under sentence of death, and I would not now be hiding here in the dark, my cheek pressed to the back of a chair, listening, waiting.

The clock went tick, tick, tick.

Outside there, past the door, the third step from the top snarled all at once, as when you nudge a sleeping cur lying in your path. That was the sound it habitually made, a canine simulation. Then its queerly warped surface relapsed into silence again as the pressure quitted it.

I flung out my hand quickly, struck out the red ember that had been held in it against something. Then I drew myself together, made myself smaller, cowered there, and watched the telltale knob from low down around the side of the chair back.

Nothing happened for a while. For a while that seemed much longer than it probably was. Tick, tick; tick, tick; tick, tick. Hundreds of them, it sounded like. If there was anyone out there at all, he must be standing with his ear close to the door seam, listening to hear if there was anyone astir in here. Or perhaps exploring the door, gauging its surface with stealthy finger tips. He would not think, at first, that it would open at trial, and yet the instinctive thing to do was test the knob; that would show him when he did.

I was frightened, for I knew violence was at hand, was coming in here with me.

Tick, tick; tick, tick; tick, tick. Oh, was it that loud always, or did it just seem so now? Like a small-sized trip hammer hitting against something.

Suddenly the knob gave a warning flash, a coruscation, as its facets slowly began to revolve and the light glanced off each successive one. He *had* been out there and he was coming in. It turned so slowly, and yet somehow so remorselessly, as though there were no power on earth could keep it from completing its appointed orbit. With not a forewarning sound to go with it. If I had stayed in that bed, if my eyes hadn't already been wide open and fixed on it, there would have been no way of detecting that entry was being gained. I would have gone from sleep to deeper sleep with scarcely a fluttering of eyelids, and *our* story, Kirk's and mine, would have had an ending not very dissimilar to theirs after all.

I couldn't even tell very accurately when the door parted from the frame, slanted inward. By the time a sluggish current of air, a displacement, had eddied toward and reached me, to show that something, some-one had come in, the door was back in place again and there was a shadowy, blurred outline between my-self and it, so that I could no longer see the knob.

This blur, this new darkness against the old dark-ness, stood motionless for a while, then gradually started to shift over toward the bed. As it sidled in that direction the knob behind it came clear again, but that no longer held interest for me. Motion could only be detected in this shadowy mass by the contrasting mo-tion it seemed to give the things around it that were not moving. As when you look from a train window and the things beyond seem to be moving. Thus the white plateau of the bed seemed to sidle forward and cut it off below the knees, but it was not the bed that had moved but the figure in the background.

Again it fell motionless and stood looking down now at close range. Breathing was beginning to be audible, the strained, harsh breathing of slowly mounting, slowly unleashed rage. Deepening, thickening, stran-gling, until it began to approach the catarrhal. My own had stopped, or seemed to have.

Tick, tick, tick—

Suddenly in the smoky dimness there was a flash midway down the vague form and close in against it. Oh, not a bright flash; the flicker of a tongue of ghostly gray flame. And a burnished blade had sprung into being, with a small wooden tick.

I bit my lip and heaved soundlessly against the padded chair surface.

It went up overhead, catching more light as it did, blurring into a low-toned silvery flash; poised there, foreshortened to a point. The strained breathing choked, formed into a sob. I could hear words all run together in a bated paroxysm of torment and fury. "You dirty devil! Why couldn't you leave her with me?"

The silvery radiance slashed down and vanished, and there was the crunch of steel puncturing tight-packed layers of fabric; the bed quivered. The shadowy form crouched low above it, then straightened again, took a heavy, sodden step or two toward the door.

He'd killed the nothingness in the bed because he hadn't killed the woman. This was the final test; there could be no greater test than this.

I pulled my face from the chair back, reached out without thinking, and tugged on the chain pull of a nearby lamp. Light bloomed out, dazzling as a sunburst after the preceding gloom. I don't know if he saw me clearly or not. I must have seemed like an apparition over there in the corner in that sudden welling up of light.

He cast a single explosive look over that way that seemed not to strike me at all, only to verify that there was light there and someone there who'd seen what he had done. Then he floundered out through the door opening as I reared up to my full height behind the chair.

I thrust it aside, tried to go after him. "Marty!" I called. "Wait! Don't run like that!"

He was already lunging down the stairs, like one possessed. He must have taken my voice, too, for a hallucination of his overheated mind. It only stung him to an added frenzy of flight. I reached the head of the stairs and could see his leaping shadow glancing from the walls below. There was no light up here, but there was one down at the foot. I kept calling down, "Marty, come back! Wait, you haven't—" I was afraid to scream too loudly; I was afraid it would rouse the entire house. I don't think he would have heeded even if I had.

The street door gave an empty slap, and he had gained the open night. Something touched my foot, and the knife was lying there on the topmost step with its blade still out.

I turned and ran back into the room and across it and flung up the window, hoping I could head him off from there. I could see him flitting along down there, making a scalloping detour of each successive doorway. I leaned far out, calling, "Marty, wait! Come back and listen to me a minute! Don't run away!"

I saw his arms go up, and he put his hands over his ears as he ran along to keep the sound out. He must have taken me for an accusing voice of his own conscience resounding against the night. He darted over to the other side, where the shadows were even thicker, and was lost there. In a moment the street was empty.

I turned slowly back into the room. The knife lay on the bed where I'd thrown it, atop the punched-in mound of clothes. If he'd only taken time to look at it, I thought ruefully, he could have seen there was no blood on the blade.

The night was empty and quiet again, just as it had been before. Inside the room something was going tick, tick; tick, tick; tick, tick.

I had to find him and I had to tell him. So I went back there to that place of the unburied dead to seek him out, to sit beside him for a moment or two, to say: "You didn't kill anyone in that room last night; don't be frightened. I lied. No one knows who did it, Marty. We'll have to let it go at that." I had a ten-dollar bill with me. I was going to touch his hand in parting, leave it behind. At that, it seemed a paltry enough thing to do. But what could I, what could anyone, do for him? Give him back his love, give him back his life?

The barman looked up when I came in, and I could tell he remembered me, knew me from the time before.

But he was busy just then, so I made my own way back through the place unaided, looking for him among the wan, hopeless faces that were raised to me as I went past. There was that same strange hush as when I'd come in here the first time. Life walking amid the dead. Empty eye sockets looking up at me with no light behind them. A hand, a hand that didn't belong to a living man and therefore couldn't be resented as such, even reached gropingly toward me as I moved by, fell short, dropped back again. Asking some sort of help; it knew not what.

I found myself all the way at the back of the place at last, beside the same table he had been at the time before. "His" table, I suppose, that he always sought out when he came in here, for habit is a strange thing, surviving even reason. There was a clear place there. Two empty chairs and an empty jigger standing before each one. His drink and hers. I knew then that he'd only recently gone.

I stood there looking down in silence, two fingers touching the table top, the frustrated ten-dollar bill still held tucked under my palm by my thumb.

The barman had come down and was standing beside me. "You looking for Heartbreak?" he said. "He *was* here and he went away again. Just a little while ago, not very long before you got here." He adjusted one of the chairs, picked up the two jiggers by the fingers of one hand. "Yeah, I seen him get up and go out."

He wanted to make conversation. I was as close to being carriage trade as this place would ever see. "He did a funny thing. I couldn't make him out tonight. He only had two bits left on him. I know for a fact it was his last two bits, because it's what I gave him back myself after the last two drinks. Then on his way out he stops and has me break it up into nickels. Four of them he hands to the four guys that are standing nearest to him, without even looking to see who they are. Then the fifth one, he goes over the the juke box and stands picking out a tune. Takes his time until he's found just what he's looking for. They never do that around here, you know; the house has to feed them things. He puts it in and starts it up, and then instead of waiting to hear it out, he goes on out right while it's in the middle of playing"—he swept his arm toward the darkness out before the entrance—"walking real steady, much straighter than usual, and with a kind of a halfway smile on his face. Like he got good news or was going to meet somebody who had good news for him. We was all looking at him by that time."

"And the song?" I murmured quietly, staring at the table without seeing it much. He didn't have to tell me.

" 'Always.' "

I knew then.

I remembered what I'd thought to myself the first night I'd come in here searching for him. The lower depths, this place was. The lowest depths of all this side of the grave. There was nothing beyond this, nothing further. Nothing came after it except—the river.

The girl was dead, and now the boy was too. That story was over, the story that began on a dance floor ten years ago to the strains of "Always."

"He may be back a little later on," the barman tried to suggest. "They come and they go—"

I knew he wouldn't be back. Anywhere. Ever again.

I turned and walked slowly back toward the entrance again, the scene around me fading out as my thoughts turned inward. The thing that preoccupied me was this: Did *I* kill that man? Was it I, by what I did last night?

And the answer was obvious, undeniable. I shook my head slowly and without hypocrisy. No, I was kind to him. I gave him something to die for. That was more than he'd had before. It is better to die for something than to live for nothing. I gave him completion, vindication. He did not hear me call out to him there in that dark room last night. In that bed lay the assassin of what he held most dear, brought to justice by his own hand. I gave him that much to take with him: the kindly illusion that he'd requited her loss.

No, I did not kill him. All I did was give him something worth dying for.

I stopped beside the juke box and took out a nickel. I searched the slots and found the one that I was looking for. I dropped the coin in and stood by there, waiting for the strains to come. Then when they had, his song and hers—

> *Not for just an hour, not for just a day,*
> *Nor for just a year, but*
> *Always*

I quirked my finger from the temple in a parting salute to someone they could not see.

"Good-by, Heartbreak. Better luck some other time, some other where—"

I turned and walked slowly outside into the dark while the cheap music, the costly, precious music, softly ebbed away behind me.

7

Atwater 8–7457 . . . . . . Mordaunt

THIS ONE WENT EASY; this one took care of itself. I found out all my self-rehearsing had been super-
fluous when a young woman's voice, immediately upon
answering, said pleasantly: "Dr. Mordaunt's office, good
day."

He was a doctor, then. Her doctor. She hadn't had it
that way in the book, though; "Dr. Mordaunt," the
usual way of putting down one's doctor's name. Just
"Mordaunt," like any other man she knew.

For a moment, because he was a doctor, I was almost tempted to hang up without going any farther,
without speaking at all. Saying to myself, "A doctor
cures his patients; a doctor doesn't kill them." But, I
reminded myself, he may not have been her doctor in
that sense; he may have been just a doctor whom she
knew. A doctor who was a friend. A doctor who was
even—something else.

A doctor is a man, after all. A doctor loves or hates,
fears or avenges himself, just as anyone else.

All this within my mind in the space of an outward
second. And meanwhile the young woman's voice was
waiting.

"May I speak with the doctor?"

"Are you one of his regular patients? May I have the
name, please?"

"No, I'm not."

"Then I'm sorry, I can't put the doctor on. I can give you an appointment, if you'd like. Would you care for an appointment?"

I'd have to do it that way then. I told her yes, I would.

"Thursday at four?" This was Wednesday. I said that would be all right. It gave me twenty-three hours' grace. "The name, please?"

"Alberta French." French had been my name before I married Kirk. And now, thanks to the state, I was once more as I had been then. So why not in name as well?

"Miss or Mrs.?"

She wanted to know everything, it seemed. I chose Miss, for obvious reasons. Mia Mercer had been unmarried too.

"Can you tell me who recommended the doctor to you?"

I had known that was coming. I could have said she did. I intended to eventually. But not to her. I wasn't going to waste any possible surprise value it might have on a third person over a wire. I was saving that for him, direct and to his face.

I said, "I'll give the doctor that information personally when I see him."

I was afraid she might argue the point and even end up by cancelling the appointment, so to forestall her and keep the appointment valid by default, so to speak, I hung up on her without further ado.

I sat and thought about it for a good long while there by the phone. Trying to map out something that would at least carry me safely past the preliminary consultation. This was not going to be as easy as the Marty matter, for instance. There was an arbitrary limitation imposed here. I had to work within the framework of a single visit, little better than half an hour, forty minutes at the very outside. Within that I might possibly find some means of extorting a second one; from the second one I might extract a third, and so on. But had to have *some* surface reason for going to a doctor in the first place.

There was nothing the matter with me that I knew of. I had a badly wrenched heart, but that didn't show. Since I had no legitimate symptoms to offer I would have to produce some ersatz ones. Yes, but if he were any kind of doctor at all, wouldn't he see through them at once? It might put him on his guard. If there were only something I could swallow to derange my system for a while without permanently impairing it. If there were only something I could rub onto my skin that would cause an irritation, produce an evanescent rash. I even thought of holding my hand for a moment or two under the hot-water tap to scald it more or less sufficiently to require treatment, but with clouds of steam already rising from the drain vent my courage failed me. The stray drop or two that leaped upon it stung so vengefully.

I was still pondering the problem unsolved twenty-two and a half hours later when I alighted from the bus around the turn from my destination and struck out the remaining short distance on foot. It was too late now; I would have to rely on improvisation, summoning up my symptoms as he explored for them. And yet perhaps that would be the best way after all, I now realized; an intangible something that he could not immediately pin down might give me more stay with him than some minor blemish that could be cleared up at a single prescription.

I rounded the turn, told off numbers—nearly faltered to a halt for a moment. I was stunned at my first sight of the place. The telephone exchange covering this entire district had fooled me. I had expected a swank, towering apartment house on one of the avenues, or a smaller but still ultrasmart one just off them at the very least. Instead, it turned out, it was an old-fashioned, high-stooped brownstone house. Badly weather-worn, and not even very clean at that. People like her, when they had a doctor at all, had one of these modish, bedside-manner practitioners, I had always thought. It occurred to me there was an anomaly here: a show girl, a woman in night life, with an old-fashioned family doctor. Well, I still had no proof that he was *her* doctor. He might have been a friend.

The whole aspect of the place was that of one of these houses forgotten by time, even to what might be called the details of everyday occupancy as they showed themselves from the street, let alone the structural signs of age. The very curtains on the parlor-floor windows, which was what they had called the first floor above the street in the days of this house, ended in a row of ball fringe.

There was no brass plate affixed to the doorway, nothing like that. A small black-lettered placard thrust into the rim of one window, inside the pane, gave his name: "J. Mordaunt, M.D."

I climbed to the top of the stoop and I rang the bell. How strange, I thought, to go into a house like this, at what to our modern eyes really amounted to second-story level. To stand there waiting admittance as I was now, as on a perch, well above the heads of passers-by or the roofs of passing vehicles, looking down on the street from above.

A flicker of motion snagged my eye, and I turned to look along the face of the house to one side of me. Someone had just been watching me through a gap between curtain edge and side of window. I was too late to see them. It was the fall of the curtain back into true, after the figure was already gone, that had caught my notice.

It struck me as a rather untrustful way to be admitted to a doctor's consulting room, where, at least during visiting hours, the door is usually open to all comers.

The inner door behind the vestibule had opened, and a stocky, better-than-middle-aged woman of Finnish or some similar northern Mongoloid descent stood looking at me.

"Is the doctor in?" I asked deprecatingly.

"You godt an appointment to see, yas?" she said surlily.

"I have an appointment for four."

I must have neglected to nod along with the remark, thinking it unnecessary. She heightened her voice: "You speak louder, yas? I cannot hear goodt."

I spoke louder. "I have an appointment for four."

"So, come in. I tell."

At first glance her hair had seemed white. It was whitening, but the process had not completed itself; what gave the all-over impression, I saw, was that its former natural color had been a straw blonde, almost white in itself.

I wondered what had become of the assistant; this was definitely not the voice that had spoken to me yesterday.

She ushered me into the front parlor with a rather browbeating sort of imperiousness. "Go in. I tell." She went toward the stratified dimnesses at the back of the hall, herself dimming, tone by tone, as she drew away from me, until she was all gone. But whether upstairs or down, I couldn't tell.

The place was stale with that stale smell that only old houses can attain. It was not a question of dust; it exuded from within the very walls themselves. It was the ichor of the dwelling's bones. This room where I sat waiting was, decoratively speaking, a sort of port of last call. It was filled with flotsam and jetsam of bygone eras, all mixed in together, a piece from this one, a piece from that one, but even the most recent items stopped well short of the first Great War.

I saw things that I recognized only by hearsay, had never seen with my own eyes before. For instance, on a center table there stood a platter of waxed fruits under a glass dome. Then there was a phonograph with a crank handle protruding from the side and a great tulip-shaped horn rearing over it and threatening the middle of the room. Against a shield on the wall hung two mallards in high relief, complete with natural feathers, under convex glass. At the small of my back, until I dislodged it to find comfort, was a lumpy, battered mass that had once been a leather pillow with a decorative motif burned into it.

What had *she* to do with anyone like this? What had been the connection between them?

He must have had to come down from above. I heard a fairly audible masculine tread coming down a staircase, although at some distance to the rear. Then it approached along the hall toward where I waited. Slow and unenthusiastic, as though finding in the summons only a wearisome, unwelcome task. It stopped short of the room I was in, however, and a door opened and closed to admit it close by.

He had gone into the next room. An unsuspected seam that had lurked unseen until now down the center of a pair of sliding doors glowed silver with high-powered examining light, and there were vague sounds of fumbling preparation from the other side of it. Disquietingly audible to me.

What sounded like an enamel panful of loosely rolling instruments was shifted sleazily aside to make room. Water ran, and there was even the suck of soap, produced by the suction between two hand hollows.

I found the whole thing terrifying. Had I been a bona fide patient, I suspected, I should have run forth into the street without waiting to be accosted by this wretched sloven.

The floor kept creaking as he moved back and forth; I imagine he was drying his hands on a towel. Evidently it was too tedious a process to pursue through to the end. A moment later there was a patting sound against starched linen or some similar stiffened fabric. He was completing the act by patting his hands down his sides!

The woman, the housekeeper, must have looked in at him. I heard the other, lateral door creak slightly and suddenly heard her voice in there with him. "You liff you glasses oppstairs."

I heard him say, "What'd she do with that appointment pad of hers?" He had to speak loudly because of her deafness. I heard him quite clearly out where I was. At least there was no conspiratorial whispering.

The housekeeper answered with that same congenital surliness she had displayed toward me: "That I godt nodding to do with. You ask her. You don't ask me."

It was the assistant's day off, apparently. Or else she only worked for him on a part-time basis.

It might have been an unfair test I was subjecting him to, judging him by his surroundings and by sounds overheard through a door; he might very well have been a genius, a savant of medical science, unrecognized and unrewarded, in spite of all this, but I found myself insisting: "This man is no good. He is no good as a doctor."

And the inescapable corollary to that, of course, though I failed at the time to take sufficient note of it, was: "Because he doesn't want to be. Because he's not interested in being." But then, if you don't want to be a doctor, if you don't care, why be one?

The doors parted with a grunting and wobbling; the seam of silver became a four-square flash flood pouring in on me, and he was ready for me at last.

He stood there, and I looked at him and he looked at me.

Antagonists for a coming duel, though only one of us was aware of it yet. He was lumpy and yet powerful with it. Bent at the shoulders and neck, but not from weakness, from lack of regard for holding himself upright, straight, all his life through. His hair was dark, and there was that most objectionable type of baldness to be discerned through it; the strands brushed straight across the scalp from side to side, with pink interstices alternating with their pitiful attempt at concealment.

His by-courtesy white jacket had stains of iodine on it, some of them worn to faint yellow by age, and his bared ankles were thrust into crumbling leather house slippers.

I said, "How do you do, Doctor?" and rose warily to my feet.

He said, "Come right this way. By all means. Come right this way."

Even that bit of phrasing smacked of the musty, the old-fashioned, somehow. Why "by all means"? That was what I was there for. It was as though there had been some imponderable objection and he were effacing it. Had there been—in his own mind?

I stepped past him, and he smelled a little. Doubly. Of some old-fashioned antiseptic, carbolic or something; it might have been the soap he'd just used. And the other component was bodily uncleanliness.

A thrill of repulsion ran its course through me and spent itself again as the broad table intervened between us.

He said, "My assistant has mislaid the record of your appointment. Do you mind giving me your name again and all the rest? I have to do this, you see."

Yes, I thought, you have to. "Alberta French."

"I believe I have never treated you before, Miss French?"

"No, you haven't. I'm not often ill."

He left the notation on the desk before him. It was obviously uncompleted. He hadn't come to whom it was had given me the recommendation yet. And I knew he surely would before I was through.

"Ah," he said about my seldom being ill. "And what do you complain of now, Miss French?"

I'd decided upon a fairly vague symptom. That is to say, one that could not be easily disproved, centered upon any particular cause at sight. "Doctor, I've been getting spells of dizziness lately, more and more often, and I don't like them."

"Hm," he said. Which might have meant anything. Which probably meant nothing.

"The other day I was coming home, and the whole street got black; I had to hold my hand out against a wall and stand still for a minute until it passed over."

"How long since you first began to notice this?" He was looking at me, but somehow the expression on his face matched the tempo of his tread as I had heard it before: complete disinterest in this case. And all other cases as well. "That," I thought, "will change at mention of a name presently. I hope."

"For quite some time now. Several months. At first I didn't think anything of it—"

He took something out of a balky drawer beside him that he had to wrench open; he curled his underlip; he stood up.

"Take off your coat, please. Roll up your sleeve. There, that's high enough. No, just that one."

I wondered why his simplest instructions, such as this, seemed to quicken a little current of fear in me. Maybe it was the atmosphere here. Or something about his own personality.

"Make a tight fist." He was dangling a rubber tube. He tied it excruciatingly tight and took my blood pressure.

I kept watching his hands while he was about it. They were strong, sinewy; the veins on the back stood out like whipcord. Those filthy, yellowed nails. Those brutal, lumpy fingers, almost looking swollen with their own bulk. They could have smothered someone to death under a pillow so easily, those hands.

It seemed to me he was doing it unnecessarily—yes, even vindictively—tight, as though not he but his hands themselves, autonomously, detected my dislike and unspoken accusation. As though his brain were down there in those two lumpy pads.

I drew in my breath, cold, and closed my eyes.

Finally he unwound it. The blood burned, struggling to get back into where it had been.

I didn't ask him and he didn't tell me.

He resumed his seat, made a steeple of his hands. "You sleep well?"

"No, very poorly."

"You eat well?"

"No, I scarcely eat at all."

A sudden little gleam of interest lit up his eyes at this point that I failed totally to understand. It was the first interest he had shown throughout the entire proceeding.

"Tell me." He stopped, as though arranging the way he wished to phrase it. "Do you eat poorly because you have no appetite or because—" He slowed a little. I wondered what he was going to say; what other reason was there for not eating well than lack of appetite?

He finished it. "Or because your circumstances will not permit you to eat as well, as fully, as you would like?" But why that mischievous little eye glitter with it? Was that funny?

I didn't answer, feeling that there was a fork in the road here and, rather than take the wrong one, preferring not to take any.

He seemed to accept the silence for an answer. He looked down again at the form or whatever it was that he still had before him. "I see here that I have not yet completed— Tell me, who recommended me to you? In what way did you hear of—?"

"Here it comes," I said to myself.

I got a grip on the lower leg of my chair with the turn of my instep. "A friend of mine. Mia was the one who told me." Then, as though in recollection that her given name might not be enough, that he might not recognize her by that alone, "Mia Mercer," I expanded. A trick of speech to suggest the closest intimacy.

We looked at each other a long time, long and hard, both of us. I said to myself, "The duel is on."

He said, "She's gone now, isn't she?"

He seemed not to know, said it as if he had heard it vaguely somewhere or other, wanted me to confirm it.

"Yes, it was in the papers." I said it vacantly, distrait, as if still mildly sad about it even this long after.

"By some man named—"

"Somebody she knew, I guess," I said, looking down, still saddened.

"Some man named Murray."

There was something almost obscene about it, having my own name thrown at me like that in a place like this. It was good he didn't have his stethoscope to me just at that minute; he would have heard it jump.

"Did you know him?"

"I didn't know anyone she knew. I just knew her."

He nodded, thought awhile.

"Those she knew, in any case, are scattered to the wind," he went on. "The fabric of her—how shall we say it?—acquaintanceship is all tattered and no good any more." I couldn't make out what he was trying to say to me, except that he was looking at me quite intently.

Then he said, "Tell me, how did she come to speak of me? Were you ill at the time?"

"Well, I suppose I must have been feeling—low, depressed."

"And she said—? Tell me, what were her exact words? How did she—?"

There was something here. I had to be careful; I had to be vague; I could sense that without understanding why. "Well, it's quite some time past. She said, 'Why don't you go to see Dr. Mordaunt? He might be able to do something for you.' "

The choice of phrase seemed to be satisfactory. His eyes enlarged, then became their normal size again.

"But it's quite some time since. Were you working in the meantime?"

"Oh yes, I—"

"But you're not at the moment?"

I took the cue offered for what it was worth. "No, not just now—"

"Yes, and when one doesn't work one's appetite—suffers," he said in sanctimonious reflection.

"And then these dizzy spells—" I began, to lend a little plausibility.

He waved that aside, as though we were both too intelligent, knew too much, to waste any more time with that. That was the translation I got from the flip gesture.

"You live alone?"

I said yes, told him where.

He danced the point of his pencil awhile. "Have you ever taken anything to steady your nerves?" he asked absently, upending it and looking at the lead closely.

I moistened my lips, uncertain of direction. "Not that I—"

"Not yourself? I see. Many people do, you know."

From a consultation this had long ago become a rambling conversation. Or was it as rambling as it seemed? Now even that dwindled; from a conversation it became just meditation.

He seemed to be looking down. I received quite a shock, suddenly, when I saw that he wasn't, that he was looking at me from under his thick, creased lids without seeming to.

He leaned forward again, this time did look at the paper below him on the table. "Come back—let me see, this is Thursday—come back Saturday, two days from now."

Then he sort of died out, looking down.

"At what time, Doctor?"

"Oh, any time after dark. Ring the basement bell. In case Sophia—in case my housekeeper—is out that night I may not hear you if you come to the upstairs door."

So he was going to be alone and he wanted me to come after dark, when no one would be likely to see me enter! What had I said that was wrong? What had I done? What trap had I fallen into, unknowing, during that long, rambling, seemingly innocuous conversation.

He pried apart the sliding doors with a horrid grating sound.

The last thing he said was, "I'll see what I can do for you then." He gave a funny glance over one shoulder as he did so, as if to see whether anyone was around.

I carried that away with me, memory of that self-betraying little backward look. That and a grisly, *unclean* sort of fear, as unclean in sensation as his office and his instruments and his person had been in contemplation. And this unshakable conviction, reiterating itself continually in my mind: "If you go back into that house again the doctor's name may not be Mordaunt the second time; the doctor's name may be death."

So I wasn't going back, and oh, I wasn't going back, and no, I wasn't going back, and in between each recurrent resolve not to go back I'd see his face, Kirk's face, or think of him, or say his name down in my heart, and when nine o'clock on Saturday came I was back; I was creeping, inching, down the darkened side street toward that darkened, waiting house. Frightened and helpless and alone, yet moving steadily forward, slow as it was; mincing, as though feeling of the ground first each time I brought my foot forward to set it down, yet getting nearer, nearer all the time.

It never occurred to me that there was someone, somewhere in a hollowed-out concrete block, could have been proud of this. I had no leisure to think of it that way.

There, it was three away now. There, it was two away. There, it was the next one. This foot was trying not to move, to stay back where it had been. Now the other one was trying not to. Smart feet. But they weren't married to Kirk Murray; just my head and heart were.

Oh, it was so dark along this street. Just that hooded, half-dimmed light on the other side, too far behind me to do any good any more. Looking downward into the little pool of its own reflection, like a discreetly retiring eye refusing to see what happened to me. And that little cross of punctured green pin points down the other way at the corner below, like a spark floating a little above the curb, that sometimes turned red and then came back to green again. A car passed once in a while, but even that was nothing, just a swift black shape hastening along on the black tide with a glint of silver at its prow.

I was up to it now, and there it was waiting: black eyes in triple rows, protruding teeth formed by the stoop steps, seeming to say, "I knew you'd come; I knew I'd get you."

I hadn't even told Flood; I don't know why. I hadn't even taken the most elementary, most ordinary precautions—to let someone else know I was coming here; I was going into this place. So that in case I didn't come out again—

Because I had nothing definite to tell him as yet, I suppose, other than that Mordaunt had told me to come back a second time after dark. Because I was afraid of ridicule, I suppose, and would almost have rather faced this thing, whatever it was to be, alone than have him turn up the palms of his hands and say: "Almost every doctor you go to see asks you to come back a second time." Or shrug and say: "Then if you're afraid to go there don't go there. No one's making you. Why come running to us? We can't give you a police escort to every doctor who makes evening appointments or happens to look across his shoulder as he's seeing you out the door."

Now I was here, and the time for what I should have done and what I shouldn't have done was over; this was how I was going to do it.

The parlor floor and the two above it were dark. But now that the impediment of the preceding stoop was out of the way, I saw that the double window in the basement, deep within the areaway, niched within the projection of the two stoops, was showing a sullen brown-orange through a thick, almost opaque, shade. So he was waiting down there, as he'd said.

I didn't even have anything on me to—well, in case anything happened. The lack was only relative, after all. A protective knife, for instance, was only as strong as the wrist behind it. A gun? I had no gun. A whistle, perhaps. Yet what chance would even a whistle have of

reaching out here to the street from the deeps, the unsuspected recesses and keeps, of that jealously sealed
house? Less chance than my own unaided scream, and
that had little chance enough.

I played a forlorn game that kids know well, pro-
crastinating, marking time, saying; "As soon as this
next man coming along on the other side goes by I'll
go down the step and ring the bell." Then, "He didn't
count; he passed too fast. Well, as soon as this *next* one
goes by, then I surely will." And then, "He didn't count
either; he turned in somewhere before he got here."
Until, in sudden helpless discovery, "There's no one
else coming. Now I have to go!" And through it all a
grown-up voice, the voice of me grown up, scoffing in
my ear, "Coward! Coward! Then why did you come
here at all? Why didn't you drop the whole thing when
you got safely outside the other day?"

I forced myself down into the coal-black sunken pit
of the areaway at last. "Kirk, look after me. I'm going
in." I knew he was helpless many miles away, buried in
steel and concrete, but I had to have *some* talisman to
see me through.

When I'd found the bell I rang it in such a strange
way, had anyone been able to see me through the layers
of dark. Collared my wrist with my other hand and
thrust it home by that means, as though in itself it were
atrophied, had no power to move.

Yes, it was childish, I know. It was the last lingering
childishness in me giving up the ghost. There would be
no more of it left in me after this. This was Alberta
Murray, growing up as she stood before this house
waiting to go in. Making her debut into an adult world
such as she had never dreamed she would enter, such as
she had never dreamed existed: a world of jungle violence and of darkness, of strange hidden deeds in
strange hidden places, of sharp-clawed treachery and
fanged gratitude, where compunction and conscience
were just other words for weakness and used as such.
Strange debut.

It made a faint sound far back inside, not the usual sound of a bell, a sort of angry, wasplike buzzing. These basement entryways in New York had, or have where they have still remained unaltered, a single common feature: a grilled iron gate giving in under the stoop structure. Then within that, at right angles, comes the wooden house door itself. This, I suppose, was to make access more difficult in the old days. The gate itself is a full-sized door in every sense of the word: it reaches from top to bottom of the embrasure, save that it is slit, can be seen through when it is daylight or where there is a light within the inner passage.

There was no sound of the inner door opening or of anyone coming out. He must therefore have already been in position, standing there concealed in the dark, watching me through the grille the whole time. His voice when it sounded, though it was low and meant to be reassuring, was so close to my face just the other side of the barrier and came so unexpectedly, it made my heels go up. "Good evening. I've been wondering how much longer you were going to take."

Then, and then only, there was noise enough as he unfastened the heavy obstacle and swung it back for me. A little carbolic, a little uncleanliness came out unseen in the dark.

"You should never do that," he said. "For fully five minutes you stood up there on the sidewalk, as if you couldn't make up your mind. It—it doesn't look right, gives a bad impression. When you are coming anywhere, especially when you are coming here to see me, go right in, don't stand around like that outside."

So he'd been watching me the whole time, probably had been on the lookout since before my arrival, like—like some sort of anthropoid lurking behind those iron bars.

I couldn't help commenting to myself, "Where would you have been now if Flood had sent someone with you as an escort, for instance, and you had parted from him within sight of the house? Or even exchanged some unobtrusive signal with him from a distance?"

I dredged up what I thought a plausible enough excuse to cover the hesitant behavior that he didn't approve of, though whether he believed it or not, I couldn't tell. "Oh, I'll tell you why that was, Doctor. I found out from a clock that I passed on the way over here that I was five minutes ahead of time, and I didn't want to be too early. I'm funny that way. I like to keep an appointment to the minute, so I waited outside to—"

"Well, as a matter of fact, you're five minutes late."

"Then the clock must have been slow."

He had not, meanwhile, stood back to admit me. He had instead come out past me to the sunken rim of the areaway and peered out over the two upright brownstone slabs that formed a sort of guard for it, first up the street in one direction, then down it in the other.

It was done with an assumption of casualness, even inconsequence, as though he were no more than an ordinary householder who, once summoned to the door, takes the opportunity of savoring the fresh air for a moment as long as he is out that far. But it didn't mislead me. He wanted to make sure that my ingress should pass unobserved.

"Go ahead in, don't stand there." In itself the remark was innocuous enough; it was the way he uttered it without turning his head toward me, keeping his gaze steadily forward on the street, that made it a conspiratorial something else again. Everything he said and did, he did so— I didn't know what the exact word was myself. Sinisterly.

I would have to go in in another moment anyway, I knew, so long as I was this far, but I grasped at any delay, no matter how fleeting. "But I don't know where the light is, Doctor. I can't see my way."

"Go in without it. It's just a straight hall; you don't need it. I'll be right there." Again he didn't turn his head. He wanted to be sure the street was sterile.

I knew. Oh, I knew; any fool would have by now. What doctor receives his patients without a light, scans the street after her as she goes in? The Finnish woman was out of the house, as he had known she would be, as he had planned she should be, and there was something grim going to take place here.

I was too frightened to back out of going in any more. I was too frightened to do anything but go ahead. There are times when that is no figure of speech. I was afraid if I balked now he would overpower me and drag me in with him by main force. And I had at least that little slack left yet to my rope; I was still a free agent for a moment or two longer, provided my direction was forward and inside.

I sidled in backward, feeling of the wall with my hands, shifting my body along it under the stoop embrasure like an ebony portcullis that blacked still further the already seemingly impenetrable darkness there had been beyond it. Through the second door opening, until my feet found wood under them instead of cement. The carbolic was stronger in here; he had lingered so long and it was so confined.

His tread scraped the gritty areaway, returning; the iron barrier creaked, clashed into its frame, and riveted closed, and all further freedom of choice in the thing had been taken out of my hands.

I was in now. Good and in.

His foot came down heavily on one of mine in passing. It felt for a minute as though several of those brittle little bones out at the end of it had been pulverized. He didn't apologize, though he must have felt it.

"It's so dark, Doctor. I can't see."

He was already ahead. "Just follow me," he said ungraciously. "You can do that much, can't you?"

I moved after him along warped wooden flooring. I thought from footfall to footfall he'd stop and turn without warning and I'd feel those cruelly powerful hands closing in a pincers movement at my—

The shaftwall of an enclosed basement stair sidled

past to one side of us. I could feel the lathe and plaster encroachment it made on our right of way and guess what it was by its shallowness and yet continued length.

"Aren't we going up to your office, Doctor?"

"What for?"

That clipped "What for?" sent a redoubled chill through me. He wasn't even making a pretense of continuing the other day's consultation, sketchy as it had been. Whatever was to happen to me was to happen down here, safely belowstairs, where no marks of struggle—or accomplishment—would as readily meet the eye of the Finnish woman or anyone else.

Suddenly the passageway was at an end; we had arrived. I had a single moment in which to notice a difference in texture of the flooring underfoot—the foot can be wonderfully acute in the dark. It was rotted as before, but perhaps the planks had been laid in a different direction or there was a thin layer of worn-out oilcloth covering them. Without any further warning than that a light suddenly flashed on, and his hand came down again to his side, leaving it swaying restlessly to add to its blinding effect.

A protector of ordinary brown wrapping paper had been rigged around it, and this helped temper its devastating suddenness still further, once the first shock on the eyes had worn off. But it also created a curious tidal mark of shadow evenly around the walls, at about half height, giving a macabre overtone to the scene. Above all was gloom, and we were as in an illuminated pit or fish tank. Then, too, unless we stood directly centered under it, it cut off our heads and upper parts at varying lengths, so that I had the additionally terrifying experience of confronting a half being with a pair of disembodied eyes glimmering wanly in the dun oblivion above the rest of him.

We were in a windowless room at the back of the basement, used either for storage or debris originally and now both. It was impossible to tell which purpose had preceded the other, since there was an equal amount of both categories in sight. There were cans and small sacks of provender, empty glass jugs filmed with dust that must have once been receptacles for the more common medicinal ingredients and solutions, rusted in tin olive-oil drums, broken chairs. I noted, among other things, a discarded sewing machine rusted to a spiny reddish skeleton that once must have made leg-of-mutton sleeves and skirts that trailed along the floor under the diligent fingers of some long-gone feminine dweller in this place.

"Close that," he said tersely. "Where's your head?"

I drew the door after me and shut us in.

There was a small table there, grimy with age, but apparently still reserved for use down here where it was, for it was placed right side up and stood clear. He made several short, swift trips to the outer dimness, so that the shadow severed him like a guillotine knife each time, returning with what looked like a shoe carton, which he placed up on it. And then a slip of paper, which he retrieved from some safekeeping place known only to himself in the surrounding litter and too quickly for me to detect where it was, had I been intent on doing so. And finally, moving between me and the table briefly but in such a way that I couldn't tell whether it had come from his person or from some shallow drawer beneath, as it cleared into view again it suddenly bore a revolver where there had been none before. It lay at his cuff's end as he seated himself, and, perhaps by accident, its vicious snout was pursed directly at me.

He saw the rotary swirl of panic the pupils of my eyes gave, then glanced at the gun as if identification of the cause were necessary to him. "I always have that in here," he said. Which, if intended for explanation, was no explanation at all.

He shot his sleeves back to more comfortable length. "Now," he said. He said it flatly, as though: "The preliminaries are over; now we begin."

"Sit down on something. That packing case." The shoe carton, if that was what it was, had descended to his lap, out of my sight. The small oblong of paper he held in one hand; tattooed it diagonally on one point, as though seeking to blunt it against the table top.

"Do you know anybody?"

I moistened my lips, unable to answer. It might have seemed, though, as if I were racking my memory.

"Anybody that would be any good to us?" he added.

I still couldn't find my voice.

"Well, you said the other day that you didn't know anybody she did. I simply wondered if you had any— any contacts of your own."

This time he answered for me. "No, you haven't." Then, "It doesn't matter. I can keep you busy."

From the unseen shoe carton, apparently—though I had no direct proof of this—he took a small envelope. It was the diminutive size that a visiting card or a gift card would be enclosed in. Or perhaps a doctor's prescription, written on a once-folded leaf from a small tab. It had not, however, been left open. The flap was sealed. And so firmly sealed that the mucilage had rippled the edges of the flap a little in drying. It was lumpy with some uneven content, the envelope, so that it was rather bloated at the bottom, squat, but at the top paper-thin, flat, as it was meant to be. Yet as he tendered it to me its gravity of weight shifted so that, receiving it upside down from him, in my hands it became clogged at the top, paper-thin at the bottom, with a sensation of granular shifting.

"How often should I—?"

Sometimes you are saved by the slightest things. He answered me too quickly; that was all that saved me. I had been about to ask, "How often should I take this?"

"As often as you conveniently can." He was already extending a second one to me.

Simply to free my hand of the first I opened my handbag and mechanically prodded the packet in.

"What're you going to do, carry it in there?" His tone was irritably uneasy, I thought.

There was a semihidden compartment in it, as in

many bags, controlled by a zipper running along under the frame on the inside. I drew the zipper across to show him. "Will this be all right?"

"Let me see it." He took the bag from me, probed with four fingers down within this newly provided orifice. Then he removed the entire bag from my sight, lowered it to his lap in company with the carton. I saw his upper arm moving slightly in its socket, as though its lower extremity were engaged in some transaction. Then I heard a familiar snapping sound I knew by heart, as if the jaws of my bag were being closed by him.

A moment later he had returned it to me, inscrutably shut. "There," he said, "that'll do for now."

When my head came up from replacing it on my own lap he locked eyes with me. "Two hundred fifty dollars, understand?"

I didn't. I looked at him.

He said sharply, "Well, don't look at me! Two hundred fifty dollars, understand?"

My mouth said, "Yes, Doctor."

His finger tips left the slablike handle of the gun; it was only as they quit it they first revealed to me they *had* been on it, so deftly had they sought it.

He handed me the slip of paper. "Now memorize this list a minute and then burn it." I righted it and looked at it. I heard him say, "After a while you won't need it."

He waited. "Got it? Now say it back."

I cleared my throat, recited uncertainly like a kid in school: "Spotless Cafeteria on Canal Street, between eleven and twelve, shredded wheat, the last table against the wall as you go toward the back—"

"You know how to eat shredded wheat, don't you?" he interrupted. "You crumble it up between your fingers until it makes a little pile of crumbs on the plate; don't dig into it whole with your spoon the way some people do. Now go ahead."

"The Oregon Bar on Third above Forty-ninth,

around twelve-thirty, answer a call for 'Flo Ryan' in the second pay booth."

"Go on. No, don't look at it." He pinned it down to the table.

"Ladies' room of the Mimi Club over on Eighth, near Columbus Circle, ask the attendant if she knows Beulah—"

"You left out something."

"Any time from two on."

"Just one more. Come on, get some speed into it."

I groped, finally recalled it. "The Gem all-night movie house on Forty-second, from three o'clock on, last row in the balcony to the left-hand side; 'Did I drop my scarf under this seat?' "

I drew a deep breath.

"You didn't mention the total," he said with something like a baleful threat in his eyes. He'd summed up the amounts.

"One thousand," I said.

"Well, keep that in mind. I wouldn't advise you to show up here short—" He didn't finish it.

I was supposed to come back here with a thousand dollars; I was supposed to get it at these various places. That was the most I knew; the sight of the gun there at hand, imminent, even though he didn't touch it again after that once, its reptilian little bore pointed at me from first to last, drove all coherency of thought beyond those two points out of my mind, wouldn't let my faculties mesh them into any sort of consecutive meaning.

"Give it to me." He took the piece of paper from me. He struck a kitchen match and burned it to a crisp, shifting his hold on it as it flamed so that it was all consumed. Then he crumbled it between his hands, rolling it like a sort of black meal, until there was nothing of it, just the streaks it had left on his palms. Then he cleaned these by spitting into them and stroking them down his sides.

Some doctor, I thought, controlling the grimace that tried to distort my face.

My eyes sought the gun in veiled speculation. True, it was so close to him he had only to shift his wrist, and I was at the far side of the table, but if I distracted his attention to some distant point in the room and made a quick grasp for it—

Suddenly it had sidled over the edge of the table, was gone, without, however, dropping of its own free weight to the floor, and his heand came up again, empty, from wherever it had withdrawn to, drummed there where it had been.

It wouldn't have done me any good, anyway, I realized; I couldn't force what I wanted out of him simply at gun point. As the gun point left him it would simply be retracted again. It had to come by some more valid means.

"Doctor, I—"

I didn't finish it, because I didn't know what I'd wanted to say.

He seemed to, however, "All right, here," he said grudgingly. He handed me a filthy-looking ten-dollar bill. "That comes off," he said.

He rose and his arm went out toward the paper-dimmed light. "Now hurry up and get out."

He let me open the door and cross the threshold. Then the light was gone, and the scene had never existed at all; everything that had been said, everything that had been done, the way it had all looked became a bad dream, badly remembered.

His footsteps sounded after me as I groped my way down the long, Stygian passage, thrusting it behind me with a continuous motion of one arm. I was frightened of those close-at-hand footsteps of his, fully as frightened again as I had been on the way in; I wanted to break into a run, to fly from them, but I curbed myself, telling myself there was a barrier ahead that would only block me if I did and undo me, to be brave and keep my nerve up a moment longer and then it would be past. Just a moment longer and then it would be past; it would be over; I would be out.

And behind me the footfalls crunched, stealthily surly, at my heels.

It came at last, and he opened it at last, and then as my body almost tried to lurch out, it was in such an ecstasy of impatience, he stayed me with a curt downward chop of his arm and looked carefully about first.

Then finally the brake of his arm dropped and I was free to go. "Monday night, same time," he said gutturally. "See that you don't forget to show up."

I clambered up the two steps to sidewalk level.

The last thing he said to me was, "Watch it."

It was said without compunction, without any fellow feeling of risk shared in common whatever; in a harsh, cruel, calloused sort of way; almost, it was a minor threat in itself. As if: "Be careful of yourself; you're to be the means of bringing me money; that's all I care about."

I was hurrying up the street now on curiously stiff legs. And as the numbness wore off, for that was what it was, I knew they were going to become weak, refuse to hold me any more. I must get a seat on a bus before that happened. One came to the stop without much delay, fortunately, and the two things blended: the end of my own nervous energy and the thrusting under me of a leather-covered tier to sink back on. So that momentary collapse was averted.

I'd come out of there alive. Nothing had happened to me. That was all I could realize at first. Almost, that was all that mattered. I couldn't get enough air into my lungs. I levered down the bus window beside me to breathe it deeply. Passengers around me turned their heads, annoyed; to them it was a draft, chilly, uncomfortable. To me it was free, grateful, restoring.

That was a dangerous sort of relief. It blurred the memory of many details. It cast a film over the issue. Above all, it made only that one house the focus of danger and construed all current surroundings as thenceforth innocuous, not to be questioned or looked at askance.

It made a man who happened to be waiting for the same train underground that I was the following evening and eyed me once or twice as he roamed about the tunnel platform just what such a thing would have always been to me, no more: a man who happened to be waiting for the same train underground that I was.

For danger was now foolishly locked in a watertight compartment, a cell, at Mordaunt's house and could not be anywhere else. Just a man in a nondescript suit, wearing a nondescript hat—I think it was brown; no, gray; no, I didn't know what it was—who stood before a mirrored chewing-gum purveyor clamped to a post and eyed his own face. Only his face was a little too far over to one side to be contained entirely within the mirror, and I was in the distance beyond, seated waiting upon the bench, so that his range of vision must have automatically taken me in.

He disappeared when the downtown train came fuming in; there were many cars to choose from, after all, but this was *post factum* in any case. He had already disappeared from my thoughts some time before; in fact, had never entered them.

And if, on changing over to the East Side line to get down to Canal Street he materialized a second time, in the closer confinement of the shuttle train, my quarantine of all danger within Mordaunt's house made this nothing, made it just a coincidence. Hundreds of people a day, every hour, changed from the West Side to the East Side lines. Why shouldn't he?

There were more cars to choose from again, once the shuttle was done with, and again he disappeared.

My decision to go down there, to carry out the unsavory expedition that had been assigned to me, was predicated upon the following line of reasoning: I needed at the very least another interview with Mordaunt, if possible several more. I had obtained nothing the first time, and yet I had obtained the promise of everything. He had known Mia Mercer; he had *not* acted in the capacity of personal physician to her but in

some illicit relationship. There was every hope of a
motive lurking there if I was just given time to unearth
it. A motive, and perhaps even proof itself. A man who
would interview an intended accomplice with a revolver
bared upon the table would almost certainly not hesitate to smother one to death who had crossed him or
jeopardized him in some way. Very well; I could not
hope for a second interview with him unless I first dis-
charged his errand. Therefore, I was on my way to
discharge it this Sunday night, this night of peace and
rest in New York.

Oh, I was under no illusions as to its basic nature.
And yet I was curiously naïve, even after the lengthy
scene that had passed between us. I realized perfectly
that it was some sort of criminal enterprise; the sums of
money I was to receive told that, and, above all, the
elaborate precautions taken to preserve anonymity both
on the parts of those I was to contact and on the part of
myself. And yet, difficult as it is to believe, I was still
unsuspecting of its exact category. I thought it must be
money owed to him for some sort of unlawful services
rendered—and this could have been anything from
falsifying records to performing criminal operations—
and that he could not safely collect otherwise than in
this indirect manner. My mind, in the torrent of other
details, had developed a curious blind spot; it glossed
over those packets that had passed between us as a
meaningless stopgap offered by him solely to make our
interview plausible. In other words, should he be
brought up short and queried, ever, he could say he had
treated me only as a doctor treats a patient, had pre-
scribed for me, had given me some sedative, headache
powder, strengthener, or whatever it was, for my spells
of dizziness and would have my word to corroborate his
and perhaps some office or desk jotting to show for it as
well.

Wise, therefore, and yet blind at the same time, I
neared the Spotless Cafeteria. I looked in as one who

takes a moment to decide what food she will select before entering.

It was surprisingly well filled with people at this hour; all the choicer tables near the front had their occupants, and though many seemed to have finished their collations long ago they lingered on, chatting in groups of two and three. It seemed to be used, like many such a place, almost as much for social purposes as for eating purposes.

I thought: "He wants me to go in here. I'm to get money in here." I swung the circular door around and pulled a pasteboard tab from the dispenser that stood like a tollgate just within. A bell reverberated shrilly, but no one even turned his head to look; it pealed like that every time anyone entered.

I took a tray and trucked it along the rail before the counters. The paper that he'd burned had said "shredded wheat." I couldn't see any. When I had reached the end I even retreated back the way I had come for some little distance to make sure I hadn't overlooked it. Finally I had to call over the attendant behind the counter and ask him if they hadn't any.

"No," he said, "but I can open a package for you; we got some inside for the morning turnover."

He came back in a moment from their larder or whatever it was with two of the familiar little oblong cakes on a plate.

He said while he was punching my ticket, "We used to get calls for this late at night. A customer used to come in and ask for it like you every once in a while, but he hasn't been around in a long time now. It's really a breakfast food."

I wondered if he knew that it was a signal. I looked at him and he didn't seem to, seemed to be talking just out of friendliness, but I couldn't be sure.

I put it on my tray and went over and sat down at the very last table against the wall.

The bell chimed and a man came in and went over and drew himself a cup of coffee from the spigot in the wall. His back was to me, but he looked vaguely like the same man I'd seen twice before since leaving my own place tonight. I decided that must be just a mistaken impression; coincidences don't run in threes like that.

I'd finished crumbling the substance, and it made a little mound, like dried leaves, in the middle of my platter. I wondered whether I was supposed to eat it. I wasn't particularly anxious to. Although I may not have been gripped by fright as I had been at the doctor's house, I was fairly tense and wishing it were over.

The man with the cup of coffee had submerged into the crowd of heads. However, remote as he was from me, there was a diagonal passage of clearance still left between us, so that I could still see him where he now sat, and he could have still seen me had he cared to. But he refrained from looking in my direction, became intent on his own immediate concerns, so that all I could see was the downturned crease of his hat crown. However, it occurred to me that there *was* a striking similarlity in general vagueness between him and the person I had already glimpsed twice on the trains coming here ton—

Before I could pursue this speculative train of thought any further a newspaper had suddenly opened before me across the table, and there was someone sitting there. No bell had rung, so he must have been in the place already.

He was scanning a headline fixedly. It only takes a limited time to read a headline, but his eyes remained upon it steadily, never dropping down to the further matter below.

I could feel my heart quicken a little.

He was sitting sidewise to me, the way most readers do at confined little tables like that. I could see a segment of his profile in the gap between newspaper screen and the wall at the back of his head.

"Got it?" he slurred without twitching a facial muscle. For a minute I almost thought he was mumbling over something he'd read to himself, the way some newspaper readers do, it was emitted so deftly.

Before I could answer he had already tired of waiting. "What's the matter, didn't he tell you about me?"

"Yes, but I don't know who—"

Before I could finish speaking he had again tired of waiting.

"What's the matter, ain't you got nothing? Didn't he give you nothing?"

"Well, he only gave me—"

He was conditioned to a hairspring tautness.

"Don't take so long. I can't hold this paper like this all night. There's other people in here. You new?"

"What do you want me to do?" I said helplessly.

"Push your bag over this way." He raised one elbow from the table top to allow it passage underneath without disturbing his newspaper.

Mesmerized by the strangeness of the whole thing, I prodded it forward until it had overbalanced on his side. His legs scissored together and arrested it, still without fluctuating the outspread newssheet.

One hand left its margin, letting the table support it at that end. Though it wavered a little and threatened to crumple, it remained upright, stiffened by its own bulky width.

I heard the smothered sound of the catch snapping open. There was a sense of stealthy activity that remained invisible, was more in his breathing than anything else. Then suddenly, with vicious recoil, "Where's what he gave you?"

"He only gave me something for my— Pull that zipper across."

The catch snapped closed again. His nostrils were pinched with the receding fury that had choked them for a minute.

The bag was suddenly back where it had been; his finger grip was back at the margin of the newspaper again. The two phenomena, black and pink, reappeared almost simultaneously, so swiftly was it done, though one must in the nature of things have preceded the other.

Before I knew it the enshrouding paper was gone; he was gone with the swiftness of a dream. Only the winged doors were spinning around empty, showing black night through them where he'd flitted out a moment ago.

I drew the retrieved bag down to my own lap and examined it under shelter of the table line. One of the packets the doctor had given me was gone. There was a bone-shaped crush of money down in its depths, tight at the waist, as if from long, convulsive hand pressure. Two hundred and fifty dollars, when I had paired and counted it.

I looked sightlessly up in a sort of belated terror only striking now. There must be something in those— "You knew," I said to myself accusingly; "you knew all along, but you didn't want to admit it to yourself. You wanted to keep your conscience from hindering you in carrying through your own purpose, to which this is a necessary preliminary. So you stamped the thought down. You wanted to make it some crime you could disassociate yourself from, such as a fee for some illicit operation."

I looked around me appalled, far more frightened now that he'd gone than I had been while I was still sitting scarcely two feet away from him.

No one in the place was looking at me. The busman behind the counter was busied at his duties, eyes down. The cashier within his little glass cubicle was reading a paper while he waited between departing customers. That man with the cup of coffee was holding it very steady, looking down into it, as though he had detected a speck in it. Not at me, into his cup. Then he went ahead and drank, completing the movement he seemed to have arrested for a moment. Detected. Arrested. That was simply my mind, using the first thought expressions that came to hand without stopping to examine them.

I got up and I made my way out in turn, sick and shaken and feeling a thousand years old; my shoulders clammy and weighted down, as if all the filthy, disinterred evil there was in the world had been dumped out upon them.

My resolve not to go on to the next place, now that I knew, was short-lived. Various factors played their part in canceling it, like snatches of inner voice, rallying me each one in turn. "I'd go ahead doing even this for you, Kirk." "I've done it once already; there can be no greater harm in repeating it than there was in doing it the first time." "I can't go back unless I do." "These people are not the victims of it; they are the professional distributors, retailers, so to speak." And lastly, there was a sort of glimmering of enlightenment that seemed to come of it, this hesitancy of mine, that did more than anything else in sending me onward. *She* had refused to go to the next place—metaphorically speaking, for she hadn't tramped from place to place afoot; she had been a luxurious lady—but she had refused to go onward at some point or other, and a pillow had come down over her face, to blot out any retained memory of that "next place," to stifle any future revelation of it.

And if the very act of what I was engaged in produced the motive itself, intact, like that, so that all that was still needed was proof of the deed, how could I refuse to proceed? It would have been the grossest treachery to my own aims.

The Oregon Bar, then, on Third Avenue above Forty-ninth, in the first half-hour after twelve that same night. It was deep and narrow, like an alcove piercing the building it was situated in. It was dark with a sort of colored darkness that was the tint of it. Although there were lights, and they were dusky orange, copper-rose, and other similar feverish hues, it was the darkness you were conscious of more than them; its overall cast was dimness, a confettilike twilight.

It was not an unduly prosperous place, even of its kind. Though I was no connoisseur I could sense in its atmosphere something static, stagnant, as of an establishment keeping its head above water, no more, the moment I put my foot across the threshold.

There were only men at the bar, but on the other side of the narrow aisle that was all it provided for ingress or egress there were tables set within head-high partitions that came out from the wall like the teeth of a comb, though far fewer, naturally. At one or two of these sat women of the type, I supposed, you would find in a place like this. Shell-like and brittle and empty inside, where they were young; like those celluloid dolls they used to sell, weighted at the bottom, so that they reared upright again no matter how often you pushed them flat. Lumpy and doughy and filled with a sort of resentful despair, where they were less than young. They were not, for one thing, young or old, of the outright demimondaine type. One bloated, stringy-haired woman was obviously drinking beer with her own husband, and they would finish up the night by beating one another around the walls of their tenement flat until the police were called.

The last of these tables, in this case, was already occupied, though I had not been definitely instructed to seek the last in here as I had in the cafeteria, to the best of my recollection. The one before it, however, was vacant, and I sidled into the rather difficult crevice between fastened-down bench and clamped-down table. The rather bovine, stupidly protracted looks from the sitters at the bar that had formed a necklace of ogling strung out the entire length of the place dropped off one by one like beads falling away, until at last I had been accepted within the establishment without further visual inquiry.

The barman had a helper for the tables, and he came over to me. I said, "I'm waiting for a call," and he turned away again without resentment.

A moment after I found out I'd forgotten the name I

was to answer to, and a brief flurry of fright came over me. Then I quickly reassured myself that wouldn't be crucial in any case; I would be reminded of it when the call came, and it was hardly likely there would be two such calls in a single night to an unaccompanied woman in a hole in the wall such as this. And as I relaxed from the hunched-over position across the edge of the table that I had inadvertently thrown myself into it came partially back to me of its own accord, as is often the way with the mind when tension is relieved. It had been something with an *R*, hadn't it? Rice, I thought, Yes, that was it.

It was very hard to know where to look, for on one side of me there was just the blankness of the wall, and if I looked on the other side I might meet one of *their* looks and invite intrusion. There was nothing but the shellacked pine-board panel opposite me to direct my eyes at. Over it would occasionally peer a little blue haze, from a freshly lit cigarette, drifting slowly over to my side. And once a curious object, like the black triangular fin of a fish, thrust briefly above it, was gone again. I knew what it was; the uptilted wing on a woman's hat. On it presently, the panel, I made out a faint tracing, still visible though it had been shellacked over. Somebody, some long-forgotten night ago, had once gouged out his or her initials with the point of a knife or the tine of a fork or perhaps even the point of a pin. Like children do on tree bark. These were older children, though; infinitely sadder, wiser children.

Where was he now, or she? Dead? Still living? Richer? Poorer? Probably not. You don't change; only in the storybooks. Did he guess that some night a woman would sit here, in the same place where he'd been, carrying something in her bag that, though it was death to everyone else, she hoped would help her gain her husband's life back?

The bar assistant was standing beside me again, having grown impatient, I supposed, that I was taking this long to order anything.

He leaned over confidentially, said: "Excuse me, are you Flo Ryan?"

That was the name; now that I'd heard it I remembered it, as I'd known I would.

I told him yes, I was.

"There's a party calling you in the second booth. Straight back at the end there."

I hadn't even heard it ring. These partitions might have helped deflect it. I sidled outward as inconspicuously as I could and straightened once I was clear of the bench and table and went back there.

There was somebody already talking in the first booth, through some unfortunate mishap of coincidence, and this propinquity made me uneasy; I remembered only too well how highly audible everything is through those lathlike inner partitions. I glimpsed the turn of a neck, the back curve of a hatbrim as I passed the glass.

The bar helper had left the receiver off, waiting for me. I drew the slide closed and picked the receiver up with five sticks of ice that would scarcely bend at the middle.

There was no sound. I didn't know what to say. "This is Flo Ryan," I said smotheredly. I used my free hand to contain the sound still further.

A man's voice said, "Is the light on in there with you?"

I looked. It was so pale I'd hardly noticed.

"If it is, reach up and give it a turn."

I reached up and twisted it and it went out. I wondered how he'd known; then I remembered they went on automatically as you closed the door in most pay booths.

He said, "Okay, that's all. Put what you've got in the coin-return slot. Then hang up and go back to your table. You know what to do. Count ten and come back after something you forgot. Don't let anyone beat you back to the booth."

I hung up. I opened my bag and put one of the packets into the coin-return slot. Then I came out. The adjoining booth was still occupied, but I hadn't said enough at my end to give anyone who was listening an inkling.

I slumped back at my table. I counted, and with each numeral there came a sort of shudder, as if it had been a death knell. Then I fumbled in my bag and pretended to miss something, a coin or a lipstick or a handkerchief. I got up and went back a second time.

The first booth now yawned open and empty too. And yet no one had followed me back into the bar. I went into the one I'd been in a moment ago and probed the coin slot with two fingers. The packet was gone, but there was one of those same layered wedges of spongy currency, this time with a rubber band about it, as I'd received at the cafeteria.

I closed my bag on it, and then I came out and looked around. The narrow lane the booths looked out upon widened a little just past where they were, then ended as it widened. There were three doors there, two the doors of comfort rooms and a third one that had no designation to it. I went to this, hesitated a moment, then reached out and opened it, as if I had lost my bearings and mistaken it for one of the others.

There was darkness outside and the bite of open air. It was a walled-in alley that ran up to the street.

I turned back the other way. An odor of cigar smoke, only freeing itself now at last, hovered about the vacant booth adjoining the one I had been in. I shivered uncontrollably, as though there were some sort of malign miasma to be detected in it, as I hurried past.

I didn't stop at my former table when I had reached it; I kept on toward the front, my frightened steps quickening all the time until I had emerged from the place almost at a terrified run.

Not too quickly, though, to catch the diagnosis offered by one barman to the other as they stared after me curiously. "He musta changed his mind about where he's meeting her."

I kept running for several doorways afterward, as though the feel of the air as I coursed through it were cleansing me like a tide. Then I forced myself to slacken and bridled my instinctive repugnance to a quick walk carrying me away from there.

My emergence, had anyone been watching or waiting for it, would have been sudden enough to take them by surprise. In one of the near-by shrouded doorways, as I hastened obliviously past, I caught the lumpy outlines of two men who had been standing there as if conferring. The little red dart of a cigarette was quickly shifted rearward out of sight, as if behind someone's person, but not soon enough to strike out at my eye in passing.

I looked back once, from beyond the next crossing, simply to reassure myself, but neither one had come into view, so their being sheltered there had had nothing to do with me.

Dancers were wavering in a tight, lashed-together cluster on a small mat of floor with a colored spotlight bearing down at each end to light it, and the rest was a zone of murky dusk. They undulated like a form of marine life seen through rippling apple-green and mollusk-purple water. None could displace the others; they were so tightly packed together, and each in the same order as before would come around again in due course, but long after. It was like the turning of an infinitely slow, clotted wheel pushed by droves of chained slaves.

I came in. I went toward this pyre of green and magenta flaming in the darkness.

There is something abysmally sad about all such group dancing late at night; it is like a publicly performed ritual to mortality, and I found it grimly melancholy over and above the grim melancholy of my own errand. A bacchanalia at fixed prices. The never-ending, never-succeeding attempt to hold pain, despair, death at bay for a little while. A little while longer.

I remembered, for some strange reason, that night clerk at one of the hotels to which I'd gone looking for Marty, and the macabre cast of his eyes. "O God," I thought, "there *is* such a thing as seeing too much. As seeing too much and too clearly."

I lurched soddenly into the first vacant chair at hand, and a woman who had been sitting there with her shoulder to it turned and said, "There's someone there."

She meant it belonged to one of the dancers.

"I know," I said, without even looking at her. I shaded my eyes with my hand, but ripples of green and purple crept through the seams of my fingers nevertheless. "Just let me rest a minute. I'll get right up again."

The music stopped, and the laboring wheel stopped with it. They clapped, holding their hands up over their heads, for their was no room to clap them down below at body level. And the music began again, pushing back their fear of dying for a few minutes more.

I got up and I skirted around the outside of them, having to squeeze my way through between their backs and the nearest tables, they were so compressed. A seated man reached out to catch my hand as I brushed past him, but I threw it forward and he was too late.

I opened the door and went in.

It was deathly quiet for a minute, with the suddenness of an inverted explosion. I saw myself coming forward in a warped mirror, so that I shook a little in the middle. There was a effluvium of cheap perfumery in the air but a degree above the rancid. There was a bulky colored woman sitting on a chair, her skin the color of dark maple sugar. She had been looking idly at the fingers of her own hands, inert in her lap, when I first came in. Telling them off against one another but without mathematical purpose. She rose beside me with a sort of easygoing laboriousness as I stopped before the mirror.

"Get you something, child?"

There wasn't a mean line in her face. And yet how reliable is a face anyway? And she spoke in the softest, most dulcet, most lulling tones I'd ever heard from a human throat. Benign was the word for her. Benign and motherly and comforting. Showing that nature sometimes does copy art. For here in New York, and of New York, and probably having never been out of it in her entire life, she was par excellence the broad-bosomed, yearning Southern mammy of the songs and the farina posters.

I said, "Are—are you Beulah?"

"I've heard myself called that, child. 'Tain't rightly my name, but you just go 'head and call me that if you've a mind to. There's been others that have."

My other hand roamed to the handbag I already held in one. "Well, I was—I was told to ask for—"

She said as though she were soothing some fretful pickaninny tugging away at her skirts, "Not out here, child. That door opens straight in. Here, you come in here. Beulah'll show you."

She took it from me and went out.

I heard her opening something: her own clothes locker, most likely. I took a step forward that she must have sensed rather than heard, for I was scarcely aware of doing it myself. "No, don't come out, child. You just stay there a minute more. Beulah won't be long."

The locker closed again, and keys jingled lightly, blanketed under a skirt.

I went back to the mirror again, still quivering at the middle. But now quivering in other places as well that didn't reflect. She had placed things on the glass slab below it that I might want to use. The money was there between comb and soiled, pancakelike puff. I couldn't bring myself to touch it for a minute, just ran a little cold water and kept trying to wipe off one hand under it, as though it were—

She said, "Don't leave nothing behind that belongs to you, child. So many folks are always doing that."

I caught her studying me with a sort of indulgent fondness. She placed one hand on my shoulder maternally, the other on the fritterlike puff. "My, you're a pretty little thing. You must be just a baby. Here, let Beulah fix you up; she'll show you how."

I squirmed suddenly from under her hand and struck the puff aside, so that it exploded into a cloud of white haze. I backed all the way across the place, still shaking in the middle in the mirror, this time with aversion. "Don't touch me! You're—you're a monster! You ought to be—!"

She didn't show any resentment. I don't think she knew what it was to feel anger. She stood there looking so benign, smiling after me so indulgently. "Bless your little heart," she kept crooning, as though she were pronouncing a benediction; "bless your little heart."

I effaced her with a single back sweep of the door, like you wipe a smirch off glass.

There is nothing more horrid in crime than the failure to regard it as crime.

They were still dancing, turning slowly from green to purple, from purple back to green, like sloppy colors that run into one another. They were chanting in unison now as they danced, and that made it even more horrible.

> *"Dance, dance, dance, little lady,*
> *Life is fleeting to the rhythm beating*
> *Through your mind."*

I beat my way out around their massed fringes, actually beat with flailing arms and fists, and they scarcely noted it. The music was a local anesthetic, numbing their backs and shoulder blades.

"Oh, Kirk, what am I doing here?" shot up through me like a rocket of dazzling sanity that went right out again, but while it lasted it sent me running full-tilt down the entryway to the sanctuary of the open.

There was a man there, reading his paper, to one

side of the entrance as I rounded the turn, so close I almost grazed him. He was holding it up very high and very close to him. I had a strange optical illusion of just-then-completed motion, as if he'd been holding it lower, had just raised it that very instant to where it was now; I don't know why.

The light wasn't very good, and at another time I might have wondered why he'd choose such a place. But I didn't then.

He must have heard the little sob of gratitude I gave, I passed so close to him, but he was too intent to notice.

I hurried down the street, and the intermittent sign back there behind me kept getting smaller each time it flashed on. Like this:

MIMI CLUB
Mimi   Club
mimi   club

I could tell because I kept looking back repeatedly, almost in synchronization with it each time it flashed on, as though fearful the spirit of disembodied evil itself would materialize and come after me out of that place.

But it didn't. Nothing did. That casual bystander stood motionless there to the last, lost in his newspaper, unable to tear himself from it. That was all.

Once I thought I heard a faint whistle somewhere back there behind me. Not a mechanical whistle, one pursed by lips. I couldn't tell from where, to where, for what reason, or what meaning it had had. Nor even if there really had been one at all. It didn't come again. A thing like that didn't alarm me. The night is full of such sounds. I had my own private terrors to contend with.

And this they called the Gem Theater, and it had a history, a past, I suppose, like men and buildings all do. Once tight-waisted ladies in ostrich-plume hats must have stepped from high-bodied, square-topped limousines to attend opening nights here. Then later, for weary seasons, lines of indifferent, underdressed girls had pranced back and forth across its stage, four, five, six times a day. Then it had outlived even that. Now it was senile, nearing the death that awaits even piles of stone.

Now homeless strays wandered in here to sleep and have the soles of their feet kicked awake by the ushers at regular intervals and sleep again until the next time they came by.

It never closed. Continually, throughout the night and throughout the day and around to the night again, lines of hissing, spitting, bluish motes given off by the livid screen ran downward in the darkness like rain, and cracked, mechanical voices, sounding just like voices talking outside in a rain, echoed hollowly through it. This was the conversation of ghosts in every sense of the word, for even the photographed lips that uttered the phrases were never even with them, moved long after or long before.

I stopped and bought a ticket for twenty-five cents. They had a man in the booth. They weren't allowed to use girls this late at night. Another man took the ticket from me at the inner entrance, and that ended the formalities of admission.

I went into the dark and glimpsed the pale blue opening the screen made in it, like a window, ahead of me, and a scattering of somnolent heads, buried low among the seat backs. Then I turned aside and went up the stairs that led to the balcony. The branch on the left-hand side, for there were two, facing one another. He'd said the left-hand side of the balcony.

The carpeting was still on them from former days of glory but worn to a pulp and clinging to the feet almost like something spongy now. The stairs turned, and just past there I met an old woman feeling her way down. She looked like a charwoman. She came very cautiously, holding to the rail and exploring the turn of each step well with the toe of her foot before she would trust herself down. She left a tracery of alcohol hovering behind her all the way to the top.

I heard a knell-like sound just as I gained it myself, and when I looked back she had stood an empty bottle very primly, very tidily, in the exact corner of the turn, out of harm's way. I saw her moisten her finger tips, touch them to the side of the bottle, as if in affectionate farewell, and then go on.

I came out on the balcony floor at the back of the seats. The "window," the flow of ceaseless-falling light lines, was below me now, and a stout shaft of fuming white light, swimming with dust spirochete, was slanted downward over my head from a glowing eye at the rear to strike at it.

The majority of the scattered heads up here were in the first few rows. The last row, at least on the left-hand side, held no one in it. It was divided, like all the others, into two segments by the center aisle, and the strip I had to do with was completely vacant. Two rows below a man sat audibly sleeping. Then no one else for several more rows. I sidled into it, stood over the third seat in for a minute, then changed my mind, shifted back to the second. Why, I couldn't have told.

I looked around me, toward the stairs where I'd just come from, and saw no one. I looked forward and watched the window into the world of make-believe for a dulled, unhappy moment or two.

A man far down in the first row got up from his seat and made his way up the terraced aisle. He seemed not to look at me, however, and after the first quickly inquiring glance I took him for somebody simply on his way out of the theater.

For several more moments I sat looking forward. Then suddenly a tendril of smoke drifting close to me made me turn my head, and he was standing directly behind me, almost at my shoulder, arms propped on the wooden bulkheads that walled off the seats from the open transverse beyond. He was, or seemed to be, unaware of me, eyes directed downward at the screen. He'd posted himself there so subtly that I hadn't even detected his presence.

I didn't know which of us was to speak first; I hadn't been told. The non-existent scarf could have belonged to either of us. It wasn't late enough in the year, however, for men to be wearing scarves yet, as a general rule, so I took my cue from that.

"Did I drop my scarf under your seat?" I mumbled half audibly.

"That's right," he said and deftly made the turn of the aisle gap and settled himself in the seat beside me.

He didn't remove his hat. He sat leaning outward, away from me, rather than in toward me, and still kept his eyes on the screen with a dissimulation that must have been second nature to him by now, I reflected queasily.

I fumbled in my bag and removed the last of the things Mordaunt had given me. I balanced it on the spindly seat arm between us and edged over as far away from it as possible. When next I looked it was gone, and I could have sworn he hadn't moved at all. His arms were folded across his chest, but they hadn't stirred.

"I hope I never, as long as I live, set eyes on another of those little white pa—" I was thinking with devout intensity, when suddenly an unscheduled interruption took place.

There was a single quick, muffled footfall directly behind us. I never saw who it was, for he must have remained crouched over there where the bulkhead opened into the aisle beside us. The whiteness of a hand suddenly spawned over my seat neighbor's shoulder from behind; a voice whispered with hot urgency: "Blow! She's a plant! I just spotted 'em coming in below!"

Then the hand and the voice and whoever they had belonged to all disappeared alike as swiftly as they had descended on us.

The man next to me was suddenly standing erect, his face, turned my way now, an almost luminous grimace of incandescent rage. I didn't see his hand coming in time. It struck like a snake. The only lucky thing was he didn't have time to close it himself; it lashed against me open. The slap echoed all over the silence like a firecracker going off, and all the somnolent heads came up higher and turned one by one. A scalding wash of pain spread out all over my face and even down my neck on that side, and my eyes watered and made me lose him for a minute.

"Wait, give me what you were supposed to!" I cried blindly and tried to grasp at him.

"I'll get you for this!" I heard him hiss. And then he, too, went. The row lay empty. After a second or two of time lag my eye caught a flurry of motion, something dark against the dark, ricocheting down the tiered outside aisle, far over against the building wall itself. A door giving onto a fire escape squeaked a little, scarcely seeming to move inward at all, then settled heavily still again.

And then nothing happened. A slap must have been a commonplace in that milieu, even against a woman's cheek. The heads slowly turned away again, took up once more the threat of the more public drama being presented in that direction.

I crouched there uncertainly a moment longer. Then I was on my own feet and out on the carpeted passage behind the seats, not knowing which way to turn. A plant, a plant, what was that? *They?* Who were *they* downstairs?

I was afraid to go down those stairs now. I was even more afraid to go out the way I had seen him go, down the outside fire escape; afraid of what I might find waiting for me when I got to the bottom of it, in the dark alley it probably descended to.

I stood there at the head of the stairs a long time, my eyes alternately on them and on the balcony seats I had left behind. No one came up. No one came near me. That bottle was still standing down there where the crone had placed it.

I summoned up courage and started down them at

last. I felt my way down almost as she had. Step by step and with both hands to the rail beside me, one following the other. How quickly you learn. How quickly you become part of the scene, fit into it.

I was at the turn now and I must either quicken my descent or not go down at all. I mustn't creep down like this, for I could be seen from below, from here on down.

I found myself almost wishing there had been something left in that bottle, so I could nerve myself with it. But I had to go the rest of the way on cold courage. I braced myself and struck out. The lower floor slowly opened into view. Those same somnolent heads, like raisins studding a dark pudding. Would one or more of them suddenly rise up, come after me, as I gained a level with them?

The steps were ticking off under me now in a quick, rippling, final descent. It carried me off them and over to the main center door. No one moved. I got out slantwise through the door, keeping it to its narrowest possible seam in order to let as little light in as I could and avoid attracting attention to myself.

Nothing happened. No one came out after me. No one was there before me, waiting on the outside. No one at all. Not even a man reading a newspaper this time.

No one seemed to be looking, only New York and the night and me.

The thought that it might be dangerous to go back was slow in coming, but it came finally: dangerous to go back to where I was supposed to. Mordaunt's house.

In the lawful world what I had to tell might have been believed. I wasn't in that world any more; I wasn't dealing with it now. In the jungle they didn't believe you. Where money was involved they would have lied to you, and they knew it, so they acted on the supposition you were lying to them. No allowances were made, no quarter given.

But then if I didn't go back—

No, I had to. He'd have to believe me.

There was nothing left of that ghastly night by the time I tottered home and barricaded myself behind the door. I couldn't have slept if there had been. I was afraid of whom I'd meet in my sleep if I did. "Let Beulah fix you up, child: she'll show you how."

I sat there holding my head in both hands—it seemed to throb and burn so with remorse—an untouched glass of water with a few drops of spirits of ammonia sprinkled in it standing beside me. After a while the world switched over to sunlight again, and that made it better, made it more bearable. I drew up the shades and hooked back the curtains; I couldn't get enough of it into the room. It seemed so healing and so cleansing. It was like God's own soapsuds, sparkling on the panes and lathering the walls, rinsing my face and tired eyes.

After a while I dozed, sitting there like that, fully dressed in the chair and with a pillow packed behind me, and when I woke up was when I first started to be afraid to go back.

It would be tonight, and tonight was coming soon. Awfully soon.

"He won't do anything to you if you go," I kept reassuring myself. "It's if you don't go that—something's liable to happen to you."

And again I was overcome by the same argument that had proved so effective outside his house the second time I went there. "If you're going to give the undertaking up now, then why did you begin it at all in the first place? You mean all last night's terror of soul is to be for nothing? No, you've got to go ahead with it now, finish it out to the end, come what may."

Night came down like a series of curtains one behind the other. First transparent, simply filming the daylight, then deeper, so that it could scarcely peer through any more, finally black with accumulated density, blotting it out altogether.

It was nearly time now. I couldn't eat, and the pits of my hands were cold.

I rose and crossed the room in the dark, and I went over to restore the curtains and shades to their normal position now that the sun was gone. Then I stopped in the act and looked intently out. I knew the look of the street by night so well already; that was the only reason I saw him there. I knew that doorway down there should not have a darkened curvature to it. It should be a straight up-and-down line, not go in and out and in again, like a projecting shoulder, then waist, then hip-bone. There was someone standing in it.

It brought back last night too vividly to mind, and perhaps for that reason rather than any current logic of disbelief I forced myself to turn away from the window. If there was someone there, it had nothing to do with me; why should it have?

"You know it does. You and no one else. You alone, of all the dwellers on this street."

I sat for a while in the depths of the unlighted room, curbing continual impulses to go back and stealthily pry again.

Someone sent by Mordaunt, to make sure I kept the appointment, didn't abscond with the rest of his profit? It must be that; who or what else could it be?

I said to myself, "Sometimes a car turns that lower corner down there on too wide an arc, and if its lights are on high enough their beam will flicker along that entire side of the street, wash over the walls and door-ways as it swings into position. I've seen that happen myself. He doesn't know that, isn't expecting it. I do."

I went back to the vicinity of the window again and waited, sheltered off side to the frame.

They seldom came. One did at last, but its lights had no force to speak of, just a dull glow.

Then one of the kind I'd been hoping for slewed abruptly into view. It was a small truck or commercial vehicle of some kind, and it had its beams powered far above regulations. In the act of turning they threw a parabola of reflection glancing along that side. It was gone again in a moment, but it had been sufficient. It was the same principle as sheet lightning on a stormy night. It threw everything into high relief for an instant. The figure in the doorway was trapped. He stood out for a brief second or two like a leaden soldier, then was gone into the dark again.

I turned away with a mental shrug that was insincere. I had wanted to know; now I knew. There *was* someone down there, and he hadn't wanted to be seen. I'd caught the convulsive recessive movement he'd begun just as the darkness rescued him again.

There was no other way out of the house.

I saw that it was already past the time for me to have started for Mordaunt's house. To put off any longer was to have the appointment lapse by omission. I was going and I knew I was. I was dreadfully afraid, but I was going.

I thought, "I should take something with me this time." I looked around, but I didn't know what to take. There wasn't anything. Then I thought, "What good would anything be, anyway, in that basement trap buried all the way back there under the house?" In the end I left as I was, empty-handed.

I was acutely conscious of that doorway as I came out. It showed in a straight line now that it should have all along, but too late to convince me. It wasn't directly opposite my own building entrance; it was some little distance down. My way took me past it, though the width of the street over.

It was so deserted-looking now, so patently lifeless. Somehow I knew, though. All its pretended vacuity availed it nothing. I knew there was someone still in it. Deep within it, all the way back to the rear of it now, where he couldn't be seen.

It was hard to keep my face looking forward as I came abreast, then passed beyond it, but I compelled myself to. If he intended coming out at all he wouldn't come right out at my heels. From the turn below I shot a quick glance back and over. It still showed empty. It refused to betray itself.

I could see a bus coming in the distance, and I ran the rest of the way. Still no sign of anyone or anything. I boarded the bus, and if I was sure of nothing else. I was sure no one boarded it with me. So if any attempted trail had been in the forming it had been broken off short.

At the other end I went down the street toward his house, and though outwardly I may have walked far more steadily, far more surely than that last time, I think if anything there was a greater fear within me. It was a different kind. No longer the half-childish fear of a dark house and a possible maniac attack without provocation. A deeper, because more plausible, fear of the rancor I might meet with on the part of the thoroughly vicious criminal whose accomplice I had made myself and whose task I had failed to perform satisfactorily.

I turned aside and stepped down into the abyss of the areaway with the feeling of treading a quicksand whose action was delayed, was withheld, purposely to lull me, until I had crossed a certain distance over it.

His voice struck through the basement grating at me without preamble, as it had the last time.

"You took your time."

I didn't answer.

His hands fumbled, and the grating came undone.

"I was about giving you up. And I wouldn've hated to have to do that." There was a humorless threat in it.

I didn't answer.

He said a third thing as he stepped forward to reconnoiter. "Go ahead. You know your own way now."

I traveled blindly along the tunnellike basement bore like someone pacing in a dream. A dream whose foreknown outcome is doom but yet which must unfold itself without reprieve to its appointed climax.

I couldn't find the light, that macabre shaded light I've spoken of, as readily as he had. Once I thought I had it, but it glanced away again.

Suddenly it went on, and he'd done it. He was in there already, and so close to me I jumped spasmodically and I suppose my face showed it.

"You're nervous, aren't you?" he said unkindly.

He motioned to the same packing case as that other night. "Sit down." It was still said unkindly.

He sat down himself, opposite me, crouched sleepily forward on his elbows. Though I didn't see his lips move I received a mental impression of his tongue licking over them; I don't know why.

"Did you go to those places?"

"Yes, I went to those places." I'm not sure, but I think this was the first thing I'd said since I'd entered.

I put one of the crushed nuggets on the table. "This was given to me in the cafeteria by a man who sat down—"

"I know, I know." A sweep of his hand stifled the details.

"This was given to me in that bar."

Each one disappeared as the next appeared.

"This was given to me at the night club."

He waited a second or two. "I think there was a fourth place, wasn't there?"

"Something happened there. You'd better let me tell you what happened there first." I was starting to be frightened already before I had received any cause to be. I could feel it while I spoke. My own voice had a sort of resonance to it within my chest.

His expression didn't change, and if anything I liked that less than if it had.

"You made delivery, and then somebody whispered to him; he jumped up and ran off." He sounded as though he were mulling it over. He shook his head slightly, as if there were some flaw of motivation there. "He's no fool; he knows what would happen to him if

he—" he started to say. Then he changed that, said:
"He wouldn't do that—"

"But he did; I even tried to hold his arm."

He kept looking at me. I couldn't read that look.
"About what time was this?"

"Around three this morning."

His lips formed into a thin, compressed line. "Let's
go upstairs, shall we? We can talk better up there."

He rose and held his hand to the light, and, I suppose, because the act of darkness would have resulted if
I stayed, I moved trailingly through the doorway ahead
of him, my head turned his way and my eyes clinging to
his face until the switch snapped and blotted it out.

I groped my way up a darkened staircase enclosed
within a shaft, more by dint of trying to remain ahead
of him, clear of his oncoming tread, than through any
deftness of my own. I palmed into a door standing
closed above, and he wrenched it out for me, and there
was the feeling of his thrusting me curtly through,
though his hands failed to contact me.

This was the back of a first-floor hall, and there was
a dim light to show it.

He opened the nearest of three doors that broke it,
touched something, and it lighted to an equal duskiness
with the hall. But at least darkness was banished.

"Stay in here a minute. Don't go out of here." He
closed the door and separated us.

It was an inscrutably fitted place, so that it was impossible to tell just what its purpose was. There was an
iron cot frame in it, but this bore no bedding. It was
just a room, perhaps, situated behind the so-called ex-
amination room in which I had consulted him on my
first visit, on the reverse side of it from the parlor in
which I had waited that day.

I listened for a moment, and he seemed to have
drawn away, though I hadn't heard any retreating footfall.

I tried the knob, and though it circled its socket the
door wouldn't give.

He'd locked me in there.

Panic flurried over me, and my first instinct was to batter frenziedly against it for outlet. My clenched hands were already backed to strike, but I held them frozen. "Wait, don't start anything. He hasn't done anything to you yet. If you don't provoke him you may yet be able to—"

In the silence I could hear the dial of a telephone creaking, but then after that stopped I couldn't hear what he said, he spoke so low.

Each breath was drawn from me as by a pulmotor.

I turned my head swiftly, thinking of the other door I'd seen and should have thought of sooner, the one giving into the consultation room beyond. And even as I did so I was too late; a white line sprang up around it like a ray, and a tiny white nick took the place of where its black keyhole had been until now.

The turning on of that highly powered light in there was the first inkling I had that he was no longer at the phone. I heard the slight clatter of instruments as he shifted aside the enamel pan that held them. I remembered that same sound from the first day.

I changed to the new direction, crouched down, and tried to look through the livid keyhole.

He was at the washstand, but he wasn't washing his hands this time. He was holding both hands down, seeming to draw something up *through* the one by means of the other. Some sort of plunger; I couldn't tell what. I thought I saw the shimmer of glass, like a tube or rod, glint through the intricate play of his fingers, but I couldn't be sure.

Then his figure changed focus, blurring as it came on toward the keyhole.

I reared, felt my way backward step by step, the ability to turn my body cataleptically denied me. I found the other doorknob, the first one, with my eyeless hands and, back still to it, pleaded twistingly to it. It still wouldn't open. I ran toward the cot. There was no other place to go. No other barrier, no other impediment, in the little foursquare rabbit hutch.

I flung it away from the wall and cleared a lane behind it and waded in there, covered only as high as the knees. The door was opening; the door had opened, the door had closed.

His face told nothing. His voice was guilefully moderate, matter of fact. "There's something coming to you. Here's your part of it." He was holding a bill or two in his carelessly extended hand. Lettuce for the rabbit about to be inoculated.

I breathed hissingly.

"Well, take it. Don't you want it?"

"Wait a minute. Why are you holding your other hand behind you like that? You've got something in it. What have you got in it?"

He spoke as quietly as when he'd gone out; it was just the text that had altered, not the tone of voice or the expression of his face. "You cuddly little rat. You baby-faced little squealer. Come over here a minute. Come over here to me." He actually beckoned at such a time and under such circumstances, beckoned me with fingers of his free hand in a mock-cajoling sort of way!

"Show me your other hand. Show me what you've got in it."

He came on toward me, and widened the canal I stood in by thrusting the cot out toward him. "Don't come near me. What are you going to do? Stay away, do you hear me? I haven't done anything to you."

"You haven't and you won't. I'm going to see that you don't."

He moved into the channel at one end. I moved out at the other, balancing on my two hands planted against the cot frame.

"I haven't *done* anything, I tell you!"

"No. Rocky was picked up within ten minutes after you'd fingered him at that theater last night. I just got word about it now."

My voice was all over the place. He was the quiet one. "I don't even know what you mean by fingered, so how could I—?"

"And now I suppose you've come here to poke it on me. Well, get this, you little she-louse. I'm in the clear. *You're* the only link between me and all of them. I can be out of here in ten minutes flat. I've moved fast before, and I can move fast again if I have to. But I'm willing to give nine of them up to—"

The needle was out. You couldn't see it; you could just see the V-shaped stance of his fingers, index toward point, thumb to plunger. A low scream sobbed from me, not very shrill, more of a moan. He'd left the lane of clearance again. I re-entered it at the other end an instant after. He reversed; I did too, and this horrible Virginia reel of death took a new direction.

"You won't even feel this. But it's a sure cure for your trouble. That's what you came to me for, isn't it? Well, I'm prescribing for you now. Sleep is what you need. Here it is here in my hand."

"They'll know you did it!" I gabbled. "You're only incriminating your—"

"They won't even know what was done. Morphine poisoning, my dear patient, leaves only one trace. Dilated pupils of the eyes. A drop of belladonna in each one before you're quite gone, and even that will be taken away. Death from an unknown cause. Suppose it did take place in my house? What they suspect and what they're able to prove in court are two different things."

I suddenly crouched low, shoved the entire cot frame back upon him with my entire strength. He was caught in mid-channel, equidistant from each end. It pinned him against the wall, at that most awkward point of leverage, just *under* the break of the knees, so that he couldn't use them to prod it back; they were held fast. He had to bend to it to use his own hand for a minute, easily as it shifted. And the blow must have stunned his leg bones, cramped them for a minute.

I used that minute for all it was worth. He'd locked the original opening, but there was still the door into the brightly lighted office from which he'd just come. I flung it out of the way and got in there.

From here there was only one other way out now. Those sliding door panels giving beyond into the front room. I wrenched at the finger sockets, splintering my nails. They gave with balky resistance, and before I could widen them sufficiently he was entering at the rear behind me.

There was that pan of instruments teetering beside me on the washstand rim. I picked it up and heaved it at him. Most of the things were light little things, short wands and what not. They sprayed out all over his chest and dropped without hurting him.

I gave one more wrench, and there was enough space to bolt through. The minute was compressed to thirty seconds now, to less. It was dark in there. I couldn't see my way, but I tried to remember. You went over to the left, and there was a door into the hall. If you got out through that, then the front door to the house lay straight ahead to your right.

I did something wrong. Turned toward it on too wide a sweep. He got over to it first and slammed it, and I was trapped. The minute was up now; the minute was gone. Our forms even brushed together lightly there at the door, then separated again for the last brief time. He would have caught me even sooner, I think, except that he spared his one arm, was only grasping for me with the other.

Something caught at the back of my leg and I twisted and turned to get away from him, and I fell floundering back on the sofa. He came down partly across me a minute later, pinning me there.

I didn't know how to defend myself. There was no defense. You can hope to deflect a knife; you can even manage to ward a gun aside. But this was like fending off a snake, a one-fanged snake. One strike and there was no use in further struggle.

Dimly, in the back of my own mind, I thought I heard a whistle blow. As I had that night, walking along the street, doing his errand. This one was swifter, sharper, shorter, directly outside the house somewhere. I knew it wasn't so; it wasn't real, just some trick of returning memory churned up in the midst of this death struggle. There was a sudden lisping surge of leather scuffling on stone, as if feet were trooping up the stoop outside. Then blows against wood.

He desisted just long enough to listen. "Well, I'll still get you first. They can't prove anything on me without you. They never have been able to. They never will."

I had my hands locked in the side fringes of his hair, one on each side of the semibald crown, as if trying to tear his skull apart by main force, but it did no good.

He wanted to make sure of where he— He deliberately pulled down the shoulder of my dress, clawed at it until he'd forced a bare spot for his purpose, the turn of my shoulder.

I heard the door go in. The outside one, beyond in the hall. It thudded like a wooden drum.

"They still can't—"

I could sense his arm go back in the dark. I didn't know where it was coming from, up, or down, or straight. Nor how soon, a second, two seconds, three.

I twisted my shoulder, flung it over, narrowed it toward its opposite, as in a last convulsive shudder.

His hand slapped up against it in a sort of raking blow. I heard something puncture the taut stuffing of the sofa with a little *pock!* Something wet seeped out of it, traced a stray tickling line over the unbroken skin of my shoulder where it met the sofa back.

A light glowered fiercely in at us, very hard-cored and round and silver-backed, poised down at full arm's length. It cast a pale aura all over the room. I lay there in it, and he lay prone athwart me, slowly starting to turn his head and face it with a sort of crafty, evasive delay in timing.

My eyelids began to blink more and more rapidly, and the light blurred, swirled smaller, went out.

I'd never fainted before. I never did again.

In a moment I'd come back again. Not to any rescue, not to any salvation, but to an unreality as bad or worse than the nightmare that had just preceded oblivion.

So little time had passed that it was as though a tiny segment of a progressing film had been snipped off and the continuing action had taken a short jump forward from where it had left off. Mordaunt was leaving the room, head dangling over as though his neck had been broken, though it was his own feet that supported him. There was a glint of steel from his wrist as his arm was held back for a moment by the projection of the door-frame and stayed behind him. Then it was drawn around after him and followed him out, drawing after itself in turn the arm of the man behind him that it was fastened to.

The room was lighted up now, and I could hardly place it. It was as though I had awakened in a strange place I had never been in before. The tulip horn of the gramophone was there in the background; the same mallards were under glass on the wall. Some vintage magazine or other, of a number that had been in here for his patients to read, had fallen to the floor and fluttered open. And as someone's foot trod unknowingly on it in passage it kicked free one of the leaves, carried it before it a short distance along the floor.

There were men in the room, on their various faces no sign of any compunction or solicitude for me. They were all stony-faced, truculent. One stood looking at me, waiting for my eyes to find him.

"Get up," he said gruffly when they had.

I forced my back away from the vise of the sofa joint. I righted my dismantled dress there where he'd wrenched it down.

"Your name's Alberta French," he said curtly. He

was looking at a loose-leaf memorandum pad he held in his hand that opened horizontally.

"Yes," I breathed low.

"And you live at—West Sixty-eighth."

I said yes again.

"Get on your feet," he jerked at me.

I staggered upright, thrust myself out from the sofa on one stiff arm.

He took hold of the other in two places, at the break of the elbow and at the wrist. He held it that way, like a lever. His grip wasn't gentle. I had to go in whichever way he went to avoid wrenching it at the arm socket.

"Now walk straight ahead. Out through that door in front of you."

I said, planting unwilling feet before me staccato, at his pace, not my own, "Why are you doing this to me? Where are you taking me? He— Didn't you see what he tried to do to me?"

His voice was harsher by far than Mordaunt's had been at any time from first to last. It was the impersonal harshness of official retribution, not personal animosity. "You're under Federal arrest for the transportation and selling of narcotics."

I went out with my own head dangling over, as though *my* neck were broken, just as he had. The fox and the chicken had been caught in the same trap.

Immediately following the last of the many times I'd been brought up before them for exhaustive questioning —or I should say the latest, for I hadn't known then that it was going to be the last—instead of being returned to the detaining cell, I was transported from there over to the police-headquarters building by car.

I was brought into an office, and when I saw Flood there I knew he'd had something to do with this change in the previous days' routine.

They turned me over to him, left me in there in his hands.

He was rather grim about it, like a man who has

performed a thankless task at no little trouble to himself and is still not entirely convinced of his own wisdom in doing so.

"You're being freed; did they tell you?"

I was too numb to react much at first. I'd been in custody four days by now. "No, they didn't. I noticed their line of questioning took a different turn the last time or so; that was all. It was more about Kirk's trouble and what I'd been trying to do for him than this—this other thing."

"Well, that's why you were brought up here. I interceded. I had a hard time convincing them. I'm no one, you know. I have no particular influence. It was just that I happened to be acquainted with certain factors in the background, in your particular case, and I put them before them. Put them before them for all I was worth, I might add. You're not freed technically, but you've been released into my custody, and you won't have to face Federal charges. Which is a good deal to be grateful for. It will be necessary for you to give evidence against this man Mordaunt, along with three other men and a colored woman, eventually, but that won't come up for several months yet."

He was waspishly unsympathetic. "Don't cry about it. You brought it on yourself."

I uncurled my enfolded arm and lifted my face from his desk blotter. "Can I go now?" I faltered helplessly.

"Yes, you can go now," he said ungraciously. "Take my advice and go home and rest up and stay out of trouble from now on. You see, this whole thing wouldn't have happened if you'd listened to me in the first place. I *told* you when you were in here that day—"

I'd risen and gone toward the door while he went on talking.

I was still far from admirable to him. "You've been a very dumb person, little Mrs. Murray. I'm willing to take your innocence in this mess at its face value on faith alone, but—"

I whirled on him from the door, almost aghast. If it

did nothing else, it drove all self-pitying weakness out of me forthwith. "You don't think I *voluntarily* co-operated in such a——!"

"I happen to be inclined to believe you. But I have no actual proof, you know. You could have."

He opened a drawer, took out a folder or dossier of some kind. He moistened his thumb and leafed over several loose papers contained in the seam of it. "Before you go it might interest you to know that the whole undertaking was a waste of time, anyway. His name is Mordaunt, right? And what was the date of the Mercer woman's murder? Never mind, I have it right here. May the twelfth. I took pains to look up this man's record—he has one that goes back to when I was in knee pants myself—and here are some interesting facts that I culled from our files. The most recent of his arrests took place on the fifteenth of March. He was evidently arrested on suspicion of some more serious charge, but with the help of a little adroit juggling he seems to have managed to plead guilty to a lesser charge and served time for that instead. Anyway, he served sixty days on Welfare Island for disorderly conduct and a few other little odds and ends, and the date of his release is down on the records as May the fifteenth, *three days after her death*." He closed the folder with a snap. "In case you still have any doubts, I've checked on the fingerprints and it's the same man."

My chin only went down for a minute; it didn't stay down. It came right up again, higher than before.

"That's what mistakes are for," I murmured quietly, "so you'll keep on going and not quit too easily."

He looked at me curiously. I don't know, for some strange reason he seemed to like me a little better when he saw me square off like that than he had only a moment ago."

"I like your spirit," he admitted, "but your line of reasoning is all flooey."

"You can keep me from going ahead with it, I suppose, as long as I'm sort of paroled to you, as you say."

"Do I have to?"

"There's only one way you can. By having me put back in jail again."

"Don't you see it's no use? Believe me, Mrs. Murray, it's no use. Give up this harebrained idea, quit trying—"

"No, I won't give up trying. I couldn't, even if I wanted to. I *believe,* and that's all I've got. Don't take it away from me; I won't let you." I opened the door to go. "Why should I quit trying? Because I was wrong this time? The next time I may be right. You're always wrong until the last time. And then when you're right, at the end, that wipes out all the times before when you were wrong. I'm going ahead, Mr. Flood; I'm going ahead. Whether with your sanction or without it. This very next time may be the right time, the last time of all. I may be just an hour away, a block away, from *him. He* may be waiting just around the corner. The next time I pick up the phone *he* may answer; it may be his voice I hear saying 'Hello. Who is this?' "

8

Butterfield 9–8019 . . . . Mason

"HELLO. WHO IS THIS?"

The voice was vivid, tingling; it rushed at you. It was in a hurry. Not in the sense of "I'm busy; what do you want? Don't bother me," but eager, zestful, anxious to be on its way from the last interesting thing that had happened to it to the next interesting thing that was to happen to it. The sort of voice that only interesting things happened to. And if they weren't already, it made them that way just by taking part. That kind of voice.

The first sip of a cocktail in it. The wind up at the prow of a motorboat in it. A walloping good dance tune in it, the kind that takes your feet and lifts them. The spanking bliss of the first gushing cascade when you turn on an ice-cold shower on a melting August day. The turn on a breakneck toboggan run in it. All those things in it. Everything that makes life swell in it. Everything that is life. What a voice.

I said, "I'm a friend of someone you know. I just got into town, and I'm giving you a ring, the way I promised I'd do."

The voice was open, friendly, trustful; it took me at my word. It didn't know how to be suspicious, that voice. "Who's the somebody?"

That was it; who *was* the somebody?

"Somebody you haven't seen in quite some time. Now, think."

The voice fell in with me, helping to work its own undoing, so to speak. "Let's see, whom haven't I seen in quite some time?" There was a quickly mumbled name or two, discarded before I could quite make them out. Then, "It wouldn't be Ed Lowrie, would it?"

I gave a little rill of laughter down the scale, meant to convey admission, capitulation. I let that stand by itself. I hadn't said it was; if something went wrong I could still get out of it.

He said, "Well, what d'ye know?" as if marveling at this mark of attention on the part of a long-unseen friend. Then he said, "Where is he, still out there?"

I said, "He was the last I saw him. I came sort of a roundabout way myself." But I laughed a little with it again. Not too much, just enough so I could still leave the way open, back out and say, "It wasn't he, it was somebody else," if I had to. This mustn't go wrong. These opening stages were always the most important part of the whole thing until I could make contact and fasten myself onto them.

"You from out there yourself?" he asked.

"Certainly am." Then, as if preparing to end the exchange, which was simply a trick in reverse to make him wish to prolong it, I said, "Well, now that I've done my duty I guess I may as well—" And I nicked the lip of the telephone mouthpiece with my nail to make the sound carry.

His voice quickened. "Hey, wait; you haven't even given me your own name yet."

I was becoming more sure of myself at every phrase. They say the art of being a gentleman is to inspire ease in others. Then the art of being a gentleman's voice is to inspire confidence in those who converse with it. And his was surely a gentleman's voice. "Oh, I thought you knew it," I said. "I wasn't supposed to introduce myself quite cold like this. I didn't realize I was. Then in that case his letter didn't reach you yet?"

"No," he said. "No, I haven't heard from him in God knows when."

"I was afraid of that," I grieved primly. "I bet he forgot to send it at all. And here I've been—"

"Oh, come on, I don't need a letter of introduction to be glad to meet people."

"Yes, but I don't like to just foist myself on— I might be anyone at all, for all you know; I might be some little hustler that thinks she's smart and just wants to—"

"I carry insurance against that," he said indulgently. "And one way of proving you're not, you know, would be to—"

"I'm sorry; I still haven't, have I? I'm Alberta French."

"So now we're friends. You doing anything for dinner tonight?" Then, as I hesitated, "Look, we both have to eat, anyway. If we don't like each other, well—we haven't lost anything. We've each had our evening meal."

"There is something in that, isn't there?"

He'd already rushed on past that point. "How'll I know you?"

"Well, for that matter, how'll I know *you?*"

His voice had a grin in it. "I asked you first. Tell you what. Is there a flower shop handy to you where you are?"

"Yes, I think so."

"Well, get hold of something good and big so that I can't miss it. A chrysanthemum. Put it on your shoulder."

"Yes, but that still doesn't take care of you."

"I don't think you'd like me with a chrysanthemum. Look, I'll just be the fellow that comes up to you and tips his hat and says, 'Are you you?' "

I knew what he wanted, all right. He wanted to see me first from a safe distance. If I didn't pass muster he wouldn't come near me; I'd never see hair or hide of him again. Glasses, maybe. Or a little too high up in the age brackets. I didn't blame him, really. I had him out there on the fringes. It was up to me to pull him in the rest of the way.

"That's it, then," he said. "Now I'll tell you where. I know a little room, a midget cocktail bar, just around the corner from the Ritz. Can't miss. It's called the Blues-Chaser. And it's like that, really. There's never too much of a crowd there, and that way we won't have to run too much interference. We have a date now, don't forget."

"All right, we have a date."

The last thing he said was, "Remember the password. 'Are you you?' Don't go off with the wrong guy."

The last thing I said was, "I'll let you do the worrying about that."

I'd have to play it his way. He was setting the tempo, not I. And the tempo was chaff, badinage, light flirtation. Maybe he was that age. Or maybe it was that he'd always be that age; it was a state of mind. Well, so be it then.

I didn't do much. I looked at myself in the glass before I was ready to leave and thought: "I don't know what he wants. So he'll have to get what I have."

I bought the chrysanthemum, a bursting yellow one, and had them pin it on. High enough so that I could nestle my cheek against it if I turned that way. Then I went over there about a quarter to five.

The place itself was intimate, confidence-inspiring, made to order for just such a rendezvous as ours. A regular postage stamp of a cocktail lounge; I'd never yet been in one as small. Heavily carpeted and hushed, but hushed in a relaxing, cozy way, not depressingly hushed. It was a little gem of a place, and I wonder now if it's still there.

The only discordant note was the rather wretched-looking attendant who came over as soon as I had seated myself. He was suffering from some skin disorder that necessitated his wearing some half-dozen tiny cross patches of court plaster scattered liberally all over his face and then, to cap the climax, one larger strip, slantwise, nearly sealing the outside corner of one eye. He came at a sort of shamble, without lifting feet from the carpet, and I refrained from looking directly at him after the first devastating glance. He was enough to spoil any apéritif he brought. There was a second, far more prepossessing one at hand behind the bar, but he confined himself to waiting upon those who sat directly before him, and I had drawn this one.

He wasn't in the place yet. I'd expected that. I'd felt fairly sure he'd purposely delay arriving, in order to allow me to get there first and be able to study me at leisure, preferably without coming all the way in. I made this as difficult as possible for him by selecting a seat that was as removed from the entrance steps as the limited confines of the place would allow. Which wasn't much. But at least he would have to show himself a few paces within the door to be able to get a comprehensive look at me. Even if he turned around and bolted directly out again afterward. I disposed my shoulder so that from that side I was mostly a burgeoning yellow chrysanthemum topped by an eyebrow and a hatbrim.

"Yes mum, what'll ye be liking?" the depressing-looking figure at my elbow asked with a brogue you could cut with a knife.

I rejected the wine card. "A glass of dry sherry."

"Yes mum." He went away and let me alone.

I thought: "He mayn't come at all. He may have out-feinted me at my own game without my realizing it." The mere fact that he stipulated an outside rendezvous, instead of calling at my hotel for me, shows that he accepted me with reservations. These open, hale, guileless voices can experience mistrust as readily as the more wary, evasive kind. Why not? The only difference is that they don't show it outwardly. True, I always knew where I could reach him again, but that was valueless. This was one of those cases in which, if the first skirmish was lost, the whole campaign had been thrown away; there was no use pursuing it any farther.

I couldn't call him a second time, not even with an attempted change of identity. He already knew my voice. He had retained his freedom of action. I had already lost mine before I'd even gained contact with him.

"Ah yes," I reflected, "he isn't quite the unsuspecting soul he seemed." I wondered why that hadn't occurred to me sooner than this. There must have been some magic in that voice of his.

My sherry came back, and with it, as he set it down, there was a small folded leaf of white paper inserted between the base of the glass and the platter it stood on. I thought it was the bill at first, but when I'd taken it up and opened it—

Are you you?

it said on it.

"Wait a minute, where did this come from?"

He looked down at it in stupid astonishment himself. "I don't know, mum. Sure, it wasn't there when I set the gloss onto the tray just now."

"But you came over here in a straight line from the bar to me; I saw you. It couldn't have been put on after you started over with it. It was *under* the glass."

I looked around covertly. "Wait a minute, don't move away. I want you to stand here just as you are, in front of me. Did you rest the tray on the bar for a minute before you picked it up and started out?"

"Well, just for a minute, mum, but then I always do. Only just long enough to jot the order down on my tab, so I have it on the bill later."

"At which end of the bar were you when you did that?"

"Over there by the wall; that's the only way you can come out from behind."

"Is it that man sitting there with a vacant place on each side of him?"

He looked over. About as subtly as a steam calliope revolving full blast. "Maybe it was, at that. It was by him. Shall I ask him, mum?"

"No, don't, you fool," I said with more candor than politeness.

I wondered why I let it irritate me, why I didn't take it in good part. It might have been that I didn't like the realization that I was up against something smarter than I'd bargained for. He'd been in here all along. And since no one had entered after me he'd already been here when I arrived. My face must have been naked to him the whole while, and I didn't like that thought. He must have sat there quietly watching me while I transparently sat marshaling my strategy about me.

I didn't like his looks, if that were he. And by elimination it must be. For all the others were in twos, girl and man or man and man. He was the only single.

I didn't like his looks. He belied his voice completely, but that was the least of it. There was a merciless shrewdness there, a cold sort of calculation that I could sense I was going to be no match for. Nothing came of itself. Nothing was casual, first time, unthought of. Every abstract turn of his head in some new direction than before, every lift of his glass, every draw of his cigar conveyed the impression: "Is it to my advantage to do this? Is there some gain in my doing it? Very well, then, I'll do it."

If he was playing at billets-doux with me, at hide-and-seek, then there was some motive in it other than just youthful gaiety, high spirits, I could be sure.

He'd been born old, that man there at the bar. Old and cruel. He'd never wasted a move in his life. He should have had everything in the world already by mere dint of lifelong rapacious application. But maybe there were many things he didn't want at one time, then wanted at another; that was all that kept him going.

I dropped my eyes and sipped my sherry and knew defeat ahead of time.

I wondered why he was playing with me like this. I bore the chrysanthemum. He'd sent the note, so he wasn't trying to pretend he wasn't here. He just lct me sit on there. Five minutes, ten, fifteen. Cruelty without provocation, just for its own sake.

I couldn't get up and go. I couldn't scuttle my own undertaking. I had to sit and wait out his pleasure. He had me. And if he had me this early what would it be like later?

I'd sipped to the bottom of my glass. I'd lit a cigarette and put out its fingernail-length remnant. The table-barman, taking more pity on me than he, for all his ignoble blemish-studded physiognomy, came back again unsummoned, perhaps drawn by my dejected, trapped mien.

"Would you be wanting another, mum?"

"Yes, bring me another."

I thought: "Since I know it's he and he won't come over to me, why don't I get up and go over to him and have an end to it?" I thought: "He wants me to do that. That must be what he's waiting for. And with a man like that, anything he wants you to do it's better not to do, since there's some purpose there you can't fathom."

I must have been looking at him too long. He'd turned full face toward me on his stool, now, and thcre was a sort of challenge in the cold, steady way he held my eyes.

The barman cut betwecn us just as the look was turning into something else; what, I couldn't see yet. He was lifting his feet this time as he traveled. He'd brought somebody else's order back with him, along with mine.

He put my glass down, then put the second one down at the vacant place opposite me. Then he discarded his tray on an unused table behind him and suddenly was sitting there with me in informal sociability.

"Here, what do you think you're—!" I started to say.

He grinned, called over his shoulder, "Here's your spare jacket back, Matt, and thanks for the loan of it."

I glanced over at the bar, and the cold-faced man was settling back onto his stool again. He turned away, unemotional as ever.

"That guy was slow," he chuckled.

I turned back to him again. "You *wanted* me to—?"

"Just for the fun of it."

Matt came over with his own coat, solicitously helped him into it.

"How was I?" he asked him cheerfully. "You'll find the orders I took in the pocket—if you can make out my writing."

"Not bad at all, Mr. Mason. You can have a job here any time you say the word."

"Thanks, I'll keep that in mind."

I saw them touch palms briefly. I didn't see what it was. I suppose it was quite a large amount.

He saw me looking at his face. "Oh, I forgot something," he said to me. "This is going to hurt; it was easier going on than taking off."

"I'll do it for you, Mr. Mason," Matt offered. "Just hold still. Do it quick is the best way."

He recoiled, especially at the paring of the big one across the rim of his eye. "Art for art's sake." He winced. The skin was clear under all of them as soon as the temporary irritation was gone. It had been clever of him. Though they had been individually tiny—each one had occupied no more than a minute area of his skin surface—they had drawn the eye so, as those things do, that they had broken up his face by optical illusion into something quite other than it was. Just like those photographs transmitted by radio, composed of consecutive dots instead of unbroken lines.

So that, though it had been just a matter of four or five midget wens of plaster, and he had been in the same room with me all the while, only now for the first time was I seeing him as he actually was.

My first thought was: "He looks awfully wholesome and friendly to kill a woman."

I studied him as carefully as though life and death depended on it. They did. Kirk's life and death. Here he was, then, at this first meeting of ours: the line of the table and a glass with scotch watered to straw color in it. An idle hand beside that, half curved around nothing. Not brutish, as Mordaunt's had been, yet good and strong. A gold seal ring on one finger, holding a flat square stone with a crest engraved on it. An onyx, it appeared to be. The nails neat-looking and trimmed short with a pair of scissors, possibly, but not professionally manicured, not glossy from a buffer; in other words, just as they should be in good taste.

Then, above where the lapels joined, a tie that, if it didn't come from Sulka, had the look of one that did. A tie so neutral, so integrated into the rest of his clothing, that you weren't aware it was there unless you searched it out. Again just as it should be in good taste.

Now came his face, the crux of the whole matter. It was a broad face, not one of these long thin ones, nor yet one of these round fat ones. It was broad, substantial, solid; when he became older it might grow too heavy, too massive, but that wasn't yet. The skin fitted it like a glove, without any looseness or seams anywhere. Its most distinguishing characteristic, as far as expression went, might be the adjective "pleasant." It pleased you. If, for instance, you were to fall in love with it, it must please you to a hell of a degree if it pleased you as much as it did just to look at it the first time you saw it.

His eyes were very dark brown, very alert, very intelligent. The pleasantness of all the rest of the face came to a head in them. They gave him away, not in the sense of treachery, but revealed his true inner capacity. You might think you could fool him, but if you looked directly into them you weren't so sure any more; you wondered if you were smart enough yourself.

His hair was red-brown and combed dry, so that it

didn't clot together and fasten into blades but topped his head the way hair should: good and plentiful, kept short, and, beyond that, allowed to do pretty much what it felt like doing.

There he was; that was he. And meanwhile he'd been studying me equally deliberately on his part. And, I suppose, telling himself those things about me that I was telling myself about him.

"So you're you." He smiled finally.

I nodded. "How do you find me?"

He screwed up one eye in self-disgust. "Of course it pays to look before you leap, but I shot twenty minutes of our time to pieces for no good reason. I'm just yellow, I guess."

"Well, maybe you've been stuck before," I suggested.

"There's no good reason for getting stuck, really. It's the simplest thing in the world. You see the thing through past the cocktails. I mean, a cocktail will see you through practically anything, anyway. If it's the face that bothers you you've got an olive to look at instead. Then with the soup, you step outside a second to buy a pack of cigarettes. You pick some brand you're darned sure they won't be able to bring to your table, in case there happens to be a ciggie girl in the place. Ramses the Third, or something, strawtipped. Never smoke anything else. Then with the main course comes the rescuing phone call. Somebody's dying in your house, or somebody's having a baby, or your office is on fire. You pay the waiter for the rest of her dinner—that's to make sure she'll have to stay and finish it, not try to come with you—you apologize; you'll call her, and you're out of it."

I laughed a little. "How many times have you done that?"

"Well, that, of course, is the funny part of it. I told you I'm yellow. I never have yet. I've sat and planned the whole thing out in my mind, but somehow when the coffee comes around I'm still sitting there, just suffering. They always look so trusting. The most I've ever been able to do is just cut the evening a little short at the other end." I liked the answer; it spiked the conceit that otherwise would have been implicit in the discussion.

"I must remember that; from now on all soup-course phone calls are open to suspicion."

He grinned. "Don't clutter your mind with stuff you'll never have to use. I bet the only time they leave *you* during a soup course is to put a padlock on the inside of the door so *you* can't get away from them."

"A spoonful at a time," I begged. "Not with a shovel like that; you won't have any left."

"Another?"

"No, two are enough, thanks."

"A cigarette, then?"

"A cigarette, then."

He held a lighter to it.

I said, "Do you have your initials over everything like that?"

He chuckled, as though he didn't think much of it himself. "No, that was my sister's idea. Last Christmas. I suppose so I couldn't return it or something."

He blew it out, forgot about it. "You haven't told me your name yet."

"Didn't I? I thought I did. Alberta French."

"What do they call you?"

"Alberta French."

"I'll have that worn out in a week," he promised.

"Well, you'll be fresh out of a name for me, then."

"Maybe I'll just be plain fresh, without the rest of it."

"It wouldn't surprise me in the least," I told him demurely.

He called Matt over to settle his bill. Then he thumbed a dime down onto the table directly before him. "Mustn't forget the waiter," he said to me confidentially. "That ought to be enough, don't you think? He wasn't so good."

"Oh, he was worth more than that," I urged plaintively.

He added a nickel to it with a show of reluctance.

Then in the brogue he'd affected before he said to himself: "Thank you, sorr." And out of the side of his mouth, in a seething undertone: "Cheap skate!"

I couldn't help tipping my head back and laughing.

"Come on, let's get out of here. We've got places to go and things to do." He shifted my chair for me. "You're in my clutches now."

"You mean," I thought somberly as I rose to join him, "you're in mine. Whether you know it yet or not." And I wasn't kidding as he was.

A scrubwoman on hands and knees kept chasing us around the mosaic-floored hotel lobby, out before the elevator, from dry spot to dry spot in a sort of concentric circular pattern.

"Now I'll really have to break away and go up," I laughed. "We're back where we started. Don't you remember this place with the wriggly crack in it?"

"I knew I'd seen it before. It must have been our last trip around."

The scrubwoman wrung out a cloth and grinned toothlessly up at us. "I'm catching up with yez," she said.

It was starting to get light out. There was light blue peering in through the doors. It seemed like a year ago I'd first met him, not just twelve hours. He knew how to make time fly.

"What're you waiting for?" I demanded, still laughing. "You've got me to that silly stage now, where I laugh at everything you say and do. We've been standing here like this for nearly an hour, doing nothing but laughing. That night desk man over there thinks we're crazy."

He turned to him and blurted out, "Isn't she nice? I just met her tonight."

He turned back to me without waiting for any comment. "I keep waiting to see how you look when you get tired. And you don't get tired."

"With you one doesn't get tired in the face; one gets

tired in the larynx. Mine's positively raw. Well, tired or not, up I go. This is positively it now."

He took leave of me matter-of-factly enough, when at last he did. "I'll call you." Picked up my hand, dropped it again, turned, and went out. As limberly as though it had been six the night before.

"Nice kid," the desk man offered, unasked, gazing after him.

I didn't answer. "Nice kid," I thought, going up in the elevator, "but I wonder if he's ever killed a woman?"

Upstairs in my room I sat for a long while, motionless, by the window, while the roofs below turned strawberry and then orange. Not laughing any more. Card-indexing him.

"He was just showing off because I'm new to him. No one can be that happy-go-lucky, that harum-scarum, whatever you'd call it, that brimful of life, *all* the time. No one is. Don't be taken in. There's a darker side to the picture. Patience. Patience. It will turn my way."

He called as he'd said he would. I was there when the phone rang. I'd been waiting for it to ring. I knew it was he. Who else knew I was here in this place, here in this particular room? This room had been taken for him, to give me background, a setting, for him.

I sat there in the chair without moving and let the call wear itself out into silence. That came under the heading of technique. Keeping him interested.

It came again in about half an hour. Again I didn't move. Then the next time it came within fifteen minutes. Interest was quickening to uneasiness, anxiety.

I answered it the third time.

He'd been worried. "You had me going. I thought maybe I'd lost you."

"I just came in. I was out window-shopping. You know, out-of-town girl in New York."

"Isn't there something you would like to do tonight?"

"Yes, very much."

His voice took an upcurve. "Fine. What is it? Tell me."

"Just to go to bed early and get a good night's sleep after last night."

His voice dipped again, even though there was a lugubrious laugh in it. "I meant something I could join you in. You don't want to sleep in New York. New York isn't for sleeping in."

"They tell me millions do. In fact, I've even seen beds. I'm looking at one right now, and it looks awfully good from here."

"Mason, are you slipping!" he said. "I never thought I'd play second fiddle to a Murphy."

"You couldn't get me out of this building tonight," I told him firmly. "I've got just about strength enough to take me downstairs and back for a sandwich. Then I'm going to stand up perfectly straight beside this Murphy, as you call it, and let myself go over backward."

I said to myself as I hung up: "He won't take it. He'll ring again before the night's through."

I sat waiting, but he didn't. One error out of four is permissible. After an hour, when he hadn't, I finally did go down to get myself a sandwich.

He was sitting there on a line with the elevator tier, grinning and patiently waiting. He was holding a terraced brown paper bag balanced on one knee, a bevy of paper napkins on the other.

He said, "You took an awful long time getting down. I have them already, yours and mine both. Just a sandwich before bed, you said. There's no reason why we shouldn't eat them together, off in some quiet corner of the lobby, is there? And then I'll see you back to your elevator and we'll say good night."

Which was the pursuer and which the pursued? He couldn't have told; I could.

It was on a subway car that our lips first met. Of all unlikely places. That moth-eaten expression for once is apt; no other one will do. There was no intent there; it just happened that way. His lips struck mine.

To him they were novel, and he didn't know how to hold himself in them very well. He was bringing me home from someplace; it was abominably late, as it always was when I was out with him, and it had been my suggestion. "It's the quickest way after all, even figuring on the station waits. Let's be plebeian for a change."

The train jarred to a stop at the station with one of those flounces they sometimes give—maybe the motorman up ahead was sleepy or something—and he was flung against me in the vestibule where we were standing waiting to get off. His head had been lowered to peer out, make sure it was the right station. His face went into me. Then he stayed that way.

I refrained from moving too. The weapons weren't of my choosing, but I wasn't discarding anything.

"You'd better hold that door," I had to say finally; "it's starting to go back again."

He was quiet going up the steps.

Halfway to the top he turned to me. "Stand here a minute. Let me try that again."

I kept on moving. "The staircase doesn't shake," I reminded him. "It was the train that did."

I thought he was kidding, but when I looked he wasn't. He had a pensive look in his eyes. Almost a little troubled.

I was too, for some reason.

It was like a premonition of disaster to both of us.

"Here's the street," I said.

"So it is."

He parted from me rather more hastily downstairs at the hotel elevator than he usually did. No laughing jags tonight, no shilly-shallying. "I want to leave you now. I have a lot to think about. And though you'll be there, it's better in a way if you're not in front of me."

I turned away without a word and left him.

Upstairs it kept ringing lingeringly in my ears for a

long time afterward. Not so much what he'd said as the
strange, grave way in which he'd said it. No lightness,
no banter there any longer. "I want to leave you now. I
have a lot to think about."

"Something on your conscience?" I answered to myself.

"Something about a death that comes back now and
then to plague you—particularly at the birth of a new
love?

"The death of an old love?

"A death you caused?"

From time to time I said something about going
back. I had to. Technically I was still here only on a
visit, elastically adjustable though it seemed to be. I still
didn't know where it was I was supposed to go back to,
but I felt I had to refer to it every now and again, if
only for the sake of plausibility. After all, he was no
fool.

His reaction to the test, each time it was made, provided a good barometer of his feelings. Unconsciously
he was self-revelatory about it. The first time I mentioned the subject he winced half humorously, coaxed,
"Ah, wait another week. A few days more can't hurt.
There'll still be trains running." The second time he
sobered, looked down, and, I noticed, didn't have much
to say for quite some time after that. The third time
he scowled, began moving restlessly about the room,
and when he went out later was grouchy, ill-humored,
drank considerably more than he usually did, and left
the waiters and the rest anarchistically small tips.

The fourth time he turned the tables on me. *He*
brought the subject up, not I. "I can't think of your
going back," he said. "I'm going with you when you
do." And then, when I tried to object, "I'm just as
entitled to make a trip out there as you were to make
one here. What do I do around here anyway? Sit in my
old man's chair at board meetings half the time without

opening my face. They can take my vote by proxy for a couple months just as well!"

I prudently let the entire matter lapse after that. It was the better part of valor. The elastically temporary sojourn became a permanent stay.

I changed from the hotel room, which I had used as a springboard for meeting him, to a little one-room studio place over on Fifty-third, just east of Second Avenue. He'd helped me to find it, since I was supposedly still a little green in New York. There was not only the matter of expense, which was as actual a consideration to me on the real plane of my existence as on the camouflaged, two-dimensional one in which I presented myself to him, but my former surroundings had outlived their usefulness. I felt we were now at, or soon to approach, a stage, he and I, in which I needed more privacy, more seclusion, to work effectively.

He accompanied me there the day I moved in. In fact, took me in his car.

I said to myself, "It is only right that he should be on hand from the very first day, the very first minute that this room begins. For the day *he* ends the room ends with him. It is of him and for him and because of him; it is through him alone that it has any reality. Without him it isn't there at all."

Little room on Fifty-third Street that I expected to forget so soon.

I wasn't expecting it.

I could feel his eyes on me, studying me from close range, and finally I chose to become aware, said: "What are you looking at me for like that?"

"I'm trying to think what to call you."

"Isn't it a little late for that?"

"There's something about Alberta; it's too stiff; it doesn't ride easily on the tongue. Do you remember the night we first met? I told you I'd give that up after a week, and it's long past that now. I have to find some name for you. Some name of my own. Stand up and let me look at you. I'll see if I can get one." He held me poised before him, his hands to my sides.

His eyes went deep, went lonesome. I saw that and I tried to keep it light. "This is the oddest christening. I'm a little old and tall, aren't I? I should be held in someone's arms and have on a long trailing nightgown-dress. Who's there to sprinkle the water on my head?"

"Don't," he said. Just that one word. With a haunted severity.

I shut up and looked away, waiting for it to blow over by itself.

"Turn your head this way again, toward the lamp, so that the light falls softly on your face from the other side."

His breath caught.

"That soft light, what it does to you. You look like an—"

He rose slowly to his own feet before me, his hands still to my sides.

I smiled a little, waiting.

"I've found one for you," he breathed. "You've got the face of an angel. I'm going to call you Angel Face. Angel Face I'm going to call you."

I wrenched myself away so suddenly, in such momentarily maddened pain, his hands were left there stretched out, empty, measuring off the space where I had been. And I was all the way across the room, not just a step away, a yard away, but all the far way across, as though he'd taken a knife to me and probed right there where my heart was.

I saw his lips moving and I couldn't hear what he said. I didn't want to, anyway.

He came over to me then, took my hands and drew them down from over my ears, where they'd been pressed in fierce closure.

"What have I done to frighten you?" he said. "Why are you covering your ears like that? Look, you're white—your eyes are so big—"

"Don't ever call me that name," I said shakily. "Don't even say it over a second time now to remind yourself what it was. Don't use it again, Ladd, or I'll—you'll never see me again. Call me any other name, anything you want. Anything but that."

"There was someone else once, is that it?"

He made his peace with my past.

"There would have had to be, with a face such as you've got. You weren't born yesterday."

I leaned against him and closed my eyes against his shoulder and saw a face before me that he didn't know was there.

Then later, of course, I was immeasurably glad I'd gone. But at the time I didn't dream it would profit me anything. Everything comes so by chance, so haphazardly, even in the best-laid schemes. *He* was the one I was interested in, not his background, his mother and sister, or whoever it was, as the case might be.

In addition, I was convinced there was the usual situation lurking behind it: *he* wanted me to be there; he was pulling the strings to force a sort of grudging affability out of them, considerably against their own inclinations, and in short was forcing me down their throats.

It was his sister's birthday.

The invitation, of course, I had disregarded as being something he'd been responsible for himself, even though she put an inked personal message on it in addition. "Do come, so anxious to meet you, have heard so much about you from L."

I tried all the stalls I knew to get out of it.

"I don't belong there."

"You don't belong there! You're my Alberta; you belong wherever I am. What are we, the landed aristocracy or something?"

"No, but I mean I'll have no mutual interests with anyone that's there."

"Fine, because you wouldn't have a chance to ex-

change them if you did! You're going to be with me all
evening; no one else is going to get near you. I'm just
looking out for myself in this, you see. I *have* to be
there. Don't you want me to enjoy my own sister's
party?"

Finally I even fell back on the most moth-eaten excuse of all.

"I have nothing to wear."

"You've been going around with me pretty steadily,
and you've never been arrested yet for indecent ex-
posure."

Then when the dress had come and I'd sent it back,
the next time I saw him I said: "Don't ever do that
again, young man, or when the night of the party does
come you'll show up carrying your arm in a sling!"

He only laughed. "I could have sworn it wouldn't
work. I told them so at Carnegie's when I picked it
out."

"I hope you laid side bets on it," I said maliciously.

And even when she called me herself on the phone,
just before the affair, I still said to myself knowingly:
"*He* put her up to it."

"This is Leila Mason. Now, you're not going to be
mean to me, are you? I've been trying so hard to get
Ladd to bring you. And—well, there's no telling with
Ladd; he can be very selfish about his friends. Come.
As a special favor to me, won't you?"

After I'd hung up I wasn't so sure. It didn't seem to
me that any amount of browbeating could have ex-
torted that much from a sister if she were congenitally
unwilling. She must want me herself. And I wondered
why.

I went.

It was about what I'd expected it to be. But for the
number of rooms that you kept encountering if you
were foolish enough to keep progressing, and an occasional crystal chandelier like an inverted wedding cake,
it was any party in anyone's home about the twenty-five-
thousand-a-year bracket.

There *was* a mother, but counter to all my expectations, which had run toward a domineering, bejeweled dowager, she was a shadowy, wispy little nonentity, fragile-looking as Dresden china, who weighed about ninety pounds, talked with fluttering wrists à la Zasu Pitts, and seemed to have the status of a pet Persian kitten in the household. Even the guests, I noticed, would give her a sort of pat in passing, so to speak, and then go on to somebody of more consequence.

It was the sister who counted. She was a tall, lovely girl. She was Ladd all over. She had all his charm of the individual and then some additional little facets of her own as the due of her sex. She greeted me with her two hands clasped to my one.

"Well, you did! You never can get together with anyone you really want to at this sort of thing, but at least it helps to break the ice. Now remember, no matter what happens, if the very building burns down around us, we're going to get in at least *one* heart-to-heart talk before it's over, even if we've got to wait all night. Ladd, make her stay."

"I'll make her."

She rushed off again, pointing her finger at me commandingly. "Remember, we have a date."

"She's charming," I said to him.

"She'll do," he answered with typical brotherly lukewarmness.

It was Ladd, Ladd, Ladd all evening. He was almost grotesque about it, the way he kept me to himself. We danced a little in one oversized gallery where they had four or five players working at instruments, sipped an occasional champagne cup, roamed around a little. He showed me some of the rooms.

"How many are there, anyway?" I asked.

"Oh, I don't know," he said half contemptuously. "I just sleep in one of those nearest the door and go in and out a lot."

I laughed.

And as I say, none of it amounted to anything. I had

no hopes of or for anything; I was just killing time there, so I let the evening drift by.

Around half-past twelve they started to thin out, and in another half-hour the backgrounds were once more clearly visible in all the rooms. I'd quite forgotten about her; I thought it had just been lip courtesy. He looked at his watch, said we'd done our duty, and he suggested that I get myself together and we'd go for a drive in the open air before he took me home.

He only released me from his protective custody now, at the very end, because I was going into a room where other men were hardly likely to follow me, I adduced. And at any rate, I sat there for a few moments in a preserve still piled fairly high with mink and brocade wraps and fooled around with my face a little.

I don't know whether she'd had her weather eye out and had seen me go in or had happened to look around after I was gone and had missed me; anyway, within a moment or two she came dashing in after me.

She swooped past without stopping, caught me by the hand as she did so. "Come on," she said. "This won't do. I have a special place for us." She took me into some little private sitting room of her own—it hadn't been open to the party—and rang for someone.

"We'll have a glass of champagne in here by ourselves," she said. "All right with you? I haven't had a chance to get down to the bottom of one all evening."

I said it was all right with me and meant it.

She was, now that I looked at her more closely, fully as lovely as she had seemed to be outside in the crowd, and that wasn't a test that I'd been at all sure she would pass. It was a loveliness of mind as well as appearance. She was cultured, but not in a cold, bookish way. Switzerland, Paris, the usual background, I suppose. But it wasn't just a veneer, as with so many of her kind. She had absorbed it. Young as she was, she was mellow with it. She was well baked, golden brown with civilization.

She poured for us when they'd left the champagne

and then brought out the cigarettes. Then she sat down and loosed the bands of her backless sandals. I made some complimentary remark about a diamond bowknot she was wearing, just to do my share at starting us off together, and she said it was Ladd's gift.

And then it happened. And this is how it happened.

We were looking around for a light, and neither one of us had one.

"I should have asked him just now—" she said and went over and opened a drawer.

I sat waiting.

"There's usually a lighter on this table of mine, but somebody seems to have removed it," she said. She closed the first drawer and opened a second. "I'll go out and get some," she said. Then suddenly she said, "Oh, never mind, here's an old book of them left over in here."

She came back and settled herself beside me once more and lit the cigarettes for us.

I lost track of the opening part of the conversation. I suppose it was girly-girly stuff, anyway. I kept looking at it where she was holding it absently in her hand.

It was blue and it had that single *M* on it. It was a duplicate to the one I'd taken from behind the door seam at Mia Mercer's apartment.

I pretended my cigarette had gone out. I said, "May I?" and took them from her. I struck one, but what I was really doing was looking at it hard at closer range.

It was the same, the same folder I'd sat comparing on the bed in the furnished room that night they'd brought me back Kirk's clothes.

I said offhandedly, "Are these yours?"

"Ladd's, really. I made him a gift of a tremendous bale of them one Christmas. Silly sort of gift, wasn't it? But if I remember correctly, I think I did it because I'd used up all my own Christmas funds by the time I got around to him, so I simply put in the order with Father's tobacconist and charged it to his tobacco account. He never did really use them much, and since then they've been sprouting up all over the house. I don't think we'll ever get to the end of them."

I kept them in my own hand from this point on. Absently, as she had. They were going out of here with me when I left tonight.

Success had a curious pewter lackluster to it; it wasn't bright at all.

She'd become serious suddenly. About Ladd and me, evidently, though I'd missed the original point of transposition. "You don't know what you mean to him," she was saying. "Oh, my dear, I don't know how you feel about him, and it's not my place to ask you—" She stopped a minute, and then went on: "He can't tell you this. I'll have to. Don't let him become too set on you. You mustn't. For your own sake. There are reasons why—why things with Ladd should never go beyond a certain point."

It took a moment for it to sink in. It wasn't the usual stuff. Are you good enough for him? Will you do? She was trying to warn *me* against *him*. I could sense it. It radiated from her. There was no mistaking it.

Suddenly he stood there looking in the doorway at us. He didn't look pleased. "What've you been saying to Alberta?" He sounded a little crisp about it, I thought. Even taut. "Anything I shouldn't hear? You wouldn't go deep on me now, would you, Leila?"

She tried to laugh it off. "Ladd, you shouldn't stick your head in here like that! We might have been comparing stocking tops or something."

He said to me, "Are we going?"

"Yes," I said, "we're going." It wouldn't have done any good to stay; there wouldn't have been anything to stay for now any more.

I wondered what she'd been trying to say to me.

I said hardly a word to him all the way home.

"Why are you so glum?"

I smiled wanly. "No reason," I said, "no reason."

I thought, "So I've found you, have I?"

* * *

I went to see Flood right after that, the very next day. He heard me for a while. "Well, have you any evidence yet?"

I showed him the matches.

He looked them over, shook his head finally. "They're valueless by themselves, not sufficient. For one thing, you didn't hang onto the original match cover that you found wedged behind the door up there, discarded it. It's therefore only your *word* that the two are similar. In the second place, although they strongly indicate that the party in question was up there and left them there, they're not positive proof in themselves; they could have been carried there by someone else just as readily. What you've got to have is direct—"

"I know," I said. "And it may come at any minute now. That's why I came to see you. I want to be ready for it. I don't know how to trap it, to catch it on the fly. To just come here afterward and repeat it to you—I want something stronger than that."

"You'll have to have."

"What do you advise me to do?"

He thought about it. "Are you by yourself in this place?"

"Entirely."

"And you feel fairly sure that something's coming?"

"After these matches—yes, I do."

"I'll have something made up for you by our carpenters. Make sure there's no one there with you when they bring it around."

It was installed before the week was out. He came over with them himself to supervise.

I said, "What is it? It looks like an old victrola cabinet."

"That's what it is," he told me. "It's built into one. It's the same principle as these machines they dictate into in offices sometimes."

I said, "Oh, I understand; right here in front of it, is that the idea?" I felt a little crawly; I don't know why.

"Anywhere around here in front of it. I'll give you

the range approximately. You won't be hollering, so anything farther out than here, say, is liable to blur." He traced an imaginary line with his foot along the floor. "Keep him inside that."

He rearranged things. "This divan ought to go over closer, right up against it. I imagine it'll come in handy to you."

I could feel a little red stop light burning on each cheek; I don't know why.

"Now, so you won't have to go over to it each time, I've had this cable starter rigged up for you. See, there's a plunger on the end. Flatten it with your thumb when you want to take. I'll pay it out along here, behind the divan, and bring it up here between these two cushions, the green and the orange. Remember where it is now. That ought to be easy; just work your hand in."

"Quite easy," I thought; "just like driving nails into a cross."

He had that masculine instinct for mechanical perfection. "Now let's try it out," he said. "We already tested it over at the workshop, but I want to see how it takes here in the room."

He did something to it. Not at the end of the concealed cable but right in under the lid itself. "Say something into it. Quietly, just as though you were talking to him."

I crushed my own fingers together. "I don't know what to say."

"That'll do as well as anything else."

There was a faint hum.

"Suppose he notices that?"

"Tell him it's the water pipes in the wall, or something." He turned it off. "We can't get that out of it entirely." He did something to it again. "Now listen. The playback." He held up his hand.

It was uncanny. "Say something into it. Quietly, just as though you were talking to him."

A cottony feminine voice answered, "I don't know what to say . . . Suppose he notices that?"

"Tell him it's the water pipes in the wall, or something."

I couldn't recognize my own voice. They say you never can; you so seldom hear it.

He cut it off.

"Are you going to leave that on there?"

"He won't hear it. It'll go on from there."

"Suppose I run over. How will I know?"

"You won't run over. You've got plenty of room. Just don't waste it. I mean, don't have it on by the hour. Just turn it on when you're getting hot." Then he said, "Call me if you think you've got anything." He went over to the door. Then just as he was about to leave he said, almost by way of afterthought, "By the way, who is he?"

I said, "I'd rather not give you the name beforehand. I think it's he, but if it isn't, then giving you the name is no good. If it is I'll give it to you then. Or it'll probably be down on here anyway."

"That was a typically feminine reaction just then." He closed the door.

I stood looking over at the green and orange cushions. I wondered why I felt so low.

I took the tickets and threw them aside.

"I was scalped for them," he protested cheerfully. "That show's sold out solid until next Fourth of July."

"Not tonight, I've changed my mind."

"I see you in a new light. So suddenly cuddly and stay-homish and domestic. Look at this, the lights low. Highballs cooking over there waiting for us. Great guns, even sandwiches, for later! Say, you can do something to a place, can't you? You make me feel like I've been married ten years. Only the nice part of that, though."

"Don't make fun of me," I pleaded forlornly. That set the mood, gave the key we were to play in. Bittersweet, not wisecracking.

"Here, stretch out here. Put your feet up. No, the

other way, I want to sit on that side of you." Orange and green. "Tonight's our night for getting to know one another better. Tonight's our night for reminiscence."

I felt as though I were preparing something for the slaughtering block.

We sipped awhile and talked awhile, until the mood I wanted had grown on us, fastened on us. Our voices were low; the lights were low; slanting shadows of treachery were stroked upon the walls.

"It's bromidic but it's true," I went on, "that a woman doesn't *want* to be the very first love in a man's life. He'd be too raw yet. So don't fail me, Ladd. Don't let me down. Don't make me think you're lacking in the completeness I want you to have. I give you two, three —how many will I need to give you?—before me."

He quit evading me. "Two will do," he murmured, "if you must make mountains out of molehills." His voice was drowsy with the return to forgotten things. "Her name was Patsy and I was twenty, and it was one of those *first* things. She lived on Columbus Avenue; that was when they still had the el there, and it ran past her flat right at the level of her living-room windows. No, excuse me, they called it the front room. I remember you had to finish up what you were saying before a train came, or else it would be broken up into two parts with a long wait in between."

He groped uncertainly. "You can't tell these things very well, can you?"

"But you loved her."

"Yes, I guess I must have, or I wouldn't still remember it. It lasted about a year, I think, and it really was pretty shiny. Maybe that was because I was twenty and she was eighteen. You can't *be* any younger than that, either one of you. I used to go over to the Columbus Avenue flat for Sunday dinners. I don't think I missed a Sunday dinner in months.

"Then I made the mistake of taking her to a party. Cinderella shouldn't go to a party, the story in the storybooks to the contrary. I was proud of her; I had a good time showing her off. I remember she cried a little on the way home. I hadn't noticed anything, but she claimed they'd snickered at her. Just the girls, not the boys. She wouldn't go out with me at all for a while after that, wouldn't even see me at first.

"Then suddenly she asked me of her own accord if I'd take her to another party. Another party like the first one again, where pretty much the same crowd would be. I located one and I called for her. I remember how she came out of the downstairs doorway all bundled in a beautiful fur wrap. Cinderella to the bitter end. She said her aunts and her cousins and I don't know who else besides had chipped in and made a first payment on it for her.

"All through the party that night she kept it on. She'd open the windows when no one was looking and make the room good and draughty, as an excuse to keep on wearing it. And this time no one laughed at her. They were all pretty young there, I guess.

"She was very happy riding home with me that night, strangely happy. She kept kissing me almost fiercely, as though we'd never see one another again.

"We never did. A couple of detectives came around to her home the next day, and she was sentenced to the State Prison for Women for stealing it."

He got up abruptly and moved away. I knew. Who doesn't want to be twenty again? Suddenly he'd stopped. He was standing right by it. My heart got quiet.

"Let's have something," he said.

"It doesn't work; it's a D.C."

My voice went up too high. But I had to stop him quickly; his hand was already out to the lid. "No, Ladd, come over here. Come here by me. Don't roam around when I'm talking to you."

"I didn't know you wanted to."

I did then, God knows. I told him so. "I do now."

He came right back. He subsided beside me again with a sweeping half embrace and a stretched-out "A-n-y time."

I blew out my breath a little to myself.

He told me of the second one, then. It wasn't she, I could tell in a moment, and I hardly listened after that. It was briefer. He'd been older, and the skin around his heart had been thicker.

"And—?"

"And that's all. The rest is just—my personal laundry. You wouldn't want that."

"Only two?" She hadn't shown up.

"Only two."

"You've told me of those you loved. Now tell me of someone you've hated. A girl, of course, not a man; someone you've hated with that same side of your heart. That's all that interests a girl about a man: the other girls he's loved—or hated."

For a minute I thought it wasn't coming, it took so long. But it wasn't the fact of *trying* to remember that slowed it; it was the fact of remembering, itself. "There was one like that," he said at last.

"What was she like?"

"She was rotten. Rotten all the way through. That word hardly does her justice." There was still hate there, now that he was raking the ashes. "If she'd looked on the outside like she looked on the inside she would have been clapped into a ward for contagious diseases. But she didn't. They never do—"

And suddenly there it was, starting. I knew almost at the first word.

"She worked here in a club—"

I felt carefully for the plunger, with one hand crossed over behind my own back. It was hard to do that way.

It nearly destroyed the gossamer skein he was weaving. He said, "What's that?"

It was more noticeable in the quiet of now than it had been in the daytime when Flood was there, I thought fearfully. We were so close to it too. "Just the frigidaire. It needs defrosting. Go on with what you were saying."

"She's the only woman I ever—"

"What?"

He wasn't going to for a minute.

"Well, the only woman, I think, that I ever wished dead."

I waited.

Then he said in a curiously sepulchral voice that must have transmitted well, "Well—she *is* dead now."

"What was her name?"

"What good does that do you?" he said ruefully.

"Well, it's something that has to do with you, and when you love someone and want to learn everything there is about them, then it does do you some good." I looked up at him overhead. I put my hand lightly against the side of his face and left it there. "Tell me her name."

"She was a bum named Mercer."

"Was that her first name?"

"Mia Mercer was her name. Her stage name, probably; I don't know." It was well under way now. If I just left it alone it would come by itself. It was like pulling the cover off a furled umbrella: the first part is the hard part; after that it just peels effortlessly.

"It was just a night-life stand in the beginning. Everyone has them in their lives. Someone you meet in a place, a club, one night and then start seeing off and on from then on. It had nothing much to do with love, believe me, from start to finish. But at least I didn't hate her at that stage yet. I thought she was a good enough scout. She was a little heavy on the—expense roll, you might say. They have no souls, so they must have things they can see and feel and touch; that's their only heaven.

"Then one night she found out something about me."

Again there was a snag in the unraveling skein.

"What?" I said without joining lips together.

"Oh, nothing to speak of—I was taken ill in her place one night and—she got a little frightened, wanted to send for a doctor—something like that."

I didn't understand what he meant, but I thought I'd better not sidetrack him too much.

"Unfortunately, she'd found out about Leila. Leila was engaged to someone at the time, someone who'd come over from England, and—well, it meant her very life to have had anything happen to it. And Leila was an innocent party to— She'd been in Europe for years going to school, and she didn't know very much about me even as my own sister. That was what made it so damnable. I don't think this mutt would have been willing to believe that, but whether she had or not, I doubt that it would have made any difference to her."

I still couldn't understand at all. I could sense he was being purposely vague about it, and that was helping to fog me too.

"Well, suddenly this woman, this devil—I think she had some doctor friend and he first put the idea in her head—I noticed a change coming over her. First she became too sweet to me, sweeter than I cared to have her be. I hadn't minded it as a place to stop by and have a drink in at three in the morning, but she started to get too twiny and whiny to suit me. Above all, she became too interested in Leila and her approaching marriage. Finally I felt I had to tell her bluntly, "Goodby, you won't be seeing me any more after this.' She changed a second time right after that. Still sweet, but discarded the build-up. Started mentioning some fantastic amount, twenty-five or thirty-five thousand dollars; did I know where she could get that much?

"I told her flatly no, I didn't.

"Well, did Leila know, perhaps? she wondered.

"Leila neither, I let her know.

"Well, then, did I think the Honorable So-and-so, the Earl of Such-and-such's eldest son, the man Leila was engaged to, did I think perhaps he might know?

"I started to smell a rat, and I forced a showdown. She was still very sweet and innocuous about it. He wouldn't want to be told that Leila could be taken ill, as I had on that one particular occasion; it might worry him a lot.

" 'You try that,' I said, 'and I'll kill you!' "

I could hardly breathe. I could feel my heart going so, it was a wonder he couldn't feel it from the back, where he was pressed against me.

"There was no threat mentioned, you understand, just what I've told you. On her part, I mean. She pretended to back down very prettily. Oh, I hadn't understood her. She'd simply been wondering aloud whether either one of them, or myself for that matter, had known where she could get such an amount. She hadn't meant anything by it, anything in the world. I shouldn't jump to conclusions like that. We'd forget about it, should we? She took leave of me very amiably. She said, 'I'll see you again in two or three days. I'll expect you then, shall I?' That was the punch line right there. 'I'll expect you in two or three days.'

"I told her I wasn't coming near her again, to get that into her head. She just smiled at me very forgivingly and said, 'Don't drop me *now*, Ladd. I couldn't bear that; I wouldn't let you do such a thing.' That 'now' got over what she wanted to say. She let me take the seed home with me, to give it time to sprout in the hothouse of my mind.

"She put me through a night of hell. The next day I told Leila. I felt it was the only decent thing to do. They were two such beautiful kids. He was only a boy himself, one of those apple-cheeked English youngsters. I pleaded with her not to pay any attention, not to let it affect her. I said, 'Don't let it frighten either one of you. It's nothing; it has nothing to do with you, believe me. Once or twice I haven't been well; that's all it amounts to. You've never been ill, have you? Well, that shows it has nothing to do with you. You're going back to the other side, anyway; we probably won't see one another again for years at a time. If you speak of this now you'll only be creating something between you that doesn't exist, that's imaginary.'

"It was hard work convincing her, God knows, but I finally got her to believe there was nothing to it, got her to promise me she wouldn't say anything, wouldn't smash up her whole life for no good reason. I didn't tell her that I was going to pay for her immunity. I didn't tell her of the woman. I only told her enough to make me feel I'd taken the woman's weapon away from her, robbed her of any chance of ever using it again.

"Then I broke my neck scraping together everything I could lay my hands on, and I went over there. That was about noon on the day she died. I had a hard time getting in, and when I did she acted frightened. Something seemed to have happened in the meantime that made her change her mind. I thought it was of me that she was frightened at the time, but now that I look back I'm not so sure that it wasn't of something or of someone else. I told her that I'd brought a considerable part, if not all, of the money that she'd hinted she needed, and she backed away from it, wouldn't touch it. She insisted I'd misunderstood her; she hadn't meant anything like that; she'd only been talking at random. She was good and scared, whatever the reason. I tried to put it down there, and she forced it back on me, insisted I take it away with me again. The only explanation I could find was that she'd suddenly lost her courage, was afraid I was setting some trap for her, going to have her nabbed for blackmail if she accepted it.

"I didn't like the way she was acting. She couldn't wait for me to go, and I could tell by her expression that she didn't intend letting me in if I came back later, so when she wasn't watching I did something to the door, put a little wedge in it, to make sure of getting in again if I came back.

"When I got back to our own place Leila was standing there waiting for me. Just standing like a statue out in the middle of one of the rooms. She'd changed her mind and decided to tell him after all, but she'd waited too long; she'd been too late. He'd already known it from some other source; he'd already been told.

"I asked her if that was the kind he was, ready to shy away at the very first.

"She smiled a little and said no, he wasn't that kind. All he'd said to her from first to last was, 'I would rather have heard it from you first, my dear.' She said, 'I released him. He didn't want me to, but I had to. It was dead. It was gone already. He would've stuck, but I didn't want him that way, just the outside of him. Mother and I will make the announcement, Ladd. Love is like an eggshell, isn't it? It can never be put together again.'

"I never saw Leila shed a tear, or mope, or wilt. She held her head up. Then in a little while, a month or two afterward, she went away on a long cruise down South America way. She'll never love again, I know.

"Two lives smashed up. He threw his away flying for the Chinese a few months later.

"Anyway, that day, the day it happened, I went back there again. I didn't have much trouble guessing what the 'other source' was he'd received his information from. There'd been some flaw in timing, some slip-up that she hadn't intended. I thought I could understand now why she'd been so frightened the first time. I'd warned her what I'd do if she did that to me, and I went there to do it."

"You went there intending to kill her?"

"I went there to see that she stopped living. I would have killed her if there'd been twenty witnesses in the room."

I couldn't stand it; my chest was going up and down so. "And—?"

He laughed a little, bitterly. "She was dead when I got in there. Somebody'd beat me to it. She was lying there on the floor with a pillow over her. I bent over her and pushed back my cuff, like when you touch something unclean, and put my hand on her heart to make sure. She was dead all right. The way I wanted her to be. So I straightened up again and I tipped my hat to whoever it was had done it, for saving me the trouble, and I went out and closed the door after me and left her there just the way she was. Her cat got out, I remember, along with me. Even her cat wouldn't stay with her."

"So you didn't kill her."

"I would have, but I didn't have the chance."

A deep sigh drifted from me; I wasn't aware of it myself until it was gone. So deep it never seemed to end.

He said, "I wouldn't ask anyone else but you to believe that, but it's the truth."

I believed it. Yes, to the ones we love, in a room alone like this, we tell the truth.

I felt my thumb go down on the plunger, almost as if of its own volition. The slight hum we had become used to faded away. There was a long silence. I felt like a spent swimmer who has reached the shore, is incapable of further movement, lies there amid the debris of his recent struggle.

I raised my eyes and cast them around me, in strange first-time glimpses, as at a new scene that I hadn't seen until now. I wondered what made the lights seem brighter than before all at once. Why, look, they shone; they sparkled. My heart was like a cork bobbing around in champagne, it was so light. The silly thing, it was trying to fly up through my throat with a pop. And where was that music coming from? Ghost trumpets all at once sounding allegrettos. Maybe it wasn't there, but just the same Harry James would have been jealous.

He didn't do it; he didn't do it; he didn't do it!

He'd been very quiet for a long time. His hand felt very heavy on me. I moved it a little, and it started to drop of its own weight. I caught it in time and eased it down gently the rest of the way. Then I disengaged myself and stood up.

I stood looking down at him for a minute. Then I moved slowly away. I put my hand on the lid of the cabinet, let it linger there a moment. Then I drew it away.

"You're getting out of here," I ordered myself sullenly. "You're getting out of here, hear it?"

He shifted a little to a more comfortable position now that he was freed of me.

"Do you want another drink?" I said softly.

He didn't answer for a moment. Then he looked at me in transient awareness. "Sweetheart, I'm so sleepy. May I take a little nap here? Just for a little while? I'll go later. Put something over me, sweetheart, and I won't be in your way."

His eyes dropped closed again.

I walked quietly about. I picked up the thing or two I had, from here, from there, unhurriedly, and dropped them in the cheap, lightweight little case I'd originally had with me in the hotel room for scenic effect. I stood it by the door and went back toward him again.

I hate writing notes. But I didn't want him to wait too long. He might think I was coming back. And I never was. Just—

> Good-by, my dear.
> You never knew me.
> I never knew you.

I left the light on so he wouldn't be too lonely when he woke up. He'd be lonely enough, but at least he wouldn't be in the dark.

His face was the last thing the light fell on as I eased the door closed, squeezing the light in there to a slit. I took that away with me. I didn't want it, but I couldn't seem to get rid of it, shake it loose. It stuck to my heart like flypaper.

I came out into the night with my lightweight case in one hand, and I started walking down the street. I didn't know where to. Just in one direction—away from there. Good and away. All the way away. Away from where there might have been love if I'd stayed any longer.

9

Columbus 4–0011 . . . . . . McKee

"**M**CKEE'S GONE OVER TO his club. Won't I do jist as well instead?"

I made myself sound cordial. "Well, almost. But not quite. By the way, I've forgotten. Won't you tell me where it is?"

"If you don't know where it is, then you don't know McKee, sister."

So the voice wasn't a butler's or he wouldn't have dared call me that. My momentary vision of a pompous figure sitting puffing a cigar and drowsing over a newspaper in a bay window overlooking Fifth Avenue thinned away. A night club. Or, more likely still, some sort of social-political club where they played cards, that sort of thing.

"Oh, I know McKee all right. He told me to ring him at the club. And I've lost the number. That's why I rang him up here instead."

The voice said, "How'je get *this* number? He never gives this number to no one."

"Oh, I've got a way," I said lightly.

A change of voices took place. The new one was deeper in pitch, breezily ribald. "Whadd'ye looking for, a dancing job? Come over here and we'll audition you."

So it was a night club. He'd said "his club." He owned it, then.

They were still having a good time with me, both voices. They were taking turns, displacing one another. "Yeah, c'mon over; until you've been auditioned by us you've never been auditioned at all."

The other voice cut in, "And bring your practice trunks."

I became a little dancer about town, hail fellow well met. It seemed to be about the best ground to meet them on. "Ah, please, boys, have a heart. You know how it is. A girl has to work. And there are so many of those darned places."

One voice asked the other in a confidential aside that still reached me, "Sh'I give it to her?"

I couldn't get the answer—that was still further aside —but I got the result. "Okay, it's the Ninety Club." Then a curious cackling chuckle that was somehow terrifying, almost simple-minded. "Now don't say we never guv you nothing." He actually said that in all seriousness: "guv"; I'd thought until now they only used it to parody illiteracy in comic strips and on the stage.

Its actual street number was eighty-eight; I think the reason for this curious flaw in designation was that ninety took up less room, saved light tubing over the entrance.

You went in the side way. A beetling-browed individual hanging around at the entrance, as though he had just emerged for a breath of air, pointed this out. "Looking for a job? Then you go round the alley and in through the second fire exit."

I went around the alley and in through the second fire exit. I knocked, and a disembodied hand pushed open the heavy metal slab without any accompanying face being interested enough to look out and see who it was. I went inside into semidarkness. A white gash stayed open behind me a moment or two; then the heavy metal slab went *whongg!* and closed it up.

Fear flickered over me—I didn't know of what or of whom—and then rippled away again. I think the closing of that door. I was coming into a new world.

The place was barren-looking and musty. Tables huddled in a corner, piled atop one another two and three at a time, and the whole thing threatening to come down. One had been left out where it belonged, and there was a man sitting at it, his coat turned inside out over the back of his chair. He wasn't doing anything, just sitting waiting in the gloom. There were eight or ten girls there, grouped about. They weren't doing anything either. They, too, were just standing waiting. Some had jumpers over their upper bodies. All were bare-legged.

There was something hideously naked about it. Obscene, almost. Pleasure, turned inside out to show its lining, always is.

The man at the table said, "You an applicant? Awright, drop your dress."

"On the floor?" I quailed.

They all roared. He said, "The maid'll be right around to pick it up for you. She ain't here right now. Makes it very inconvenient."

I compromised by rolling it into a neat oval and packaging it on top of a fire-extinguisher cylinder clamped to the wall.

They were all smirking about something. I still had on more than most of them, so I couldn't see the point.

A rather gaunt-looking brunette sauntered over finally and stood looking me up and down as though I were something curious to her.

"You'll never make it," she said. "You may as well get dressed again and save yourself the time."

"Why? What makes you say that?" I answered docilely.

"Anyone that comes to an audition without having her practice trunks already on under her street dress has never been in this business before. Look around you; where you going to change *here?*"

I stood there huddled helplessly in my white rayon briefs.

She finally took a sort of contemptuous pity on me. Turned her back and made herself into a screen. "All right, make it fast and keep down."

While I was doing it I said from behind her, "Give me a hint, will you? Where'll I say I worked before? I need this job."

"Pick an out-of-town joint someplace." Then she added, "If it'll do you any good." The last thing she said as she turned away to rejoin her more experienced fellow applicants was, "I'm telling you again, you'll never make it. I c'n tell 'em just by looking at 'em."

I felt great.

A door opened and men came out. First there were five of them, all talking at once. "Here's an angle, boss. For three or four days ahead run a little square place in all the papers with nothing in it, blank, just the number ninety by itself in the middle of it, until they start wondering what it—" "Yeah, if I can get that kind of red you want, but it ain't going to be easy. I've already been all over—" "I told him if he won't meet our price we'll let somebody else supply us, but he's holding out till the last minute to see if—" Then they started to break up, until there was just one left. A looming figure, blank in detail, little better than an outline against the light filtering out of the office behind him. Tall, almost grotesquely tall, but that might have been partly due to the uncertain dimness in which they kept this outer place.

He said, "Okay, Dolan. You ready out here?"

The man at the table said, "Give us a couple of lights out here, Harry."

A sort of flare path swept into being between me and him, and there was a lot of shuffling around. It seemed that way, anyway: as though I were at one end of it and he was at the other and it was a path that I had to travel. Sooner or later I had to traverse.

I missed most of the rest of it. I looked over at him

hard. He slowly lit up, came into existence, came into this funny story that was my life. I guess the lights went on slow, but that was the way it seemed: as though he were gradually brightening from the floor up.

Tall. Over six and something. Carrying it without trouble, as though every joint were newly oiled. Black-pitted eyes and hair almost as dark, brown only in the superficial sheen that hovered over it. A face with an Irish cast to it. Handsome, I suppose. But hard. Not hard in a brutalized, vicious way, if you can understand the distinction, for that bespeaks heat, even though a warped heat; but hard with the passionlessness of concrete, of a steam roller that flattens you impersonally if you happen to be in its way.

I looked at him hard. Looked at his hands: one at a pocket, one to the knob, ready to close the door he had just come through. Sure, they could have. Sure, they already must have—not once but many times. I looked at his eyes. Sure, they could have watched that other thing, unflinching, as they watched this line of girls now. I had to get up that flare path that stretched between us, to where the answer waited.

Someone shoved a piano out away from the wall, sat down at it, rubbed his elbow along the keyboard to dust it. It had a panel missing, and you could see the wires move each time he struck notes over on that side.

The man at the table said, "All right, line up for a time step."

I tried to get up *his* way. All the others seemed to have the same idea. I got in third from that end. Then I got crowded back to fourth, side-stepped to fifth, elbowed to sixth, detoured around to seventh, while the line wriggled into straight like a worm. I wound up third from the wrong end, away from him. My face must have been just a pinkish dot to him.

This was to weed out the obvious incompetents before they interviewed and passed on the remainder individually. I was the first one to be weeded. Every time he said left I raised my right leg and every time he said right I raised my left. I didn't know how to change over once I'd got started wrong.

Finally the man at the table said, "Hey, you, number three. Step out. You're tangling up the whole line."

I stepped out. I looked up *there*, not at him. He thumbed the fire exit. "Get dressed," he said wearily.

The tall figure lounging by the closed office door spoke. "Give her a chance," he said. He was more lenient than his hired man. I suppose the latter wanted to show how conscientious he was.

"What do you do?" he asked me with a sort of aloof kindliness. "You got some sort of specialty or solo? Is that it?"

Thus for the first time McKee had spoken to me. Even though my face was still a pink blob to him. I had edged one foot forward along the flare path.

If I said no it meant the fire exist. "Yes," I said, "I—I do a solo."

"What'll you have?" the man at the piano said, spitting out a loose leaf of his cigar.

I couldn't think how anything went. I remembered something that Kirk used to like, but by name alone, not how it went. " 'Moonlight and Roses,' " I stammered.

He started it, and only then I realized it was too slow to do anything with. I didn't know anything about dancing. I could only think of two things to do. Pirouette; that is, swing around. And kick high. So I pirouetted. And I high-kicked. And I pirouetted. And I high-kicked. The third high kick was too high. I sat down. Straight, in a vertical line, almost with economy of movement.

A howl went up. Even the face by the doorway joined in it. I scrambled to my feet, and this time I started over for the fire extinguisher where my dress was cached without being told.

Suddenly his face froze. His own hand started up toward it, as if to touch it, then dropped again. He asked the man at the table in surprised discovery, "Wait a minute, was I laughing just then?"

"Who wasn't?"

"I don't laugh easy. I never laughed in one of my own clubs yet. Or anybody else's. If she can do that to me and to everyone else in the place here, what'll she do to an audience with fizz under its belts?" Then he said to me, "Stay where you are."

I stayed. He thought about it for a minute. "Can you do that every night? Sit down like that every three or four kicks you take, for about five minutes straight?"

"Certainly," I said.

"Pretty looks, you've got a specialty. She's in for seventy-five a week."

A hiss of reptilian antagonism went up from the line behind me.

Even after I'd given my name and address I didn't go right away. I hung around. It didn't do me any good. He didn't look at me again.

I left when it was all over and they were milling around getting dressed. He'd gone by then by the front entrance. On my way out I cut across the brunette's path and nicked her with my elbow. "*Who* wasn't going to make it?" I said softly.

I never got near him all that week. I used to see him sometimes in the distance. He never watched rehearsals; that wasn't his job. His show was set and he let Dolan beat it into shape.

I rehearsed wearing a sort of protector of quilting on wires around my hips so I wouldn't injure my spine. I would have been in the hospital in forty-eight hours if I hadn't. Then later, when they made up the gown, they put heavy pads into it down around there. It was one of these spreading, hoop-skirt things, so it couldn't be detected. It was a lovely-looking piece of business, clouds of filmy black like mist. Then there were two long streamers attached to my wrists, and when I moved my arms they opened out like wings. And for the head there was a sort of silver arc that went halfway around on the order of a halo. You got the most unexpected allies.

I was getting a little better at it. The falls came easier once they'd waxed the dancing floor for the opening. But Dolan warned me not to get too good. "If you get too good it looks like you rehearsed it; it takes some of the funniness out. Try and keep it looking accidental, like it was the first day."

We had a dress rehearsal around five in the afternoon, the day the show was to open. I put on the finished dress for the first time. Until then we'd just used practice shorts and things.

I started to notice something; something was coming up as far as I was concerned. I kept getting signs that I was starting something. Something I only hoped I'd be able to finish.

The first one came from the old woman who had charge of the costumes. That was her job, and she was old and tired and didn't care one way or the other how we looked, only how her stuff fitted us. She helped me into the thing and fooled around a little down at the bottom. Then she happened to look up, I suppose to see if it was on right, and she stopped dead, stayed like that on her knees.

"What's the matter?" I said.

She sounded out of breath. "It's a sin to say it around here, but you look like—like a vision up above the altar of a church." And she almost acted afraid to come very near me and finish putting in the tacking and the pins.

Then one of the others came in. I was the first one in there because I was the green one. It was the same brunette of the first day. She did something to her head; it gave kind of a quirk around my way, and her feet locked where she'd last put them. She stayed like that a moment, and then she fought it off and grunted: "You're the first Jane I ever saw that looked better with her clothes on than with them off. They better have stretchers outside this place tonight: the casualties are going to be terrific."

And the third sign that I was under way came from Dolan himself, whom I'd overheard saying once that he was so sick and tired of looking at pretty girls that it was a relief to go to the zoo and stare at a cageful of the ugliest monkeys they had there. He dropped his lower jaw when my cue came up and kept it that way for a minute. He started to say, "Are you that same skinny little—?" Then he didn't go any farther. He didn't have to.

I said to myself, "If I hit *him* like I'm hitting them I'm as good as at the other end of the flare path already."

I'd heard them all saying over and over, to explain their own difficulties, that there was no tougher audience to gain the attention of than the opening-night audience at a night club. I saw what they meant as soon as I'd stepped out there. With me it didn't matter as much, because I had no lines to speak, no song to deliver. And the show I was giving had nothing to do with this crowd out here; it was a show for one.

There was a blur of lights and faces. It was like a machine shop going full blast. Nobody was looking at the floor space. People talking from table to table, waiters cutting between me and ringside, dishes and glasses going. Even the cigarette girl was getting more attention than I.

Somebody saw me at last. Someone at one of the back tables gave one of those long, drawn-out corner-loafer whistles. Then the commotion started to taper off. All of a sudden there was less noise. Then all of a sudden it was quiet. Then all of a sudden it was deathly still.

You can feel things. I didn't know what I looked like, and I wasn't there to find out at this late date. All I knew was something about me was doing something to them. And since I wasn't doing anything as yet, it must have been just the way I looked standing there.

I heard a drunk say close by me, "Is it real? Boy, I'm getting good ones now for a change!"

A mantle of oddly attentive silence seemed to have fallen over the entire place that had something nostalgic about it, pensive. Only the music went on, subdued, decorous, a little melancholy, for that was the way we had arranged it. For perfection of contrast, I was to fall to stately, muted music, not the raucous, laughing kind.

I kicked and I fell, and a gasp went up. Then I did it again. The laughter was slow in coming, but it came finally, dragged out of them by sheer repetition of the grotesque. I knew I was destroying something, but I didn't care. It was something I hadn't sought, didn't want. I was no performer.

I had only one thing to ask, when I went off, of Dolan, the director, who was standing there looking on. "Did Mr. McKee see it? How did he feel about it? What did he say?"

"He was there until a minute before you came out," he said. "Then he got called to the phone, someone wanted to congratulate him on his opening. He's been in there ever since. You're the only part of the whole show he muffed seeing. There he is; he just came back now."

I turned and slunk back toward the dressing room, and even the gown couldn't make me anything but a skinny, whipped little thing now. All those days and nights of drudgery for nothing. All those black-and-blue marks for nothing.

Each time I'd come off the floor I'd ask: "Was Mr. McKee out there tonight? Did he see me?"

Sometimes they said, "He hasn't been here tonight yet. They expect him a little later."

Five nights went by like that.

The sixth night I kept the dress on after I'd come

off the floor. I sat there in the dressing room in it, waiting, and when the wardrobe woman came to take it from me I said, "I'm staying in it."

"You ain't supposed to," she said. "I'm rissponsible for it; it's got to go away. Now gimme it here."

"I'm staying in it awhile!" I snarled threateningly.

They all came spilling in. "Hey, what're you waiting for, an encore? The show's over; didn't you know that?"

Yes, I was waiting for an encore. Or rather a première. But not the kind they meant.

The old woman kept badgering me. "I gotta go home; gimme that dress!"

"If you want it you'll have to pull it off me piece by piece."

The brunette stopped at the door on her way out, gave me a look. Then she changed her mind, came back a minute. "I think I get it," she said. She gave her head a hitch toward the door. "He's out there now. He just came in before the finale."

I acted as though I hadn't heard her, didn't move.

When the last of them had gone I got up. I warded off the old woman's shakily interfering hands and opened the door and went out. I stood there for a minute at the mouth of the dressing-room passage, looking into the club room proper. He was at a ringside table over at the left, on the other side of the bandstand. There were two men with him, the same two that were always with him.

There was a small table far back against the wall that had been recently vacated. It wasn't a very good one, but I made my way over toward it at an obtuse angle— by way of his table.

They were talking avidly as I went by.

They stopped talking on the down syllable.

"I've made it," I said to myself.

I heard him ask in an undertone, "Who's the angel with the folded wings?"

I sat down all the way over against the wall and didn't look at anyone in the room. A couple of minutes went by. Then a light-toned shadow blotted some of the cloth's whiteness.

"Haven't I seen you before? Now please, before you answer, I know that's old, but I'm asking it in all sincerity; it's not a wisecrack."

"I work for you here, Mr. McKee."

"How much do I pay you?" Then before I could answer he said to someone, "Call Dolan over here a minute; is he still around?"

Dolan got there fast.

"Double this young lady's salary. By the way, what's her name?"

"Miss Alberta French."

"What does she do?"

This time I answered. "I sit down on the floor, Mr. McKee. From where I come in, all the way across the room in a straight line, over to where I go off. Don't you remember me? I did it by mistake the first day, and now they have me doing it every night."

Something about it made him sore. It was his own idea, but he'd forgotten that. "You did it for the last time tonight. What's the matter? Haven't they got any sense around here?"

Dolan got out of the way fast.

He said, "Come on back to my table. It isn't often that I have a chance to sit with an angel. I want everyone to see."

He didn't waste finesse on the two men he'd been with. "All right," he said curtly to one, and "See you around" to the other, and they both got up without delay, drifted away.

I caught something one said to the other, though, before they'd quite gone beyond earshot. "It was about due. It's been a long time now." It wasn't said maliciously; it was said philosophically.

While we were waiting for the champagne I thought a little about Kirk. A voice penetrated my thoughts dimly. "Gee, you look so sad. I've never seen anything so lovely." The voice of somebody or other from out-

side my innermost thoughts; they couldn't exactly identify who it was at the moment. I sat and thought a little
about Kirk while we were waiting for the champagne.

It was excruciatingly hard to get rid of him at the
door.

"Words are curious things, aren't they?" I said
through the narrowing gap I'd finally achieved. "Their
meanings are so often just the opposite to what you
think they are. To like someone, to think a lot of someone, then, that means to force yourself on them, to
make them unhappy and cause them distress, to harm
them and make them ashamed. Doesn't it? I must remember; I didn't understand that until now."

He looked down at the floor. "No," he said almost
inaudibly. And all of a sudden he was sober, penitent;
all the champagne was gone.

"Good night," I said with warm friendliness. I closed
the door slowly and cut his face in half, in quarters,
into nothingness. I drew the finger bolt across.

After a long time I heard someone go away on the
other side of it. I'd been thinking of Kirk; my innermost
thoughts couldn't remember who it was for a minute.
Someone outside their pale, someone out there on the
other side of the door.

It was effortlessly easy to get rid of him outside the
door.

"Don't stand there looking at me like that, McKee. I
have no answer for a look like that, and you know
it."

"Don't be sore at me. You're like an angel fading
from view. Just smile at me once more before you close
it. Is that asking you so much, a smile through a door
as you close it?"

I closed the door slowly and cut the smile in half, in
quarters, into nothingness. I drew the finger bolt across.
After a long time I heard someone go away. I'd been

thinking of Kirk; I wasn't sure who it was. Just someone on the other side of my door.

The sit-down falls had ended since the night I'd first met him. All I did was stand there now with a line behind me doing the work. Not literally stand there, but that was all it amounted to practically. He'd got hold of someone to teach me a few simple turns and dips and bends. Just enough to give the illusion of dancing. "No one looks at anything but your face when you're out there, so just if you move across the floor a little, that'll do," as Dolan had said.

Not a word was breathed in the back room. The combustive violence of the suppressed thoughts, however, made it dangerous to strike a match in there. Once somebody wrote in eyebrow pencil "Du Barry" across my section of the glass. I hadn't known there was anyone that literate in there. I didn't care; what did I care?

And then one night this arrangement ended too. As dramatically as everything else that happened with him.

We were in the middle of it, and he'd just come in. With Skeeter and with Kittens, of course, never alone. He stood there for just a moment, looking at me. Something got him. I don't know what it was—jealousy, some possessive instinct or other.

Suddenly, in the music-underscored silence, his voice boomed out, shattering the illusion like a hand grenade tossed onto the floor. "Kill that music! Kill that spotlight! Hey, you back there, take that spotlight off her, hear what I say? If you don't I'll come back there and make matchwood out of your whole booth!"

The music died. The spotlight dimmed. The girls behind me stopped, knees elevated. I stopped, and the swirling black mists settled about me.

He was wild-eyed and I was scared; I couldn't tell what was the matter. It wasn't drink; though his face was mottled, his hair, his tie, his clothes still retained the perfect grooming of sobriety.

His voice was a bay that shook the walls of the confined place. "Get 'em outta here! Clear the tables! Never mind settling their bills; get rid of 'em! They're not gonna look at her any more! I won't let 'em look at her like this every night!"

Skeeter was trying to hold him back by one arm. And yet trying not to be too obtrusive about it too. I think he was afraid he'd draw a gun.

In another minute there would have been a full-fledged panic on. Already a two-way rush had started in, was gathering headway. Some of the more timorous customers were making for the front entrance; the floor girls all started spilling toward the back, in toward the dressing room.

"What is it, hop?" I heard one of them breathe frightenedly to another, directly behind me.

I heard the answer too.

"No. Love."

That cold slug of fear I'd experienced the first day I walked in here bedded itself in me again. I stood rooted there where I'd been originally, almost the only one in the place who wasn't on the run.

The club manager was pleading, "Mr. McKee, *don't!* We're doing a landslide business. Mr. McKee, think what you're doing. Take the young lady out of here if you want—I've sent someone back for her coat—but at least let me go ahead serving them; let them dance with each other. What harm is that?" And then he kept wheedling interrogatively, "All right, Mr. McKee? All right, Mr. McKee?" over and over.

"All right!" he raged back at last. "Let 'em dance; let 'em drink till they can't see straight; I don't give a— what they do! But they're not going to look at *her* any more! Nobody's going to look at her any more—but me!"

The club manager snapped his fingers in an urgent aside. "Boys! A quick rumba. Hurry up, before we lose any more of them!"

Somebody put my coat around me from behind, just the way I was, angel outfit and all, and I was gently but insistently pushed toward him by about six or eight hands at once. The way a noontime meal is prodded gingerly toward a raging lion's maw.

Those few straggling steps I took across the floor— that was the flare path leading to him that I was crossing at last. And at the other end of it he stood waiting with his arms extended to receive me, to shepherd and take me in tow.

And as I reached him, as we came together, there in that crowd around us, suddenly—I don't know—he was so docile; he was so contrite; he was all over again just what he'd been all along, someone I could wrap around my little finger.

He adjusted my coat about me, put his arm around behind my waist. "Come on, Angel, don't be frightened," he said with husky solicitude. "It's only that I'm taking you out of here with me."

I'd made it all right. But it occurred to me to wonder how I was ever going to manage the return trip—away from him again—when the time came.

It was a strange place he had. A fantastic place. High up on a turret on Central Park West. New York has more than a few such, I suppose, but not more than a few people ever get into them and see them. It was hard to say what there was about it that called for the adjective "strange." Hard to put your finger on what it was. It wasn't its size; the Mason apartment had been even larger. It wasn't any definite freakishness or bizarreness of appointment; he seemed to have turned over the entire job to a decorator, and it didn't sin particularly in that respect, although it may have been a little too coldly formalized, as such jobs usually turn out to be. The trouble was there was a certain discord to it. The setting and the occupants didn't blend, clashed at every turn.

You would stop before this impeccable, carefully atmosphered drawing room, and at a glance the whole thing would fly to pieces around the figure of a man sitting there coatless, shirt sleeves flowing through the armholes of his vest, a bottle of beer standing on the floor at his feet, playing solitaire upon a knee-high inlaid table.

Or you would come upon a guest bedroom, tailored for masculine occupancy, perfect in every detail, and he'd widen the already partly open door to display it to you with pardonable pride. "This is one of the boys' rooms."

And the boy in question—Kittens or the other one—would be sprawled sidewise athwart the bed with a pipe cleaner in one hand, a loosely dangling revolver in the other. He'd flip it up by the trigger, blow through the bore. And on the wall, superimposed along with the carefully chosen hunting prints that had originally been placed there, a startling photograph of a nude, clipped from some art magazine.

Whereupon my host ejaculated testily, "Cover that thing up—what's the matter with you?—I want to show her your room!"

The room's owner got up from the bed, went over to it, planted one outspread hand strategically in the middle of it, and stood there like that, waiting for our visit to be completed.

I felt neither embarrassed nor yet secretly amused, but only supremely silly. I worked in a night club, after all.

That sort of thing. A certain discord between the occupants and the surroundings.

He didn't try anything.

He only said, unobtrusively at one point, "You could have all this."

I didn't pretend not to have heard. I merely closed my eyes briefly, opened them again.

I stayed there about an hour.

There was a slight crackling sound from the pocket

of my coat when I got back and took it off and threw it carelessly down.

I put my hand in and found a check that hadn't been there yet when I went up to his place. It was signed "Jerome J. McKee" and endorsed on the back, as a sop to my scruples: "For one year's salary in advance, for professional services to have been rendered, Club Ninety." It was for ten thousand dollars.

I had become the most highly paid performer in New York in one night.

I knew how to use it most effectively. He was putting my own weapons into my hands.

I put a stamp on an envelope and addressed it to him. I put some red on my lips and made a print of them just under the endorsement. I wrote beneath that: "But no." I put it in the envelope and mailed it back.

That meant I would be getting the highest possible return out of my money.

Twice a day, for several days past, he'd been calling me up about this party, reminding me I'd promised him to be there, urging me not to fail to keep my promise; I didn't quite understand why. That it was to be more or less in my honor, I gathered, but his insistence almost seemed to go beyond that, as though I were actually sponsoring it along with him.

"I want you here good and early. I'll send the car for you, say about six; how will that be?"

"You don't have to do that. I can get over there all right—"

"I should say not. I wouldn't think of it. You're coming in the car."

Then he went on: "Will you do something for me? Wear the angel dress again. Have you still got it? I want them to see you just like I do."

I said to myself, even while I was still on the line, talking to him, "The safe is built in above the fireplace in that little study or whatever it is; I saw it in there."

"All right," I said.

He was like a kid; I'd never heard anything like it. "I can hardly wait until tonight. Gee, it's still so long away until tonight; what am I going to do until then?"

"It will come," I said evenly. I thought: "It always does."

He was in a dinner jacket when I arrived, and the place was swarming with florists and caterers. He was standing there supervising a great long table they were arranging in the dining gallery for about twenty or thirty people.

He was still like a kid. Skeeter had been standing unobtrusively by, looking on with him, and as McKee came forward to greet me Skeeter crept a stealthy foot nearer the table. McKee immediately whirled on him in a sort of righteous fury. "You touch another one of them salted almonds after I told you not to, and I'll bust your jaw so you won't be able to use it at the meal!"

Skeeter retreated guiltily to where he had been before.

I had to tell myself: "These men have killed people."

"What is it, your birthday?" I asked him.

"Better than that, much better. I'm not going to tell you ahead; you'll find out when the time comes."

The other one, Kittens, came in harassed. "Hey, I can't get this tie on right. I must be nervous or something. We never gave a formal party like this before, just brawls."

"Here, I'll do it for you," I offered, so McKee would find me charming.

He stepped up close to me. His face smelled a little of tangy shaving lotion. "How strange," I discovered to myself with a sort of wonderment; "they're no different from other men, except that the moral sense is gone, and you can't see that from the outside."

When I finished McKee was crowding at my elbow. His face had a slightly sulky look to it, and his own tie, which I could have sworn had been intact a moment before, was drooping invitingly down. He was jealous of his own henchman!

Within the next half-hour his past came to life before me, came in the door in twos and threes. No, not the past. Who knew where that actually was at this moment as he stood beside me greeting arrivals? A lumpy torso huddled ankles to throat in a rotting sack in a lime pit somewhere. A wavering, undiscovered thing down under the waters of the harbor, feet in a cement cast. A skeleton under a cement garage floor that would be dug up some far-off day when this lawless age was a forgotten moment in a distant past.

His present, then, came to life before me, came in the door in twos and threes. In a sort of strained demureness that was their new-found respectability still sitting uneasily upon them. The men were too meek and brittlely polite; you couldn't move but what they moved a chair to accommodate you. The women were too subdued and kept porcelainly smiling at nothing, just to keep smiling for the sake of smiling. Dolls that the men had brought with them. That slightly heightened excitement of voice and vivacity of movement that women ordinarily bring to a party that *is* a party were entirely lacking in them. A faux pas would have warmed the rarefied air, but they were all alike in dread of one.

He had me at his right.

I kept thinking, "The safe is in the study, over that way, to my right. Tonight is the time, with all of them here. Far safer for it than if I were alone."

His voice broke in upon me: "I didn't get you one because—you're more than just a guest. And I have something else for you later on."

I looked around, and they were all exclaiming over little gold powder compacts. I hadn't even missed not having one.

The conversations were ludicrous, but I wasn't there to be amused, to take social notes. Who was I, after all?

I asked myself. Just a desperate, stealthy creature sitting in their midst, less secure than they were even.

Then from one of the wives, in tactful arbitration, stemming perhaps from some long-haunting memory of a small dispute that had once grown beyond bounds and ended in a tragedy: "Oh, don't let's talk politics. It's not nice at the dinner table. After all, we're all good Americans here, I'm sure. Don't you agree with me, Miss French?"

"You're right. Of course we are." I smiled cordially.

They had so many taboos, their new state of grandeur must be hell for half of them.

He had risen.

Kittens went "Sh!" to the person next to him. Skeeter went "Sh! The boss is going to say something" to the man across the way from him.

He looked at me privately, then at them. "I'd like to make a little speech to you. I suppose you wonder why you've all been brought together here on this particular night. Well, it's like this. Everyone finds someone. But most men, they just find women. I'm a man in a million. I've found an angel."

They all looked at me and applauded delicately.

"Give me your hand, Angel."

I stretched it out mechanically, already beginning to be a little afraid even before I knew what was coming next.

It hadn't been there a minute before. I don't know whether somebody had just passed it to him from behind his chair or it had been concealed underneath something on the table itself. Suddenly there was this plush box. There was a snap and the box split open. There was a flash from the satin lining for just a second, and then the box was empty.

Something cold, cold as death, that struck a shudder into the very depths of my heart slipped down my finger.

The flash came from there now. Kept coming from there. Came from there permanently. I'd never seen a diamond that size before.

It went up to his lips and down again, and the kiss now struck the same cold shudder into me that the ring had.

"I want to announce my engagement to Miss Alberta French. Our engagement to be married."

The pupils of my eyes felt like taut exclamation marks stretched from lid to lid. Under cover of the hand clapping and din of congratulatory ejaculation that churned around the table he leaned over toward me. "Say something to them. What's the matter; did I startle you? Look at her, how white her face is. Was it too sudden for you? Don't be frightened—"

I kept saying to myself, "This isn't real. This isn't so."

They were subsiding now. They were waiting. He was waiting. I had to do *some*thing. What did you do when you were suddenly told you were engaged? Jump up and run from the table? Say "No, I decline the honor with thanks"?

"Say something to them. Come on, say something to them." He had me by the elbow now.

If Kirk's face would only get out of the way—

I found myself standing suddenly, so I must have risen. I didn't look at him, nor at them. I raised the champagne high until I could see the ceiling lights turn gold through it. I didn't point it at him. I pointed it upward, through the lights, through the ceiling, toward —whatever it was up there.

"To my husband," I said in a steady voice.

"Keep it on," he coaxed in the study. "Are you supposed to take it off like that? I think I once heard somewhere it brings bad luck."

"That's the wedding band," I improvised, "once the ceremony's been performed. Not this. I'm worried about it. There are so many people here—and you never know. Look, it's a little loose, and I don't want anything to happen. Let me put it in your safe while I'm here. I'll put it on again when I'm ready to go."

He found me charming. If I'd stood on my head he'd have found me charming. "So that's why you wanted to get me alone in here. You're a sentimental little lady, aren't you? I didn't know you thought that much about it. All right, give it to me; I'll put it in for you."

I continued to work at being charming. "I want to put it in myself. It's my ring."

I put my hand on the dial, stood waiting in an attitude of trustful helplessness. "Tell me what I have to do."

For a moment his innate caution held out against his heart. He cast a brief look of sober speculation at me, hesitated almost unnoticeably.

I opened my eyes a little. "I thought it was an *engagement* ring."

He raised my hand and put his lips to it in amends. "It is," he said. "Wait a minute till I close the door."

He came back again.

"I wouldn't do this for anyone but you. Steady it so that little arrowhead points straight up first of all. That's it. Now go around this way until you come to eleven—"

He came back from seeing the last of them out.

"Well, how'd you like it? What sort of a party did I give you? I'm glad you stayed to the end like you did; I was afraid you'd—"

"It was my party. I couldn't leave before all of them did." I hooked a finger to an inadvertent yawn.

"Tired? Shall I take you back now?"

"I'm almost too tired to *go* back," I said languidly. I hooked a finger to a second yawn. "It seems so much trouble to go all the way over—"

An idea hit him, born of his solicitude. Or perhaps my yawns. "Say, you wouldn't want to—? I don't suppose you'd feel right about staying over here on account of me being in the place? Because if it weren't for that—"

I looked around me as if in sudden attentiveness to

the proposal. "You know, that's not such a bad—I don't think I'd mind doing that at all, if I could only be sure you wouldn't misunderstand me."

"How could I ever misunderstand anything you did?" he protested with an almost luminous sincerity. "That stage ended long ago with you and me. You shouldn't say things like that to me. You ought to know me by now. You'd be as safe here in my place as you would back at your own."

"Then I think I *will* stay," I acceded impulsively. "After all, we are engaged, and I'm too tired to care about the looks of it."

His bustling, enthusiastic reaction showed how complimented he felt by this mark of confidence I was showing him. There was a brief undercurrent of ordering and telephoning, and one of these prepared toilet kits containing everything necessary for the night arrived—I don't know where he'd been able to obtain it at that hour, possibly from one of the hotels—within fifteen minutes.

I took leave of him at the door of the room I was to grace. The last thing I said to him was, "Now you won't do anything to make me regret this, will you?"

I knew he wouldn't. I could tell just be looking at him. He would as soon have thought of desecrating a church.

To be worshiped, though I didn't realize it at the moment, is a far more dangerous situation to be in than simply to be desired.

"Pleasant dreams," he said with abashed tactfulness, refraining even from kissing me, lest that seem to be an attempt at tilting the delicate balance between us.

I heard him go back to "the boys." I could hear him say, from where I was, as he went in, "Now listen, cut out the drinking, you two. There's a lady staying here in the place tonight, and I don't want her disturbed by you guys getting loud."

There wasn't a sound. They knew enough not to smirk or say anything out of turn. They must have

known him well. They must have known when he
wasn't kidding, when a thing was just what he claimed
it was.

First you steadied it so that the little arrowhead
pointed straight up. Then around *this* way until you
came to eleven—

It came open quite easily. Quite easily and quite silently in the slumbering, plushy silence of the apartment.

I shifted the boxed ring out of the way first, over to
one side. Then I eased out a metal strongbox that stood
at the back, careful not to scrape it against anything. I
took it over to the table, tipped up the foresection of
the pleated lid. Bonds, whole packets of them. They
weren't his; they were registered in the name of Michael
J. Dillon. Under them an assortment of legal papers,
deeds, or liens, or something; I couldn't make out. I
rifled through them rapidly. I didn't want any of them. I
closed it up again. There was a smaller fitted-in box in
the upper compartment of the safe. I took that out,
brought it over in turn.

Currency, tight-packed little bricks of it, taped in
strips of manila paper with the amounts of denomina-
tions serialized on them, the way banks do. I disregarded them. Under them, sheaves of clipped together
checks, perforation-canceled. I rippled through them,
scanning the payees.

Her name suddenly flickered up at me as I went on
too far past. I toiled back to it again, retrieved it. "Mia
Mercer." Two hundred and fifty dollars. Salary or
something? There was nothing there at sight—

Suddenly I went into reverse, crushed the lid flat on
them, started the box hectically back into the safe. I
misjudged the upper slot, couldn't slip it in right the
first time, had to withdraw it partly and aim it over
again.

I was too late.

"Mr. McKee won't like that," he said in a sort of grieved remonstrance from the doorway.

I'd drawn the door even to the frame, but I hadn't fitted it in tight, to avoid a possible betraying latch click. Now it was wide again. It was the one called Kittens. In a dark flannel robe, fists to pockets.

The bleached skin in my face felt like cardboard, it was so stiff.

"My ring is in there; I just wanted to see if it was all right. I had a bad dream just now and—"

He was simple-minded. But dangerous and shrewd as only the simple-minded can be. "But there it is in front of you, and it's those other things you were taking out. I watched you through the crack of the door first."

I died a little more than I had already.

"I didn't mean anything by it. You know how curious women are. Don't—don't tell him about it."

Instantly I realized what a bad mistake that was.

His face twisted into a grin. He came in and returned the door to where it had been before, flush with the frame. "Okay, it'll jist be something between you and me." And suddenly that high-pitched cackle that I'd heard the very first day of all on the telephone wrenched jarringly from him, stopped short again.

He came over close. I pushed the safe lid back into true, trying to efface the marks of my own guilt.

He was looking at me, not the safe.

There was something wrong about him. I'd known that all along. I couldn't tell just what it was. Something that went beyond just ordinary cruelty. I remembered now that I'd seen him one day. There was no time to review that now. Suddenly he'd caught me to him.

"Don't you know what McKee'll do to you if I tell him you tried to kiss me? Don't—*please*—ah, please, don't! Don't let's have any trouble."

"I ain't trying to kiss you. Look, am I trying to kiss you? I don't like kissing myself."

"Then what're you holding me like this for? Let me—"

"Just let me twist your hand a little, like this. I'll stop if it hurts you. Even since I first saw you I've been dying to—"

I threshed around a little. "Sh! Somebody'll hear us. Don't!"

"Jist the skin on the back of your wrist, where it's loose; the wrong way around, like this. Don't do that now; don't scream!"

I screamed more in stark terror of the pain to come than at any pain he'd actually caused me yet. I knew now what was the matter with him. He was a pain worshiper. Something out of the nether world of twisted impulses. Cruelty for the sake of cruelty. Cruelty that was not punishment but love.

He was becoming enraged. "I told you not to scream, di'n't I? When anyone tries to stop me like that I can't stop at all. Now I can't stop, myself! Now you're gonna get it!"

I'd never seen anyone hit so hard before. He went into the table, took that with him, until it had overturned, and then toppled backward over it, legs bucking briefly in air, to lie there floundering on his back and with it partly over him.

McKee didn't go after him, continue the assault, as ordinary rage would have dictated; he held back, froze there where he'd first struck him. The hardness of cement. The implacable steam roller pulsing in leashed motion.

He said to me in a breath-choked voice, "Get out of the room here; hurry up. I'm going to shoot him as soon as I come back with my gun, and I don't want you to see it."

Then he turned to accomplish it in cold blood, as if he'd said: "I'm going to get a handkerchief."

The palpitating huddled mass in the corner said, "She was going through your safe—I caught her—" Then ran out of further breath.

The other one had come in belatedly.

He said to him with a complete lack of emotion that was almost insane: "Get me my gun, Skeeter. You know where it is."

"You can shoot me, but it's true, McKee; she was going through your safe." Blood peered at the corner of his lip.

"Did he see anything like that?" He was waiting for me to say no. That was all I had to do, and it wouldn't have gone any farther.

Something locked in me. I knew he'd kill that man within the next thirty seconds if I said no. That was all I had to say. I couldn't, couldn't bring myself to. One's better instincts can show up at the damnedest times, to one's undoing.

He repeated it, phrased even more prejudicially. "He didn't see anything like that, did he?"

Then suddenly it was no longer necessary to say anything. The wind had subtly changed direction. I'd lost my chance.

"Look, boss," Skeeter purred almost inaudibly. His hand was on the safe front; he'd tilted it out from the frame, showing it to be unlocked.

Then after a while he closed it again.

"He doesn't know the combination," McKee murmured. "Neither of them do." He didn't say it to me. You couldn't tell whom he was saying it to. To himself, maybe, in a sort of sad confirmation.

He didn't say anything more than that; he let it go at that. But I could sense a slow change taking place in him; he was drifting away from me; I was losing him, like someone standing on a shore loses a boat carried out on the tide, and I couldn't do anything to stop him.

"I'll take you back to your room," he said to me. His voice was still intimate, considerate; there was still that special quality left in it he'd used for me alone.

I slipped my arm through his and I turned and walked out beside him. I saw his lower lip tremble a little and I was afraid to look any more after that.

Halfway there I suddenly stopped, planted both hands against him in appeal. "McKee, you've got to believe me. I didn't see anything I shouldn't have."

"Not even about the Sabbatino affair?" he said dryly.

"No."

"Or the stuff about Conway?"

"No. No. Nothing but some bonds belonging to a Michael J. Dillon, and I hardly gave them a second—"

He'd trapped me. And I knew that was the name he'd wanted; he'd only made the others up as he went along.

"Even the middle initial," he mused wryly. "You know I could be sent up for that, don't you, if it ever came out? You know that Michael J. Dillon, 'Crooked Judge Dillon,' the 'Corkscrew Judge,' as they called him, disappeared eleven years ago and I could be accused of something even worse just as well as not?"

I'd heard of him. Everyone in the country had. The "Michael J." had thrown me off.

He'd spoken quite gently, in a tone of indulgent remonstrance, but somehow I knew, in unshakable premonition, I'd signed my own death warrant.

"I'd never tell anyone on you."

"I know you wouldn't." He took my hands, which had been fastened on him all this while, and stripped them off like empty gloves. He wasn't obvious about it; there was simply an inattentiveness there, as if to say, "What are these things doing on me?"

He held the door open for me, to show me as a silent order where to go in.

"Good night, Angel," he said caustically. "Angel in Black."

I was badly frightened as he closed the door on me. I crouched there listening. I couldn't hear anything. I hadn't expected to. They must have been talking it over quietly among themselves, if they were talking at all. Or maybe they weren't; maybe he was just doing the talking within himself and they were waiting silently to be told what the outcome was to be.

Then suddenly I heard a morsel of consolation from one of them. He had perhaps come into a position, just then, from which I could hear that and no more, opposite the room opening or something.

"Don't take it that way, boss."

From him no answer.

I could feel the blood leaving my face there in the blue dark. The verdict must have gone against me or he would not be mourning. I wanted to rush out then and there, throw myself at him in one desperate final appeal, before judgment had been inalterably passed. I knew it was too late for that. It wouldn't do any good. The idol had toppled; it couldn't be put back on its pedestal again. A remark Ladd had once made came back to me. "Love is like an eggshell; it can never be put together again."

A further long, breathless wait. Then suddenly another bowdlerized remark reached me. "The place on Long Island." It was as though somebody were making a suggestion to him.

The suggestion must have been taken up. There were a number of blurred, diverging treads off at a distance, as though they were in the act of dispersal. From nearer at hand, but in a guarded undertone, I heard a voice ask: "Are you coming with us?" Again I failed to detect the answer; perhaps he had just shaken his head.

Finally there was the snap of a light switch somewhere immediately adjacent to the room I was in, and then the elliptic remark: "—just get my things on a minute."

An alarm bell was ringing in me wildly, hurting my chest with its brazen clamor. "I've got to get out of here!" the voice of inner panic shrieked above it. "Oh, how am I going to get out of here?"

The bell stilled suddenly; it's clapper hung breathless. He had just knuckled the door.

I spread-eagled myself against the door in a violent convulsive movement, arms out at their widest. "Don't come in; I'm—I haven't got much on!"

"I won't come in. I just wanted to talk to you for a minute."

I opened it on a crack, kept back behind it, as if afraid to look at him.

"I'm sending you home with the boys."

"Home," I thought; "home into the ground."

"I thought you said I could—"

"I know, but I have to leave; I just got word, and you wouldn't want to stay here alone. I think it's better if you go back now, don't you?"

What could I say? He could have come in and dragged me out bodily if I tried to resist. "Just—just give me a few minutes. I'm all undressed. I'll have to—"

He flung them in at me with a sort of contempt. The night was so long; death was so sure, I suppose. "Don't take too long, baby. The boys are waiting, and I need them for something else—afterward."

What a horrid word that was, "afterward"; it seemed to give off vibrations, like a knell, long after he'd turned and gone away again.

I ran across the room to the triple casement. Frustration eddied through me like a form of nausea as I stopped short by them. We were so high up that perspective became a crazy guilt, lost all coherence. That string of beaded lights trailing across the dark was not Manhattan any more but the Long Island shore across the East River. The East River Drive, on the near side of the channel, seemed closer at hand than the concealed crevice hidden somewhere deep underfoot that was Central Park West. To scream out was to launch my voice futilely across the night at Astoria, not toward the base of this monstrous monolith.

I tore myself away. There was a bath to my room, and I went in there. Then there was another door that led out on the other side of it again. It had been locked on my side when I was still a goddess. I unlocked it now, listened, drew in daring through raptly parted lips, cautioned it open, and looked out.

The room beyond was dark and unoccupied. For a moment hope shot up again. There was only one further door other than my mode entrance. Only one way out of it. It must be through there or not at all. But as I reached it and softly pared it away, knob crushed to silence, a crevice of light ignited along it, like a noise-less but livid fuse suddenly set off.

Hope went down again with the sickening suction of a whirlpool draining through me. A figure in shorts and undershirt was revealed, foot to chair, attaching a gar-ter to his leg. Even before I could withdraw the vignette had altered, he was moving so fast. The leg went down, and there was the flurry of an outspread shirt, sleeves without hands sticking up in air like an X-shaped scare-crow. A muffled voice said to someone, presumably in a room beyond, "Bring a little chloroform along, in case we have trouble with her in the car."

I smoothed the door closed again, stealthily as I had dislodged it. Its silent docility of hinge and latch had been my only salvation.

"Like a rat in a trap," kept beating through my brain; "like a rat in a trap."

There was a telephone in the room I was in. As I widened the bath door to re-enter, light fanned out, caught it for me, pinned it against the wall like a beetle, licorice-black, glistening black.

How could I hope to use it undetected, with just a flimsy door between me and him? The first word out of my mouth would resound in the magnifying silence in here.

I crushed myself against the wall, as if trying to smother it with my entire body. Such a loud clatter the release of the hook gave. Sh-h! The police? I didn't know; I wasn't sure of whom I was calling until I al-ready held it cupped to my lips, like a sort of chalice of salvation. I only knew I needed help, wanted it fast, in the worst way.

I thought she'd never get on, answer the signal, and I daren't touch that hook again.

And then, when she had, suddenly it seemed to come by itself; it was my heart speaking out in its fright to the only one it remembered.

10

Butterfield 9–8019 Again (and hurry, operator, hurry!)

A SLEEPY VOICE GOT on, one of the servants.

He couldn't hear me, I was so strangled with caution. Oh, the fool, he was killing me! I had to do it all over again.

"Quick—Ladd! Only Ladd, not you! Only Ladd will do! Don't stand there—"

"I know, miss, but it's after three o'clock. If you'll only give me an idea of who you are I'll see whether—"

"Tell him Alberta. This is an emergency. Tell him to come quickly to the phone if he loves me. If he ever loved me."

I didn't know what I was saying any more. Already some of my life had gone by, and nobody could bring it back.

If he loved me; if he'd ever loved me. Oh, he must have, all right, to come so fast. I could hear the floundering rush of unshod feet and something go over, like a chair that had been in the way. I could hear the fright in his voice, needling sleep to pieces.

"What is it? Where are you? What's happened?"

And like the squeaking of a trapped little mouse in her hole, "Sh! Listen carefully. I have only a minute. I'm in an apartment on Central Park West. They're going to do something to me. Some men. They're taking me out of here in just a minute. Ladd, find some way of helping me. I have only you to turn to—"

"The police. I'll get them there right away. I'll come over with them my—"

"That'll be too late. They won't get here in time. I won't be here any more. They'll deny I ever was. No one'll ever find out where—"

It's hard to think fast when your heart has just received an uppercut. Fast and clear. He did it. He had to. "Where are they taking you, got any idea at all?"

"I heard one of them mention Long Island, but I can't be sure."

"That means the Queensborough Bridge, nine chances out of ten. Where is the place you're in right now, Park West and where?"

"In the upper Sixties."

"They'll take you through the crosstown cut in the park at Sixty-seventh, then. That's quicker than going down to Fifty-ninth and over, no lights. Maybe I can cut in on them—"

"Oh, Ladd, don't miss me, whatever you do. They may hold me out there for days, or I may never get there. Ladd, his car—the license plate is 072-027. Try and remember that."

I heaved, elongated as if I were trying to climb up the bare wall.

"Ladd, he's knocking at the door, inside in the other room. They're ready for me—"

Even having him just on the phone, all the way across the city from me, was better than nothing at all.

"Ladd, Ladd, are you still there? Oh, don't leave me—"

He was already gone. He hadn't waited to hang up.

I got back to the bath outlet on the far side just as McKee re-entered the room from the other door. His face was dangerous for a minute, as if threatening something imminent, here and now, because of the delay. Then it smoothed somewhat. "Are you ready?"

I moved across the threshold ahead of him. "Why are you sending me home in disgrace like this?"

He didn't seem to hear me.

I tried once more, between my room and the one where the two men were waiting for us. "McKee, you wouldn't let them do anything to me, would you?"

This time he gave me the oddest smile. I could translate its message so clearly: "There *was* a soft spot there, in that place, until a little while ago. You're just too late; it's sealed up now. But how well you remember its location, don't you?"

We came into the room and he said to them, "She's a little frightened, boys; don't drive too fast."

If I hadn't known already, it was a dead giveaway the way the two of them flanked me. They didn't exactly stand one on each side of me like sentries, but somehow they were there, closer than they'd ever walked beside me yet.

Suddenly his voice caught up with us, pulled us back like a lariat. "Wait a minute. I want to say good night to her. Wait outside there."

I went calmly back toward him; they went on. It was the strangest thing I'd ever witnessed. And though I was a participant, I still could witness it, for I wasn't involved. How could I have been?

His arms went around me; he strained me to him. I turned my head aside, and he missed my mouth.

"Good night," he said huskily, "good night."

I'd been yellow until now, all the way through, from the moment he'd first trapped me at the safe, whining and whimpering. Now I could feel a cold, low-burning flame of contempt licking through me, fusing a little courage into me, stiffening my back against him. I was glad. I'd have that much to look back on afterward, at least, no matter what happened after I left here.

I smiled as his arms fell away, releasing me. "Who gets the ring now?"

"Oh—wait, take it with you. I want you to have it on you."

He got it out and put it on my finger.

I let him.

I turned and went back toward where they were waiting, just past the doorway.

It had been a little loose from the beginning. I gave my fingers a disdainful downward fling, as though ridding them of some clot of mud or dirt that had adhered. It flew off downward, like a raindrop, and lay there winking in the plushy carpet nap.

Our eyes met for the last time in this life, his and mine.

I stepped on it, ground it under my foot with supreme contempt, as I moved on.

"Come on, gentlemen," I said, "take the lady home."

Skeeter had me in the back beside him, Kittens at the wheel. We skimmed through the Sixty-seventh Street transverse, the park a rippling black desolation on either side of us. They were going fast even for that unobstructed and unfrequented thoroughfare at three-thirty in the morning; they wanted to get me over the bridge quickly, I guess.

I was holding the cigarette they'd given me—as executioners are wont to do—fast in my mouth without benefit of hands. It shed sparks backward on the buffeting wind of our progress.

We hadn't spoken, any of us. What was there to say?

As we neared the Fifth Avenue exit on a long, slow curve that hid the roadway ahead from us, a stalled cab came into sight, hugging the westbound lane, vis-à-vis to us, motionless there where it had no right to be. This was just clear of the last overpass; that is, before we reached it. These overpasses, carrying lengthwise park-roadways overhead, form tunnels for all practical purposes, wherever they occur. Every New Yorker is familiar with them.

The cab's headlights, whether accidentally or intentionally, flared up as we came within range of them, drenched us in a momentary spray of light, like a mist of calcium. While it splashed over us it must have been vivid enough to catch our license number on the wing, if that was the purpose, though in another instant we had torn through it and plunged into the tunnel. Three long, spaced blasts of the cab horn, I noticed, chased us into the tunnel and beat us through to the other end, as sound does even the fastest-winging car.

There was no time to analyze all this; before one could it was already all a terminated fact. I *had* thought, for a moment, that it might be he in the cab, but there was no one to be seen in the rear of it, only the driver up forward.

The tunnel ended and we came out into the light, the last lap of the defile continuing to unwind semicircularly before us. Suddenly the black shape of a lightless car impinged itself into mid-thoroughfare dead ahead of us, gliding out in low, slantwise to the right of way, narrowing it to a bottleneck that every moment grew slimmer.

I heard Skeeter scream something: "Look out, he's cutting us off down there!" Kittens slewed us over, trying to get through between the curbing and the impediment while there was still time, before the space had closed entirely.

The offender immediately and effortlessly ebbed back again, as though it had been but teetering on open brakes, but it was too late to do us any good; all it could ensure now was to avoid a catastrophic fender-to-side collision between the two machines. We were already off course. The two inside wheels had struck up onto the pedestrian lane with a sickening pitch. A moment later there was a series of dragging concussions as we skimmed the retaining wall.

He stopped us short of overturning by a miracle of adroit brake graduation, and we lurched motionless, now on the far side of the erratic jaywalking car that had caused all the trouble.

The three of us sat there dazed for a moment from the cushioned buffeting we had received. Kittens was leaning his face down upon the wheel, cushioned by both arms, his senses evidently doubly dislocated by this shaking up coming so soon after McKee's frightful blow.

"Son of a—! Did you see what he tried to do?" Skeeter muttered numbly.

Suddenly the door on my side, which was the only one of the two still usable, wrenched open, and Ladd was standing out there beside it afoot. I recognized him even in the dark.

He didn't say anything. He didn't have to. I made an abortive movement to lurch out through the opening and join him, then swayed back into place again, like something dangling on a loose string.

"I can't, Ladd; he's holding a gun against me!" I croaked hoarsely.

"Stay where you are, you out there; don't come any nearer!" Skeeter warned him over my shoulder.

The cigarette was in my hand. I don't know how I came to do it; I don't think I would have found the nerve if I'd thought about it consciously. I didn't; I just acted on instinct alone. His hand was against my side, just over the hip. I simply swept my outside hand around, under the arm on that side, and burrowed the live cigarette deep into the veined back of his hand.

He barked like a seal and snatched it back, and the gun fell loose on the seat. I sprang down and was already on the ground beside Ladd. I think my abrupt movement dislodged it even farther, and it fell from there down to the floor, but there wasn't time to see exactly what happened.

Ladd closed in and sent his fist crashing through into the open side of the car. It caught Skeeter off balance, bending down to retrieve the gun, his face thrust forward to meet the blow almost gratuitously.

I saw the face there one moment, then the fist, then just empty space under the car ceiling. The shank of Kittens' leg was coming out through the front-door opening, without the rest of him showing yet. I turned and ran back along the walled-in chute, back along the way we'd just come. "Up this way, quick! I've got a taxi waiting at the other end of the tunnel," I'd dimly heard him say.

"Look out, Ladd, they're going to shoot before we can get in there!"

"Keep in front of me," he said tersely. He could have outdistanced me; he didn't, of course—hung back, propelling me forward with an arm about my waist. We were like that statuette group of shepherd and shepherdess fleeing before the storm. Angel in a high wind.

A moment later the shot came. There was something unreal about it even after I'd heard it. A shot right in the middle of a New York traffic by-pass. It wasn't very loud. I'd thought they were louder than that.

The first car, his, provided us with a measure of shelter, once we'd rounded it and streaked for the tunnel entrance up ahead. But I could hear their feet beating up fast on the other side of it.

"They're coming after us. We'll never get in—"

A truck had slowed on the eastbound lane, blocked in turn by the snarl we had wrought between the lot of us. I screamed out toward it at random as we raced by: "Stop those men; they're trying to hold us up!"

A deep masculine voice blared accommodatingly from the towering driver's seat: "Police! Holdup! Poli-i-ice!" A moment later I heard what sounded like an empty pop bottle on the wing strike something with a bell-like bounce and shatter on the ground. There was the sound of a long, dragging fall. One pair of footfalls kept pounding relentlessly on after us.

We were nearly at the tunnel mouth now. "There he is; he backed up like I told him!" Ladd gasped. A red taillight glowed out in welcome to us. He flung me inside just as the second shot came, and I landed sprawled on hands and knees. There was a dull, whacking sound from some part of the cab structure, as though somebody had hit it with a stick. He clung to the outside of the door handle as it swept off with us into the gloom, then finally floundered in after me. "Get us out of here!" I heard him grunt to the driver. "Just keep going and never mind looking around!"

A police whistle was starting to blow, faint and querulous, somewhere out on Fifth Avenue, now that it was all over.

I crawled up onto the seat by means of my hands. Then I just lolled against him while he panted down into my hair from overhead.

I don't think we said anything as far west as Amsterdam Avenue, two blocks beyond the park.

Then I said, "Did that really happen to us? I'll never doubt anything like that I read in the papers again—"

He said, "Where do you want me to take you? Back to my place?"

I said, "No, they'll find your car and they're liable to come after me there. Take me back to my old place; I'll be all right there. They don't know about it. That is, if it's still available."

"It's still there waiting for you," he said. "I made sure that it would be. I wouldn't let them dismantle it. I've been going around there nearly every day, hoping that sooner or later you'd—"

"And now I am," I sighed with inexpressible content.

"For good," he added, low.

It would be light in a little while. New York was a night older. I couldn't hate the town. I forgave it. It was easy to, with him there with me. Tender there with me.

"Over it now? Better?"

"Over it now. Better," I answered with heavy-lidded eyes.

"How'd you happen to get mixed in with such a bunch in the first place?"

"I was trying to find evidence that might help Kirk."

"Kirk? Who's Kirk?"

"My husband." I wasn't watching what I was saying. Then I thought, "Oh, he may as well know now as any other time; he's got to sooner or later." I was too tired.

"I'm Kirk Murray's wife. He's under sentence, you know, and I've been trying to help him; that's all it is. I found his name—McKee's—I found all your names in a little book of hers, and I've been going down the list—"

I saw I'd hurt him, so I stopped.

"Then it was sort of a police assignment—on your own?"

"Yes, but— Don't look at me that way; don't feel that way about it," I said contritely.

"Then that was all you wanted with me too. I was just a name on your list. I was just a suspect and you were just an informer. Then I didn't really meet you, know you, *love* you—"

We both fell silent. What could I say to that? We both stopped talking, and I thought perhaps it was better so. I saw I'd hurt him very badly, more irreparably than I knew.

He'd been holding a small glass in his hand for some time before. That was the first sign of anything, that glass. His face hadn't changed; his body hadn't moved yet. There was a crunching sound, like someone crushing nuts with his teeth. A little white stuff like coarse sugar trickled out of the hollowed curve of the hand he'd been holding it in. Then the brown liquor dripped out. It slowed, attenuated, changed slowly to red. Became drops instead of a continuous line.

I said, "Oh, you've—"

He was looking at it now himself, without seeming to understand what it was. Then he looked up at me, as if to ask me what it was. His eyes looked funny; they weren't right.

First a trembling started. Then retching. That went down deeper than the throat. Deeper than the chest. The stomach. Down through the very legs. Until—it was all of him.

He bolted to his feet, as if his first impulse was to get out of here. Then he checked himself. He leaned against something, as if he couldn't make it. Then he straightened again. Leaned again and straightened again.

I was on my own feet now. "What is it? What's happening to you?"

He kept doubling and straightening again; it was hideous.

"You brought this on," he heaved. "You should have loved me. Should have loved me, as I did—you. The shock. You brought this on. You brought it on—"

I tried to help him. "Lean on me. Let me get you over here to—"

"And I said *she* was low! Even she left me some guard against herself at least; you crawled into my blood, into my brain. Now I can't get you out and I can't have you either. Well, I *can* get you out, if I have to. There's one sure way that never fails."

Before I realized what was happening he was trying to get at my throat. But something was the matter with his reflexes; they were faulty. Fluctuations, like a sort of alternating current passing through him, would interrupt the clutch of his arms each time; yet they kept coming back, coming back, as I retreated before him, at first only fighting him off passively, then, as necessity slowly mounted in me, struggling more and more strenuously against him.

"Don't— Not you, Ladd! No, not you! Ladd, you're ill; you don't know what you're doing—"

Foam was suddenly flecking his lips.

"I'm ill," he said in a terrible, hacking voice, "but I know what I'm doing. I'm going to"—and then he lunged for my throat again—"if I die a minute later myself."

He had me pressed back against some sharp outline —I think it was that cabinet Flood had brought into the place—and the whole thing rocked in company with our combined weights.

I tried to reason with him, even at this pass. I don't know; terror wasn't absolute, as it had been with Mordaunt or even McKee. It could never be with him. "Don't—haven't I been through enough for one night?" The thing gave behind me, shunted aside, and we were wedged in there, in a little space. A little space, but big enough for dying in.

I kept trying to hold his swollen eyes with mine. "You can't. Look at me well. You loved me, didn't you? You can't do it!"

"I've done it before. I can do it this time too. I'm going to kill you as I killed her."

"You didn't. Don't you remember? You went there and she was already— It wasn't you. No, Ladd. You said it wasn't—"

"I did. It was. I never told anyone, not even you. I was afraid it would stand between us. Now know it and be damned to you. You've broken me all open."

I went down on one knee.

"I can't breathe, Ladd. Can't—breathe—"

The room was darkening intermittently, as though fleeting banks of clouds were passing over it. Then it would clear again in between.

"Air—give me air, Ladd. One breath more—only one—"

He held the words down in me; he wouldn't let anything through.

He was swinging my body from side to side now, like a rag doll. I could feel my legs sweeping bonelessly far over one way, then far back the other way again.

Suddenly he let me go, and I was all limp, but alone, without him. A dim point of light flickered, like a spark in straw, threatened to go out. Then the straw caught, kindled into renewed brightness. Life was on again.

I kept coughing strangledly and pulling at my own throat, and blurred figures moved before my eyes until they were able to focus properly again.

He was at the open window, on the *outside* of the open window, one hand grasping the frame, wavering there, so ill, so stricken, so alone, against the night. My heart went out to him, the heart he had tried to founder.

The door had sprung open, and there were figures deployed about the inside of it in bated attitudes, frozen still, where each had fallen to a halt at instant of entry. One of them was Flood, though I couldn't think who he was for a moment.

I only knew I had to speak, had to speak quickly; they must hear me in time. I clawed at my own throat to free it.

"Don't shoot," I pleaded raspingly. "Don't shoot that man!"

I heard their breaths all go *Ihf-f-f!* together in sharp ascent. I turned slowly, and by the time my look had reached it my eyes only told me what I knew already. The window was empty.

Later they had me sitting there huddled, lonely in a chair, one side of my face pressed to the back of it, my eyes staring sightlessly down toward the nothingness on the floor. Oh, I heard all the things they did and said; sometimes they even said them to me, but I seldom answered.

"It's a good thing we got over here when we did." That was Flood, I guess; I didn't move my eyes to see. "That ownerless car left standing there earlier tonight, when those shots at the Sixty-seventh Street transverse were investigated, was traced to him, and I got word of it. We've been keeping him under fairly constant surveillance, anyway, ever since that first transcript was taken out of the thing here; there was enough on it to warrant that, if nothing else. He's been seen coming around here pretty steadily, even after you'd left, and when we were unable to locate either of you at his own address, for questioning about that McKee business, we thought of this place."

He gave up and turned away again. I could sense that he was shaking his head to them to express futility.

At one point I heard somebody say to him: "What

was that? He acted like he had the bends just before he went over."

"Epilepsy, I think," he answered in an undertone. "That's what it looked like to me, anyway."

I remembered what he'd once told me: "I got ill there one night up in her place. She got frightened and wanted to send for a doctor—" And his sister, trying to say something to me: "He can't tell you this; I'll have to—"

It didn't matter; I would never remember this last scene; the heart is kind that way. I'd only remember a cheerful face across from mine at the Blues-Chaser a hundred years ago, a minute ago, forever.

I got up abruptly and drifted toward the window. Flood didn't understand. "Don't look down there," he tried to warn me.

"I wasn't going to. I was going to look up—" I didn't finish it. That's where they go in your memories of them; up, not down.

Suddenly, behind me, they brought him back again for just a moment or two. Unwittingly, without intent at cruelty; somebody's idly straying hand must have done it.

"I've done it before. I can do it this time too. I'm going to kill you as I killed her."

"No, Ladd, it wasn't you. You said it wasn't—"

"It was. Now know it and be damned to you!"

"It's on there!" I heard Flood exclaim.

For only a moment or two, but I couldn't bear it. I arched my back away from the sound as though a knife had been put into me, then deflated again.

Flood was standing by me, shaking me so I would listen. "You've done it! You've saved your husband. It got on there without your knowing it. It's on there, all you need. Do you hear what I'm saying? Do you understand? You've done what you wanted. He'll be back again. Inbound through Grand Central one of these days—"

I said after him, like a parrot, so he'd stop shaking me: "I've done what I wanted. He'll be back again."

I turned to him in sudden fearsome supplication, quickened now in turn, but not by the same thing he was. "Please go. All of you. *Please!* Hurry. I can't hold out much longer. Something's going to happen to me, something I don't want you to see."

He gave a quick order or two. "All right, that's all for now. Carry the whole thing out with you, the way it is. She's been through a lot; she's all in." He cleared them out and went after them.

I got the door closed, but they didn't go away quickly enough on the other side of it. Two of them were slower than the others.

The tears weren't just wet. They were heavy. They pulled me draggingly downward against the door, face pressed inward to it, while they stormed and raged from me.

I could hear their voices in surreptitious inquiry of one another out there as the sound reached them.

"What's she feelin' bad now for? It came out all right. She got what she wanted, didn't she?"

"I dunno. Unless maybe—say, d'you suppose?—she musta loved him."

"She must have," kept echoing through the freshets of my woe; yes, oh yes, she must have. She must have, all right!

11

CLOSING SCENE

THIS MORNING HE WAS leaving me again. He always leaves me. I don't know where he goes, but each time he goes I'm afraid I'll never have him back again. Then when he does come back it's only to leave me once more.

He was leaving me like he always does. Slowly, lingeringly, in that most poignant, hurtful way of all. Each time he goes like that I hear the barman's voice again that night of our first meeting at the Blues-Chaser: "Do it quick is the best way, Mr. Mason."

Everything that was ever said, that was ever done, that had to do with us at all, like that, keeps coming back again, over and over all the time. They are so few; they must be made to last.

This morning he was leaving me again, drawing away slowly, moving softly backward out of the room, thinking perhaps I was asleep and trying not to disturb me. He was near the door now, that recurrent door that I could never get by, no matter how I ached and strained, that I could never pass through myself. His face was turned to look back at me. Now he was drawing the door slowly closed after himself. Now he would be gone again.

I started upright, arms stretched arrestingly out toward him, to show him I wasn't asleep; he mustn't go like this without at least— "Ladd, wait!" I called out to him. "Don't go! Come back a minute!" The door was all but closed now. I could still see just the outline of his face, slowly dimming behind it. My arms strained out in helpless appeal, while I kept calling after him, more loudly, more heartbrokenly with every breath, "Don't leave me behind! Don't leave me behind!"

And then the miracle did happen; my plea was heard this one time. The cry was answered. His face grew clearer again, came back toward me. He hovered over me, sat anxiously down beside me, tried to quiet my wildly reaching hands by nursing them with his, at last drew me to him and kissed me soothingly on the brow.

My eyes flew open and I was in my husband's arms.

I hid my face against him. I felt him touch his finger to the outward corner of my eye and gently stroke it off, and the touch of it was wet.

"Why are there so often tears in your eyes, like this, when you wake up?" he asked softly. "Who was that you were calling? Who is it hurts you so?"

"Somebody I knew in a dream, I guess."

"I know you've been through a lot. There's nothing more now."

"No," I agreed sadly, "there's nothing more now."

"Angel Face, don't ever leave me."

"No. And you won't leave me either, will you? I don't want to be all alone."

"You're so loyal; you're so mine."

He's leaning toward me now; his face is close to mine. He's cost me dear, but that's the price, and I won't quibble.

"Angel Face," he murmurs low.

He always calls me that; this is his name for me. That is a special thing, from him to me, when we are by ourselves.

MURDER... MAYHEM... MYSTERY...

From Ballantine

12   TA-43

mystery and SUSPENSE